A CATSKILL EAGLE

Books by Robert B. Parker

Robert B. Parker

A CATSKILL EAGLE

A Spenser Novel

Delacorte Press
Seymour Lawrence

Published by
Delacorte Press/Seymour Lawrence
1 Dag Hammarskjold Plaza
New York, N.Y. 10017

Manufactured in the United States of America

First printing

LIBRARY OF CONGRESS CATALOGING IN PUBLICATION DATA
Parker, Robert B., 1932–
A Catskill eagle.
I. Title.
PS3566.A686C3   1985   813'.54   84-28617
ISBN 0-385-29385-2

For Joan

"And there is a Catskill eagle in some souls that can alike dive down into the blackest gorges, and soar out of them again and become invisible in the sunny spaces. And even if he forever flies within the gorge, that gorge is in the mountains; so that even in his lowest swoop the mountain eagle is still higher than the other birds upon the plain, even though they soar."

HERMAN MELVILLE, *Moby-Dick*

Chapter 1

IT WAS NEARLY MIDNIGHT AND I WAS JUST GETTING HOME from detecting. I had followed an embezzler around on a warm day in early summer trying to observe him spending his ill-gotten gain. The best I'd been able to do was catch him eating a veal cutlet sandwich in a sub shop in Danvers Square across from Security National Bank. It wasn't much, but it was as close as you could get to sin in Danvers.

I got a Steinlager from the refrigerator and opened it and sat at the counter to read my mail. There was a check from a client, a consumer protection letter from the phone company, the threat of a field collection from the electric company, and a letter from Susan.

The letter said:

> I have no time. Hawk is in jail in Mill River, California. You must get him out. I need help too. Hawk will explain. Things are awful, but I love you.
>
> Susan

And no matter how many times I read it, that's all it said. It was postmarked San Jose.

I drank some beer. A drop of condensation made a shimmery track down the side of the green bottle. Steinlager, New Zealand, the label said. Probably some corruption between the Dutch *Zeeland* and the English *Sealand*. Language worked funny. I got off the stool very carefully and went slowly and got my atlas and looked up Mill River, California. It was south of San Francisco. Population 10,753. I drank another swallow of beer. Then I went to the phone and dialed. Vince Haller answered on the fifth ring. I said it was me.

He said, "Jesus Christ, it's twenty minutes of one."

I said, "Hawk's in jail in a small town called Mill River south of San Francisco. I want you to get a lawyer in there now."

"At twenty minutes of fucking one?" Haller said.

"Susan's in trouble too. I'm going out in the morning. I want to hear from the lawyer before I go."

"What kind of trouble?" Haller said.

"I don't know. Hawk knows. Get the lawyer down there right now."

"Okay, I'll call a firm we know in San Francisco. They can roust one of their junior partners out and send him down, it's only about quarter of ten out there."

"I want to hear from him as soon as he's seen Hawk."

Haller said, "You okay?"

I said, "Get going, Vince," and hung up.

I got another beer and read Susan's letter again. It said the same thing. I sat at the counter beside the phone and looked at my apartment.

Bookcases on either side of the front window. A working fireplace. Living room, bedroom, kitchen and bath. A shotgun, a rifle, and three handguns.

"I've been here too long," I said. I didn't like the way I

sounded in the empty room. I got up and walked to the front window and looked down at Marlborough Street. Nothing was happening down there. I went back to the counter and drank some more beer. Good to keep busy.

The phone rang at four twelve in the morning. My second bottle of beer had gone flat on the counter, half finished, and I was lying on my back on the couch with my hands behind my head looking at my ceiling. I answered the phone before the third ring.

At the other end, a woman's voice said, "Mr. Spenser?"

I said yes.

She said, "This is Paula Goldman, I'm an attorney with Stein, Faye and Corbett in San Francisco and I was asked to call you."

"Have you seen Hawk?" I said.

"Yes. He's in jail, in Mill River, California, on a charge of murder and assault. There's no bail, and no realistic hope of any."

"Who'd he kill?"

"He is accused of killing a man named Emmett Colder, who works as a security consultant for a man named Russell Costigan. There are also several accounts of assault on other security personnel and several police officers. He is apparently difficult to subdue."

"Yes," I said.

"He admits he killed Colder, and assaulted the various others, but says he was set up, says it was self-defense."

"Can you make a case?"

"On the facts, maybe. But the problem is that Russell Costigan's father is Jerry Costigan."

"Jesus Christ," I said.

"You know Jerry Costigan."

"I know who he is. He owns many things."

"Yes." Paula Goldman's voice was firm and unhesitant. "And one of the things he owns is Mill River, California."

"So he doesn't have much chance," I said, "if he gets to trial."

"*If* he gets to trial, he's a gone goose."

I was quiet for a minute, listening to the little transcontinental noises on the open line.

"Did he say anything about Susan Silverman?" I said.

"He said he'd come out at her request, and that they'd been waiting for him. The interview was conducted under close scrutiny and was given very grudgingly. Stein, Faye and Corbett is a major law firm in the Bay area. We have a lot of clout. If we'd had less, there might have been no interview at all."

"That's all you know?"

"That's all I know."

"What are his chances of beating this thing?"

"None."

"Because it's an iron-solid case?"

"Yes, it's iron solid, but he also broke three of Russell Costigan's front teeth. That's like beating up Huey Long's kid in his home parish in Louisiana in 1935."

"Un huh."

"And, for crissake, he's black."

"The Costigans are not egalitarian?"

"They are not," she said.

"Tell me about the jail?"

"Four cells off the police station, which is in a wing of the town hall. Hawk is the only prisoner at the moment. The civilian dispatcher, female, and two cops, male, were on duty when I was there. As an officer of the court it is my obligation to remind you that abetting a jailbreak is a felony under the California penal code."

"It's never loosened up out there since Reagan was governor," I said.

"When the sun comes up," she said, "I'll scramble around and work on the bail. But that's shoveling shit against the tide. If you need me call the office." She gave me the number.

I said, "Thank you, Ms. Goldman."

She said, "Mrs. Goldman. I work criminal law fifteen, sixteen hours a day. I'm already more liberated than I want to be."

Chapter 2

AT SIX FORTY-FIVE IN THE MORNING I WAS AT THE HARBOR
Health Club. Henry Cimoli had an apartment on the
ground floor past the racquetball courts, and I was drinking
coffee with him and making a plan.

"I thought you quit coffee," Henry said. He was doing
handstand push-ups on the beige shag wall-to-wall carpet.

"This is an emergency," I said. I was not sleepy but I was
tired. "You get the idea?"

"Sure," Henry said. "All the years I was a trainer. I can
rig any kind of cast you want. I'll make it big, and you can
slide your foot right in it when you get there."

"We'll need to get that little walker sole for it."

Henry eased out of the handstands. There was a chinning
bar across the door to the kitchen. At five four Henry had to
jump to reach it. He began to do pull-ups, touching the
back of his neck to the bar, his arms apart to the width of the
doorframe.

"There's a medical supply house up on Beacon Street,
just past Kenmore Square. It's on the left past the old Hotel
Buckminster going toward Brookline."

Henry was wearing gray cotton shorts and nothing else, and his body pumped up and down on the bar like a small piston. There was no suggestion of strain. His voice was normal and unforced, his movements precise and prompt.

"Maybe you should work less on strong," I said, "and more on tall."

Henry dropped from the pull-up bar. "Tall enough to kick you in the balls," he said.

"Take a number," I said, and went looking for the medical supply house.

The place didn't open until eight. So I drank three coffees sitting in my car in front of the Dunkin' Donuts in Kenmore Square watching punk rockers unlimber for the day. A kid with tie-dyed hair strolled by wearing a white plastic vest and soft boots like Peter Pan. He had no shirt on and his chest was white and hairless and thin. He glanced at himself covertly in the store windows, filled with the pleasure of his outlandishness. He was probably hoping to scare a Republican, though in Kenmore Square they were sparse between ball games.

I had Susan's letter in my shirt pocket, folded up. I didn't read it again. I knew what it said. I knew the words. I knew the tone. The tone was frantic. I looked at my watch. Almost eight. There was a nonstop at nine fifty-five. I was packed. All I had to do was rig this leg cast with Henry and get going. I could be there by one o'clock their time.

I telescoped the three paper coffee cups and got out of my car and put them in a trash can. Then I got back in and drove up and was the first customer at the medical supply house. By 9:05 Henry had the leg cast made, too big, and I was able to put it on and take it off like a fisherman's boot. I put it in my Asics Tiger gym bag, under my clean shirts.

"You want a ride?" Henry said.

"I'll leave the car at the airport."

"You need any dough?"

"I got out a couple of hundred with the bank card," I said. "That's all there is in the account. Plus the American Express card. I can't leave home without it."

"You need anything," Henry said, "you call me. Anything. You need me out there I'll come."

"Paul knows to call you if he can't get me," I said. "He's back in school."

Henry nodded. "Christ, you'd think you were his old man."

"Sort of," I said.

Henry put his hand out. I shook it.

"You call me," he said.

I headed for Logan Airport at a high speed, working against the morning traffic. If I missed the plane there were other flights, but this one was nonstop and quicker. I wanted to get there quicker.

I was twenty minutes early. I checked my bag through. If they lost it on me it would be a mess. But I couldn't carry it on with a handgun in it. At nine fifty-five we were heading out to the runway, at ten we were banking up over the harbor and heading west.

Chapter 3

AT HERTZ I GOT A BUICK SKYLARK WITH THE WINDOW CRANK
handle missing on the driver's side. Where was O.J. when
you needed him. I went straight south on 101 along the
west side of the bay and at a little after three I turned off
south of San Jose and headed east, on Mill River Boulevard. A mile off the highway there was a big shopping
center built around a modernistic Safeway supermarket
made of poured concrete, with large round windows and a
broad quarry-tile apron where groceries could be loaded. A
big redwood sign at the entrance to the parking lot said
COSTIGAN MALL *30 Stores for Your Shopping Pleasure.* The lettering was carved in the wood and painted gold. I pulled in
and parked near the Safeway and got my cast from the bag.
When we'd made it, Henry had rubbed it with some dirt
and ashes from one of the club sand buckets. It looked a
month old. In the foot, indented, was a hollow space, and I
put a .25-caliber automatic in there, flat on its side. Over it I
put a sponge rubber innersole. Then I took off my left shoe
and slipped the cast on. I shook my pants leg down over it

and got out of the car. It worked fine. Comfort was not its strong suit, but it looked right. I walked on it a little and then went in the Safeway. I bought a pint of muscatel and got directions from a customer to the town hall. Then I went back to the Buick and got in. I stashed my wallet in the glove compartment. I took a Utica Blue Sox baseball cap from my bag, messed my hair, and jammed the cap on my head. I checked in the mirror. I hadn't shaved since yesterday morning and it was beginning to show. Strands of hair stuck out nicely under the cap and through the small opening in the back where the plastic adjustable strap was. I was wearing a white shirt and jeans. I ripped the pocket on the shirt, rolled the sleeves up unevenly, and splashed some muscatel on it. I poured more of the muscatel onto my jeans. Then I put the bottle on the seat beside me and drove on into Mill River. The town hall was white stucco and red tile roof and green lawn with a sprinkler slowly revolving, trailing the water in a slightly laggard arc behind it. There was a fire station on the left side and then a kind of connecting wing, in front of the connecting wing was a pair of blue lights on either side of a sign just like the shopping center sign, except this one said MILL RIVER POLICE. There was a small lot in front of the police station and a bigger one beyond the town hall that looked like it went around back. I turned into the big lot and circled the building. A public works garage was out back. Not stucco, cinder block. Not tile, corrugated plastic. One for show, one for blow. I could see the jail windows in the back, covered with a thick wire mesh. Two police cars were back there beside a blank door with no outside handle. I went on around the building and out the driveway past the fire station and turned toward the center of town. Fifty yards down and across the street was the town library. A sign out front said J. T. COSTIGAN

MEMORIAL LIBRARY. There was a parking lot in back. I pulled in, shut off the Buick, took my bottle of muscatel and rinsed my mouth out a couple of times. The wine tasted like tile cleaner. But it smelled bad. I took the half-empty bottle, put the car keys on a window ledge behind a shrub at the rear of the library, and strolled around front. As soon as I came into public view I began to weave, my head down, mumbling to myself. It is not easy to mumble to yourself if you don't feel moved to mumble. I didn't know what to mumble and finally began to mumble the starting lineup for the impossible-dream Red Sox team of '67. "Rico Petrocelli," I mumbled, "Carl Yastrzemski . . . Jerry Adair."

I sat on the front steps of the town library and took a swig from my bottle, blocking the bottle neck with my tongue so I didn't have to swallow any. What I was going to do didn't get easier if I did it drunk. A couple of high school girls in leg warmers and headbands skirted me widely and went into the library.

"Dalton Jones," I mumbled. I took another make-pretend swig.

A good-looking middle-aged woman in a lavender sweat suit and white Nikes with a lavender swoosh parked a brown Mercedes sedan in front of the library and got out with five or six books in her arms. She looked forcefully in the other direction as she edged past me.

"George Scott," I mumbled, and as she went by I reached up and pinched her on the backside. She twitched her backside away from me and went into the library. I sipped some more muscatel and let a little slide out and along the corner of my mouth and down my chin. I could hear a small commotion at the library door behind me.

"Mike Andrews . . . Reggie Smith . . ." I blew my nose with my naked hand and wiped it across my shirt.

"Hawk Harrelson . . . Tony C." I raised my voice. "José goddamned Tartabull," I snarled. Up at the town hall a black and white Mill River Police car turned out of the parking lot in front and cruised slowly down toward the library.

I stood and smashed the muscatel bottle against the steps.

"Joe Foy," I said with cold fury in my voice. Then I unzipped my fly and began to take a leak on the lawn. Provocative. The cruiser pulled in beside me before I had finished and a Mill River cop in a handsome tan uniform got out and walked toward me. He wore a campaign hat tilted forward over the bridge of his nose like a Marine DI.

"Hold it right there, mister," he said.

I giggled. "Am holding it right there, officer." I lurched a little and smothered a belch.

The cop was in front of me now. "Zip it up," he snapped. "There's women and children here."

I zipped my fly about halfway. "Women and children first," I said.

"You got some ID on you?" the cop said.

I fumbled at my hip pocket and then at my other hip pocket and then at my side pockets. I looked at the cop, squinting to bring him in focus.

"I wish to report a stolen wallet," I said, speaking the words carefully like a man trying not to be drunk.

"Okay," the cop said, "walk over to the car." He took my arm and I went with him.

"Hands on top," he said. "Legs apart. You've probably done this before." He tapped the inside of my good ankle with his foot to force my stance out a little wider. Then he gave me a fast shakedown.

"What's your name," he said when he was through.

"I stop standing like this?" I said. I was resting my forehead against the roof of his car.

"Yeah. You can straighten up."

I stayed as I was and didn't say anything.

"I asked you your name," the cop said.

"I want lawyer," I said.

"Who's your lawyer?"

I rolled along the car until I had turned and was facing the cop. He was about twenty-five, nice tan. Clear blue eyes. I frowned at him.

"Sleepy," I said. And I began to slide down the side of the car toward the ground. The cop grabbed me under the arms.

"No," he said. "Not here. Come on, you can spend the night with us, and we'll see in the morning."

I let him put me in the car and drive me to the station. At twenty-two minutes to five by the clock in the station house I was in front of a cell in the Mill River jail. Booked for public drunkenness and urinating in a public place. Listed for the moment as John Doe. There was a porcelain toilet in the corner with no seat, there was a sink, and there was a concrete shelf with a mattress on it, no pillow, and a brown military blanket folded at the foot. The arresting officer opened the door to the second cell. The first was empty. There were two more beyond.

"Wait a minute," I said. "I wanna see other guests." I lurched past him and saw Hawk in the fourth cell, lying on his bed, his hands behind his head.

"Hey, Rastus," I said. "You gonna play sad fucking harmonica when the warden comes?"

Hawk looked at me with no expression. "Maybe play a tune on your head, white belly," he said.

"Come on, come on," the young cop said. He took the

back of my shirt in his hand and shoved me into my cell. "Sleep it off," he said, "and don't fuck around with the nigger."

He went out and locked the cell and left me alone. Who said I couldn't get arrested.

Chapter 4

I WAS SUPPOSED TO BE ZONKED, AND I HADN'T SLEPT IN TWO days, and my great escape plan didn't go into effect until after midnight, so I made a pillow out of the blanket and lay on the cot and went to sleep.

When I woke up it was late. I had no watch and there was no clock in view from the cell, but there was the heavy silence that comes at two in the morning. Whatever hour, it was late enough.

I took my cast off quietly and took the gun out of the left foot. I stood and felt uneven with one shoe on and one shoe off, so I kicked off my right shoe and moved across the cell barefoot. With my shirttails out and the automatic tucked in my belt, in front under my shirt, I leaned against the bars of my cell and said loudly, "Hey, Rastus."

Hawk said from two cells down, "You talking to me, motherfucker?"

"Any other jigaboos down there," I said, "might be named Rastus?"

"You and me is all that's in here, whitey."

"Good, what time is it?"

"You wake me up to ask what time is it?"

"Niggers sleep?" I said.

"You be sleeping the big sleep, motherfucker, I get hold of your pale ass."

"You trying to sleep, Rastus?" I picked up my shoe and began to rattle it over the bars, the way a kid will drag a stick along a picket fence. "How's that sound, a little jungle rhythm for you, Rastus."

"I play some rhythm on you, you honkie bastard," Hawk said.

I began to bang with the heel of the shoe on the bars and sing loudly, " 'Bongo, bongo, bongo, I don't want to leave the Congo, Oh no, no, no, no, no! Bingle, bangle, bungle, I'm so happy in the jungle I refuse to go.' "

And Hawk started yelling at me to shut up. Then the cellblock lights went on, and a moon-faced cop with a crew cut came in from the office.

"What the fuck is going on in here," he said.

"I'm singing to the coon," I said.

"The man's goddamned crazy," Hawk said at the same time.

I sang louder. The moon-faced cop walked toward me. He had a leather sap in a low pocket on the right side of his uniform pants and he pulled it out as he walked.

"You," he said, "button it up, now."

" 'Don't want no bright lights, false teeth, doorbells, landlords, I make it clear/That, no matter how they coax me, I'll stay right here.' " I beat a sloppy paradiddle on the cinder-block wall with my shoe. Actually half a paradiddle, because I had only one shoe.

The moon-faced cop turned and yelled out into the office.

"Hey, Maury, get in here."

A second cop appeared, this one taller than Moon Face, with a puzzled country look to his face, and brown hair slicked back and parted in the middle. I kept singing. Hawk was silent. Moon Face made a gesture at me with his head and Maury pulled a switch inside the corridor door and my cell door slid back. Moon Face walked in tapping his thigh with the sap. Maury walked down the corridor and came in behind him. He was taking the handcuffs from the back of his belt.

I said, "What are you guys going to do?"

"We're going to show you how to shut up," Moon Face said.

I put my hand under my shirt and rubbed my bare stomach nervously. "I was just ragging the spade," I said.

"Turn around," Moon Face said, "and put your hands behind your neck."

I took my gun out from under my shirt and pointed it at both of them. "If you make any noise," I said, "I'll kill you."

Both of them stopped in freeze-frame.

I said, "Hands on top of your heads, walk over and stand facing the wall."

They did what I said, neither one said a word. I took the service revolver from each of them. Moon Face had a standard issue .38, but Maury was packing a .44 magnum. Good for whale hunting.

I said, "Who's on the dispatch board?"

Moon Face said, "Madilyn."

I said, "Okay, to be sure she doesn't get hurt, and you don't get hurt, you be as quiet as two tombs in here. I'm going to open the other cell and I can see you all the time."

Carrying both guns by the trigger guard, I backed out of the cell and down the corridor. On the wall inside the door to the office was a series of switches labeled Cell One, Two,

Three, and Four. I hit Two and the door closed, I hit Four and Hawk's cell opened. He came out and walked to me. I handed him the guns.

He handed me the .38 and held the .44 in his right hand. I stuck the .38 in my pants pocket.

"Bongo, bongo, bongo?" he said.

"Get the dispatcher," I said.

Madilyn was about fifty-five and not slender. She went without a word and sat on the bunk in Hawk's open cell, while we shut the door.

"We got until somebody on patrol calls in and can't get an answer," I said.

"Long enough," Hawk said.

We walked quickly out of the police station and down the silent main street to the library. The Skylark was still parked behind it. "There," I said. I got the key from the ledge and gave it to Hawk.

"You drive," I said.

"Susan's?" he said.

"Yes."

"First place they'll look," Hawk said, "when they know we gone."

"Doesn't matter," I said.

We swung out from behind the library and turned right at the end of the square. A mile up the road, we pulled right again and then left into the parking lot of a six-story industrial building. Even in the moonlight you could see that a lot of work had gone into the place. The brick walls had been sandblasted and steam cleaned and all the windows were new. There was a lot of granite filigree around the rooftop and the door lintels were granite blocks.

Hawk parked right in front of the back door.

"That her window," Hawk said, "over there. You want to ring the bell or you want to go on in through the window?"

The window was ground-floor level.

"We'll go in," I said, and started across the parking lot.

The lot had numbered slots and cars were parked in most of them. One of them might be Susan's. I used to know what her car was. Now I didn't.

"Maybe she won't be alone, babe," Hawk said.

"Got to see. If we ring and there's no answer, we got to go in anyway, make sure. May as well cut out the first step. We don't have a lot of time."

Hawk nodded. We stopped beside her window. I took the police .38 from my pocket and broke the glass at the juncture of upper and lower sash. Hawk reached through and turned the window catch. I raised the window and went in, sliding on my stomach over the sill and landing on the floor like a clumsy snake. Hawk came right in behind me. We were both still for a moment. There was no sound in the apartment. I got to my feet. To my right was a spiral staircase. Hawk pointed toward it.

"Bedroom," he said softly.

I went up the stairs quietly. Behind me I could hear Hawk move through the darkness. The stairs ended in a small platform and the bedroom opened off it. I stepped in. I could smell Susan, her perfume, her hair spray, maybe even herself, imprinted on me. The bed was to my left, parallel to the low wall that let you look down from the sleeping balcony. The moonlight coming in the high-arched window made it easier to see up here than in the living room. It shone on the empty bed.

"Hawk," I said in a normal voice.

"Nobody down here," he said.

"Nobody up here either." I turned the bedside lamp on.

The room was neat. The bed was made. It was too neat. Susan would have left makeup out, maybe some panty hose draped over a chair. Shoes on the floor, one standing up, one lying on its side. There was no sign of that here. Maybe this Susan was different.

I opened the closet doors. Downstairs Hawk turned on the other lights. I heard him come up the staircase. The closet was wall length and the doors were louvered and opened by folding back along a sliding track. Her clothes were there, again the smell of her. The clothes were very neatly hung, and spaced carefully so they wouldn't wrinkle. She was careless about what she had worn, but very careful about what she was going to wear. I recognized many of her clothes. But there were too many. I couldn't tell what was missing. Or if there were any missing.

"The bathroom," I said.

Hawk said, "We pressed for time, babe."

"I want to know if she's gone, or just out," I said. "If she's gone she'd take lingerie and makeup."

"Downstairs," Hawk said.

I took in the apartment as I went down the spiral stairs. The living room ceiling was two stories and the windows were twenty feet high. There was a kitchenette off the living room, with a counter top tiled in red Mexican tile. A huge red fan was spread high on one wall of the living room, and a Tiffany lamp hung straight down from the ceiling on a gold chain. Beneath it a glass-topped dining table sat on oak sawhorses.

The bathroom was off the living room, and next to it a den. Susan always kept her lingerie in a small bureau in her bathroom, and her makeup in the medicine cabinet and everywhere else there was room. The bathroom was white tile with black and silver trim. A small four-drawer bureau stood opposite the sink. I opened the top drawer. It was empty. There was a maroon half-slip in the second drawer and odds and ends of eye shadow, mascara, lipstick, face powder, blusher, and conditioner and things of unknown application in the remaining two drawers. All were partially used and looked discarded. I knew Susan kept the current stuff near the mirror. The stuff in the drawers was backup. The medicine cabinet was nearly empty, and there was nothing on the sink top. I turned and touched the half-slip for a moment, then I closed the drawer and went back into the living room.

"She's gone away," I said to Hawk. "No underwear, no makeup."

Hawk was leaning against the wall near the open window, looking at the parking lot, listening to the silence. He nodded.

"Two more minutes," I said.

Hawk nodded again.

I went into the den. There was a desk in there and a big sectional sofa and a color television set. I sat at the desk.

It was disorganized and cluttered with small slips of paper stuck into alcoves, and mail in piles that had been pushed aside to clear writing space. A letter from me showed among the other mail. Susan's calendar was there. There were entries on various dates in Susan's nearly illegible hand. Most of the entries meant nothing. There was no entry for today, and for Monday it said *Dr. Hilliard @ 3:40.*

The doorbell rang. I turned off the light in the den and almost at the same time Hawk killed the living room light. He was out the window by the time I got to it and by the time the doorbell rang again we were both crouched against the outside wall of the building moving in its shadow toward the Buick, fast.

There was no sign of anyone in the lot, and no sign of anyone at the door.

"This the back," Hawk murmured. "They must be at the front."

We were in the car, and Hawk drove. He went out the other side of the parking lot and turned left and drove slowly parallel to the condominium building toward Mill River Boulevard. In front were two Mill River Police cars. We turned right on the boulevard toward 101, not fast, staying under the speed limit.

"They know we're gone," I said.

Hawk said, "How you get the gun in?"

"Henry rigged me a leg cast and we hid it in the foot."

Hawk laid the .44 in his lap. I was driving barefoot. Hawk said, "They catch us, they gonna shoot us. So you be ready. This a bad town, babe."

I said, "Susan. I want to know. Tell me."

Hawk nodded. "Yeah. Some of this gonna be hard to hear."

I didn't say anything. The dashboard clock on the Skylark said 4:11.

"Susan call me," Hawk said. "She say she can't call you. But she in trouble. She say she gotten involved with this dude Costigan and he a bad man."

There was nothing on the road before us. The Skylark started to creep up past sixty. Hawk slowed to under fifty-five.

"She say she want to leave him but she think maybe she can't. She say she too involved to leave on her own."

"Involved how," I said.

"She didn't say. She sounded real tight. So I say, I come right out in the morning, and if she want to leave I take her with me. And if anyone bother her, I tell them to stop. And she tell me come to her condo, which is down here in Mill River, and she give me the address, fifteen Los Alimos. Unit number sixteen. And she say, she don't know if she want to leave, but she needs to talk with me and if she want to leave, she need to be able to."

We had reached 101. Hawk turned north, toward San Francisco.

Chapter 5

IT WAS A CLEAR NIGHT, A LOT OF STARS, THE MOON ABOUT three-quarters full. The land loomed higher in a dark mass of low hills to my left, and tabled away flat toward the bay on my right. There was nothing on the highway.

"So you went out," I said.

"Course."

"Without telling me anything."

"Yes."

The wheels made a little hum on the asphalt and now and then when we hit a seam there was a *harumph.*

"I wouldn't have told you either," I said.

"I know," Hawk said.

On the other side of the highway a big produce truck went by, heading south toward Salinas.

"So I got here and rented a car and drove on down to Mill River like she say. And Susan's there."

"How'd she look," I said.

"She looking terrific, except she looking real tired and she tense, like she frantic but she don't want anyone to know it, including her."

"How'd she sound?" I said.

"Same way," Hawk said. "Got a bow, you could play 'Intermezzo' on her."

I blew out some breath.

Hawk said, "Told you this wouldn't be easy."

I nodded.

Hawk said, "So we have some coffee, she got some new French roast, and she put out some little sesame cookies, and all. Like she playing house and she tell me she met this guy Costigan in Georgetown last year, when she in Washington doing intern. And she took up with him and he say he can get her a job at a clinic out here."

"In Mill River?"

"Yeah," Hawk said, "Costigan Hospital."

"Family business," I said.

Hawk said, "One of them."

There were unattractive shacks along the way that sold artichokes and strawberries and things. The headlights picked up the ugly hand-lettered signs in front of them.

"So Susan having her troubles with you and all, she decide she going to come out. And she really like Costigan, she say. But she don't want to let go of you. So she talk to you on the phone and you write her letters and you talk and she hanging on to you but she staying close to Costigan too."

A green sign loomed up on the right shoulder of the highway. The headlights brightened the reflective lettering for a moment. It said, SAN MATEO BRIDGE, 5 MILES.

"And Costigan, he getting edgy. He wanting to move in, and she saying no. And he saying, 'how come you don't dump this stiff from Boston,' and Susan saying, ' 'cause I love him,' and Costigan saying, 'how come you love him and me too,' and Susan saying, 'I don't know,' and they having a nice time like that."

"I know some of this," I said.

"So she can't go back to you and leave Costigan; but she can't give you up and move in with him. She say to herself, I believe I am fucked up, and she go see a shrink."

Hawk's voice was soft and pleasant as he talked, telling the story as if he were talking about Br'er Rabbit and the briar patch.

"I say to her, 'Susan, *you* a shrink,' and she say, 'I know' and shake her head. Anyway," Hawk said, "she talk to this shrink . . ."

"She mention the shrink's name?" I said.

"No," Hawk said. "And the shrink help her see that maybe she got some problems. And she begin to pull back a little and Costigan not liking that and he begin hanging around even when she ask him not to, and he come into her apartment, he got a key, even when she say she need to be alone and try to work this out. And she say if he don't give her some room she going to move, and he say he won't let her. And I say, 'what he going to do,' and she shake her head and she say, 'you don't know him.' And I say, 'you want to tell me about it' and she just shake her head, and I see she getting tears, her eyes filling up. And I say, 'why not come back with me. And Spenser and me, we fix it up, whatever it is. We can fix up anything.' And she just sit there, she not crying exactly, but her eyes full of tears and she shake her head, and then the door opens and Costigan comes in and he got a couple of heavy lifters with him."

"Only a couple?" I said.

Hawk said, "I telling this story."

The dashboard clock read 5:03.

"And Susan say, 'Russell what in hell you doing,' " Hawk said, "and Russell, he say to me, 'beat it.' "

I almost smiled. "Beat it?" I said.

"Beat it. He that kind of a slick guy. So I say something about lawzy me M'ars Russell but I a guest of Ms. Silverman. And the two heavy lifters are standing around checking their pecs in the mirror and seein' which one got the bigger tricep dimple and Russell he say, 'You ain't nobody's guest, Boogaloo, on your way.' "

"Boogaloo?" I said.

"Boogaloo. So I look at Susan and she frozen, and . . ."

"What do you mean, frozen?" I said.

"Still. She got a little half smile and she look scared and mad and she not moving or speaking or looking like she going to."

"Jesus Christ," I said.

"Umm hmm," Hawk said. "I not feeling warm toward Russell anyway, even before I know him. And he getting on my nerves telling me to beat it and all. So I expressed my displeasure by hitting him in the mouth with my elbow. I hate to cut up my hands if I don't have to. And the two gym rats get into it and I forced to quell them. And I quell one of them kind of hard with a chair and the dumb bastard died."

"And the cops came," I said.

"Yeah. About ten of them with shotguns and vests and all."

"And no one called them," I said.

"Nope," Hawk said, "they come in the door about the time the last gym rat hit the floor."

"Like they'd been waiting."

"Yep."

"You were set up," I said. "You were supposed to get

roughed up and then arrested for assault. Teach us all a lesson."

"Figure they had her phone tapped," Hawk said.

"Cops or Costigan?"

"Don't matter," Hawk said. "They Costigan's cops."

Chapter 6

Off to the right, clear in the lucid predawn stillness, I could see Candlestick Park on the edge of the bay. When I was a kid the Giants played at the Polo Grounds, and the '49ers played at Kezar Stadium and I didn't even know Susan Silverman.

"The cops take me to the pokey and last I see they giving Russell some ice in a towel to hold on his mouth. And Susan still frozen, weird little smile, and she crying."

I was silent.

"There a picture of you," Hawk said. "In her condo."

Ahead I could see the outline of the Transam tower on the San Francisco skyline.

"Boogaloo," I said.

"Knew you'd like that."

"You broke three of Costigan's teeth," I said.

"He got some left," Hawk said.

"I know. We'll get to that."

"We surely will," Hawk said.

"But first we get Susan," I said.

"We surely will," Hawk said.

"And then we'll see about the Costigans."

"We surely will," Hawk said.

"And Mill River," I said. "Might neaten that up a little, too."

"While we doing all this, be better if the cops don't catch us," Hawk said. "Be pretty soon they figure out who you are."

"And then they'll check the airlines and the rental agencies and have a fix on this car."

Hawk said, "How much bread you have?"

"About two hundred," I said.

"Jesus Christ," Hawk said. "Diamond fucking Jim Brady."

"And the American Express card," I said.

"That be a lot of good," Hawk said. "Check right into the Stanford Court with it, sit around and have room service till the cops come."

"Not my fault," I said, "you don't have rich friends."

We went down the ramp off the expressway at Golden Gate Ave past the Civic Center and turned left onto Van Ness.

"We need to get off the street," I said.

"Costigan will figure it gotta be you," Hawk said. "Get that picture from Susan, show it to the fuzz we locked up, and they got your name on the wire. Mine too. Me for murder one, you for accessory after the fact, both of us for felonious escape from a sardine can."

"Up around Geary Street," I said. "There's a hotel with an all-night garage underneath it."

Hawk spoke into his clenched hand. "All units," he said, "be on the lookout for gorgeous Afro-American stud in company of middle-aged honkie thug."

He pulled into the garage and took a ticket and cruised on down the lane looking for a slot.

"Nice talk," I said. "I gallop into Mill River and rescue you like the white knight that I am and you sit around and make honkie remarks."

Hawk pulled the car into a slot beside a green BMW and parked and shut off the engine. I got my Tiger sport bag out of the trunk and got a clean shirt and some Nike running shoes and changed in the car. I put the .25 in my hip pocket, tucked the Mill River .38 in my belt under my shirt, and got out. Hawk pulled his shirt out and let it hang over his belt. He stuck the big .44 in his belt in front.

"Hungry," Hawk said.

"There's a donut shop," I said, "across the street. Opens early as hell."

"You leaving the bag?" Hawk said.

"Yeah, less conspicuous."

"How 'bout I carry it on my head and walk behind you."

"Probably be a good cover," I said, "but it might perpetuate a racial stereotype."

We went across Van Ness. There was a bare hint of light east down Geary Street, and an occasional car had begun to move on Van Ness. A bus came down Van Ness and stopped at the corner of Post and an elderly Oriental man got off and went up the hill past the Cathedral Hill Hotel.

The donut shop was open and smelled steamily of coffee and fresh baked goods. We each had two donuts and two coffees, and stood at the little counter near the window and ate. A black and white San Francisco Police car stopped out front and two cops got out and came in the restaurant. They were young, both had thick mustaches. One was hatless. They got coffee and French-twist donuts to go and left.

"Probably looking for a gorgeous Afro-American and a middle-aged honkie," I said. "No wonder they didn't make us."

Hawk grinned. "Less see," he said. "We got two hundred dollars . . ."

"Hundred and ninety-seven now," I said. "We just did three bucks' worth of donuts."

"Hundred and ninety-seven bucks, 'bout seventeen rounds of ammunition. We three thousand miles away from home and we don't know anybody in the area, 'cept maybe that lady lawyer and I figure she can't do much now."

"I think the bar association gets on your ass about aiding and abetting," I said.

"And Susan gone and we don't know where . . ."

"Except we figure it's got to do with Costigan," I said.

"And Costigan's papa one of the richest and also one of the baddest men in this great nation," Hawk said.

Outside the hint of sunrise made Van Ness Ave look a pale gray and the still-lit streetlamps showed a milder yellow, as their influence waned.

"And we got no car, no change of clothes, no toilet paper, no champagne." Hawk finished his second cup of coffee.

"Lucky it you and me," he said.

"We're going to find Susan," I said.

Hawk turned his intense expressionless gaze on me. "Oh, yes," he said.

Chapter 7

THE SKY OVER THE BAY WAS ROSY AS WE STROLLED TOWARD Union Square. Morning, seven o'clock. Along Polk Street bars and boutiques with names that punned on oral sex were unshuttering.

"We need to get organized," I said.

Hawk nodded. "We need to get bread, too," he said.

"Part of organizing," I said. "First thing we've got to do is get off the street and get a base."

Hawk and I were walking briskly, two guys on their way to work. No loitering, no dillydally.

"We got to be on the wire by now," Hawk said.

"Yeah, but maybe no pictures yet."

"Don't need pictures. Cops can stop every black guy and white guy walking together they see," Hawk said.

"We could hold hands," I said, "and blend into the ambience."

Traffic was moving now in San Francisco. A lot of cabs. A lot of smaller foreign cars. There were people on the streets. A lot of young women, smelling of floral shampoos and scented soap and expensive perfume. They were wearing man-tailored suits with high slit skirts and carrying purses designed like briefcases. Many wore running shoes with their expensive dresses and carried their high-heeled shoes in shopping bags with Neiman-Marcus logos, or the name GUMP's. Working women, full of excitement, or vivacity, or desperation. Land of promise.

We turned the corner on Powell Street at Union Square and walked up Powell in front of the St. Francis Hotel. The cable car was not running while the system was being overhauled, and traffic moved along Powell Street better than I'd ever seen it. At the corner of Post two good-looking women stood watching people go to work. As we passed one of them said, "You gentlemen looking for adventure?"

Hawk looked at me, his face beginning to brighten.

"At seven thirty in the morning," I said.

They were both blond. The one who spoke wore a neat red dress with big white buttons up the front and white high-heeled shoes. Her hair was cut short like Princess Di's and her makeup was expert and unobtrusive. Her friend had on designer jeans and high heels and a beige cotton sweater with a V neck. The sweater was belted with thick blue cord.

Red Dress said, "Never too early for fun."

Hawk said, "You ladies got a place we can go?"

Red Dress said, "Sure. Nice apartment. Cost you a hundred dollars each."

"Hundred bucks apiece off the street?" I said.

Red Dress shrugged. "Worth twice that much," she said. "I'm Fay, this is Meg."

I looked at Hawk. He was grinning. "The Lord will provide," he said.

"Shall we take a cab," I said to Fay.

"Yes," Fay said. "Best bet is in front of the hotel."

We walked over and the doorman got us a cab. I tipped him a dollar. Hawk and I got in back with Meg. Fay sat up front with the cabbie.

"What are your names?" Meg said.

"Frick," I said.

"Frack," Hawk said.

Meg nodded seriously. "I'll remember by rhyming them," she said. "Frack as in black."

"And Frick as in prick," Fay said from the front seat. The cabbie laughed and pulled away. We went around Union Square, down Stockton and across Market. We ended up outside a four-story beige building with the stucco flaking off at the corner of Mission and Seventh. There was a video game arcade on the first floor. We paid the cabbie and followed the two women into a door to the left of the arcade. There was a narrow corridor and a stair leading up. We went up the stairs and into an apartment that fronted on Mission. There was a big square living room with a white porcelain sink-stove-refrigerator unit along one wall. There was a daybed covered with a green corduroy throw, an oak table, four chrome chairs with plastic mesh seats, and a pine bureau painted yellow. Across from the daybed a color television sat on an imitation-brass television stand. A short corridor ran off to the right, past the appliance unit.

"You boys want a drink or anything?" Fay said.

"A little early," I said. "Mind if I turn on the TV?"

Fay shrugged.

Meg said, "How about coffee?"

Hawk said, "Fine."

I turned on the TV and Diane Sawyer sprang into focus. *So close and yet so far.* I turned the sound low.

Meg was at the stove.

Fay said, "Business first, fellas. That'll be two hundred up front."

I said, "You have a pimp?"

Fay looked at me as if I were a child. "Course. Won't let you operate without a pimp."

"He come around and collect every day?"

Meg turned from the stove and looked at me. Fay smiled and stepped toward me and put her arms around me and pressed against me.

"Never mind him, honey, let's you and me get closer," she said.

I said, "You'll feel it anyway. There's a gun in my belt and I'm not a cop."

Fay stepped away. "What the fuck is going on," she said.

Meg was turned away from the stove, a jar of instant coffee in her hand.

"You guys are vice," Meg said.

"Nobody not cops as much as us," Hawk said. "When your pimp come to collect?"

"We got no pimp," Fay said. "You guys got us wrong. We're just looking for a little fun. You want a little fun?"

"No fun," I said. "We want to know when your pimp comes to collect."

"And we want to know pretty bad," Hawk said.

On the quiet television the network cut away for the eight twenty-five local news. A picture of Hawk and one of me appeared on the screen. I stepped over and turned up the sound.

"Bay area police," the announcer said, "are seeking two men wanted in connection with a daring jailbreak that took place early this morning in Mill River."

The women both stared at the screen as our names and descriptions were given.

"The two men, both from the Boston area, are considered armed and dangerous. Now this from Hoffman's Bakeries."

I shut the television off.

"They got me fifteen pounds too heavy," I said.

"That's the picture of you from Susan's apartment," Hawk said.

"How come they didn't get you fifteen pounds too heavy," I said.

Fay said, "Jesus Christ."

Hawk said, "Told you we wasn't cops."

"But we did lie about the names," I said. "You had to know sometime."

Meg said, "What do you want?"

"One last time," I said. "When does your pimp collect?"

"Mondays and Fridays." Meg had olive skin, which made you wonder about the blond hair. She swallowed hard as if her throat was tight. "What are you going to do?"

"Today's Thursday," I said. Hawk nodded. "Day and a half resting up, talking to these ladies, and the pimp comes along with a pocket full of cash."

"You can't rob Leo," Fay said.

"Pimps good to rob," Hawk said gently. "They got money, and they ain't likely to call the cops. And mostly they deserve it."

"Leo's bad," Meg said. "Leo's really bad. He set one of the girls on fire once."

"We not one of the girls," Hawk said.

"What are you going to do to us," Fay said.

"Nothing," I said. "We will just stay here for a day or two and then be gone."

"And what the hell do we do," Fay said, "while you're sitting around in here? We got a living to make."

"You'll have to take a short vacation," I said. "You can do anything you want except use the phone or leave the apartment."

"How long," Meg said.

"Couple of days," I said. "No more."

"I'm not staying cooped up in here with you two mugs for a couple of days," Fay said.

Hawk looked at her for a moment and said, "Shhh."

Fay stopped as she was about to speak.

Meg said, "We don't want any trouble. You guys want to fuck us?"

I said, "No. Take a rest for a couple of days."

Meg looked at me and her eyes widened. "You don't?"

Hawk said, "He speaking for himself. He in love."

"It's not natural," Meg said.

"It natural for him," Hawk said.

"Tell me about Leo," I said. "Does he come alone?"

Fay shook her head. "We got nothing to do with this, mister."

"Fay," I said, "you have everything to do with this. I am looking for a woman, and I am going to find her. I'll do anything I need to do, and that includes hurting a couple of innocent whores. Does Leo come alone?"

"No," Meg said. Fay didn't speak, her lips were pressed together. "He has Allie with him," Meg said. "Allie's his bodyguard."

Meg didn't look at Fay.

"Does Leo carry a piece?" I said.

Meg shook her head. "I don't know. I know Allie does. But I don't know about Leo."

"What time does he come?"

"Five," Meg said. "He comes exactly at five in the afternoon, every time."

"Does he collect other places first?"

Meg shrugged. Hawk said, "Probably, evening is heavy work time for the girls, he probably collects during the day."

"And stops here last," I said.

"With the day's receipts," Hawk said. "How nice."

There was a bath and two bedrooms down the short corridor. I sent the women down to one of the bedrooms. Hawk leaned in the doorway of the corridor to see that they stayed in the bedroom, and I called New York City Information and got the number for Rachel Wallace.

"She the writer that got kidnapped on you?" Hawk said. I was dialing 212. I nodded.

"Maybe she don't feel too helpful toward you," Hawk said.

The phone was ringing. "I got her back, didn't I?"

"That would help," Hawk said.

Rachel Wallace answered.

I said, "Spenser's the name, heterosexuality is my game."

Rachel Wallace said, "How good to know you haven't aged. How are you?"

"Bad," I said. "I need help."

"You need help?"

"Yes," I said, and told her.

"I can get there by evening," she said.

"No," I said, "thank you. There's nothing, right now, for you to do out here. What I need is research. I want to know everything I can know about Jerry Costigan and his kid."

"What's the kid's name?"

"Russell. I don't know whether Jerry is the old man's real name or short for Gerald or Jerome or whatever."

"It's all right," Rachel Wallace said. "I'll find it. It's a little after noon in New York. I'll go down to the public library, I should have something for you by suppertime. Can I call you?"

"Yes," I said, "call me here." I gave her the number. "Helping me is against the law," I said. "Probably makes you an accessory after."

"I know," she said. "I'll call you about nine tonight, your time."

"I'll be here," I said and hung up.

"She the lesbian," Hawk said. "I saw her on the tube once."

"Lesbian, feminist, gay-rights activist, probably opposes racism too," I said.

"Don't sound to me like a good American," Hawk said.

I got up and walked to the window and looked out at the Post Office Building across Mission.

"We got a couple of things to do after we roust Leo," I said. "We go see Dr. Hilliard and we visit Jerry Costigan."

"Who Dr. Hilliard?" Hawk said.

"A name on Susan's calendar. Probably a shrink."

"And where we find Jerry Costigan?"

"He must be in Mill River. I think Rachel Wallace will find his address. If she doesn't we'll just go down and ask."

"Be good to get back to old Mill River," Hawk said.

Chapter 8

THE PHONE BOOK TOLD ME THAT DR. DOROTHY HILLIARD had offices on Russian Hill, and the noon news told me that an "exhaustive manhunt" for me and Hawk had now spread throughout the Bay area.

"Exhaustive," Hawk said.

"No stone unturned," I said.

"Did you really kill that guy?" Meg said.

"Yes," Hawk said. "It was the best thing for him."

Fay was not talking.

For lunch we had peanut butter sandwiches and instant coffee. The peanut butter was Skippy. The bread was pale white.

"This is revolting," I said.

"We don't usually eat here," Meg said.

"I can see why," I said. I ate three sandwiches.

After lunch Hawk took a shower and then had a nap. I watched the women. At suppertime Meg said, "We got no more peanut butter."

For supper we had white toast and Kraft strawberry jam

and some white jug wine. The evening news rehashed most of what the noon and morning news had said. They still had me fifteen pounds too heavy. After the news we watched an animal program and then something called *Trauma Center.*

"Another day of this," Hawk said, "and I turn myself in to the Mill River cops."

At nine Rachel Wallace called.

"Jerry Costigan, his baptismal name, lives at something called The Keep in Mill River. The Keep is located off Costigan Drive, which in turn connects to Mill River Boulevard."

"I know where Mill River Boulevard is," I said.

"Good. Costigan inherited a small trucking firm from his father in 1948. It is the basis of what is now Transpan. They still do trucking, but have diversified into air freight, agriculture, hotels, television stations, and the sale of arms and munitions. Costigan occasionally dabbles in show business, investing in motion pictures, for instance. At one time he owned part of a record company and is currently involved through Russell in producing rock music videos. The company appears to be privately owned and controlled entirely by the Costigan family. Jerry is president and chairman. Russell is executive vice-president. Grace Costigan, Jerry's wife and Russell's mother, is listed as treasurer. They have offices in most cities."

"What do you know about them personally?"

"About Jerry, almost nothing. He's reclusive. He has contributed money to conservative and anticommunist organizations. He was investigated once by a House committee looking into labor racketeering. No conclusions were reached. He was linked to illegal arms dealing in the Middle East and Africa. No charges were ever brought. He is probably one of the three or four wealthiest men in the country.

He was born in 1923, and has been married to the same
woman since 1944. Russell was born in 1945. Attended
Berkeley but didn't graduate. During the Vietnam war he
was a naval air cadet but washed out of the training and was
discharged for a health disorder which none of my sources
were able to specify. Most of this is old newspaper clippings
and *Who's Who*–type entries. The discharge was honorable.
In 1970 he married a woman named Tyler Smithson. There
were two children, Heather, born 1971, and Jason, born
1972. I have no address. There is no record of a divorce.
Russell often represents his father in public. Transpan
maintains an office in Washington, D.C., and Russell
spends a fair amount of time there. He's not registered as a
lobbyist, but one of his principal duties for some years was
to influence government action on behalf of the family
business. Now that he is executive vice-president—it's a
new post, by the way, no one seems to have filled it before
him—he is less often in Washington. But he still gets there
regularly. The business keeps a suite at the L'Enfant Plaza.
Russell has been arrested several times for minor things.
Public drunkenness. Driving while impaired. Possession of
a Class D substance. He's been party to several altercations
arising, apparently, out of disputes in public places where
liquor is served. None of these arrests resulted in anything
but a quick trip downtown by one of the company lawyers,
and they didn't get much press coverage. Only an unusually
gifted researcher would have even found mention of these
things."

"But self-effacing," I said.

"Yes. That is about all I have. The only other thing is that
neither father nor son seems to have taken a vigorous public position on women's issues."

"Amazing," I said. "They sure seem like they'd be feminists."

"I can continue, in fact I will continue to dig into this. I'm a wonderful researcher. I'll get more. But more will take time. Is there anything specific you want me to look for?"

I said, "I also need the names and addresses of everyone connected with Costigan, Costigan Junior, and Transpan."

"Everyone is quite a large number," Rachel Wallace said.

"I'm looking for Susan," I said.

"Yes," Rachel Wallace said. "I'll be as complete as possible. There will be decisions necessary as to whom I research first and whom I put off. If I can't reach you I will have to make those decisions."

"You know what I'm after," I said. "Do what you think is best."

"And when you get what you're after," Rachel Wallace said, "when you find her. Then what?"

"We'll worry about that when I've found her. Right now finding her is all."

"That's how you're dealing with it," Rachel Wallace said. "It's a thing to be done. A task to be accomplished."

"Yes."

"And you won't think about anything but how to do it best."

"Yes."

"And you will try very hard not to feel anything at all."

"Yes."

"You're bound to feel things," Rachel Wallace said.

"Nobody's perfect," I said.

"Hold that thought," she said. "Call me when you can."

Chapter 9

FRIDAY THERE WAS NOTHING TO EAT. WE DRANK INSTANT COFfee and moved around each other in the apartment and stared out the window.

"It's not right," Meg said. "You can't starve us."

"You'll eat tonight," I said. "Seven more hours."

"I'm hungry," Meg said. "Let me go out and get something. I won't tell. I could go get us some sandwiches and stuff."

"No," I said. "Wait until tonight."

"Been a long time," Hawk said, "since I ate good."

"Me too," I said. "But I've been sleeping badly."

We stood at the window looking down on Mission Street. I watched the women. Not so chic down here. Overweight more often. Stretch pants that fit too tight. More of them carrying groceries and almost nobody with a shopping bag from Gump's. Young black women, elegant very often, no matter what they wore. And chicano girls with thick long hair. Women holding on to the arms of men as they walked. Tired women, alone.

"Hard doing nothing," Hawk said.

"Waiting is doing something," I said.

Hawk shrugged. "Hard waiting," he said. "Hard to not think while you're waiting."

"I'm thinking about how to find her," I said. "That's all."

Hawk said, "Umm."

The two women were watching television. A game show hooted and shrieked behind us.

"Sartre claimed that hell is other people," I said.

"He never saw no TV game show," Hawk said.

People went in and out of a pizza shop across the street. Most bought it by the slice and came out and ate it as they walked on. I envied them.

"Leo as bad as the two babes say he is," Hawk said softly, "might be better to kill him."

"He'll take it out on them?"

"Maybe," Hawk said. "Can you do it?"

"Have to," I said.

We looked out the window some more.

"You're fucked," Hawk said. "You got too many rules. Against the rules to blow Leo away cold-blooded like. And against the rules to let him burn those whores." He smiled happily.

"We exploited those whores," I said.

"So we got to fan Leo," Hawk said.

"We kill him," I said, "we'll have to kill the bodyguard. That leaves the women with two stiffs to explain."

"If they stay," Hawk said.

I turned and said to the two women, "You own this place or rent?"

Meg said, "We rent from Leo."

Hawk laughed. "Old Leo got it every way."

"You sign a lease?" I said.

Fay laughed without any hint of amusement. Meg shook her head.

"Slick," I said to Hawk. "Leo owns property, puts his whores in it, they pay him rent, use it for commerce, and split their earnings. Leo gets a nice double dip."

"Also means if these babes leave no one know they were here," Hawk said.

"Yes. They're not profitable, or whatever, he can move them out, move in two more."

Fay was watching us as we talked.

"Why do you want to know that stuff," Fay said. It was the first thing she'd said since yesterday.

"Better to know than not to know," I said.

"You're thinking of killing us," Fay said.

"Oh my God," Meg said and turned toward Fay, forsaking the game show.

"You want to know if we can be traced. You want to know who knows we're here."

"How do you think Leo will react to getting tossed in this apartment?" I said.

"We won't ever tell anyone," Meg said. She was leaning forward with her hands squeezed together in her lap. "Honest to God we won't."

Fay reached over and touched Meg's clenched hands. "What do you mean," she said.

She rested her hand on the double clenched fist in Meg's lap. She patted it slightly.

"Will Leo blame you?" I said.

"Oh holy God," Meg said. She began to rock slightly, her hands still clenched. Fay continued to pat.

"I hadn't thought of that," Fay said. She was quiet while she thought about it. Meg slipped her hands from under Fay's comforting pat and pressed them against her mouth.

"Jesus," she said in a choked voice. "Jesus, Jesus, Jesus."

"He might think we were in on it," Fay said. "He'll pretty sure know that we told you about the collection. And getting hassled in front of two of his girls will . . . He'll take it out on us even if he doesn't blame us."

"If you have to get out of here," I said, "you got someplace to go?"

Fay looked at me without speaking for maybe thirty seconds. Then she said, "Neither one of us is Little Red Riding Hood."

"Okay," I said. "Why don't you pack up and be ready to leave."

Meg had stopped murmuring *Jesus.* Her clasped hands were still pressed against her mouth. But she had stopped rocking and she looked up at Hawk and me over the tops of her hands. Then she turned and looked at Fay.

Fay smiled at her very slightly. "Come on," Fay said. "We'll pack."

The two women went back down the corridor to the bedroom. Hawk was still looking out the window. As he stared down at Mission Street he was singing softly, "Goodbye, Leo, we hate to see you go."

"It's really something about you black guys," I said. "You got so much soul."

Hawk turned from the window and grinned. "Born to sing, honey," he said. "Born to boogie."

Chapter 10

LEO CAME KNOCKING AT THE DOOR PROMPTLY AT FIVE. HAWK and I stood out of sight from the front door and Fay let them in.

"Hello, Leo," she said. "Allie, come on in."

A soft voice murmured so that it was barely audible. "You girls have a good week?"

The door closed and the two men came into view. Hawk and I pointed guns at them. Leo looked at us, and back at Fay. He was a large man with neat graying hair. He wore horn-rimmed glasses and a full Brooks Brothers costume. Striped shirt, knit tie, Harris tweed jacket, gray flannel trousers, wing-tipped Scotch brogues. Behind him Allie looked like he'd grown up watching Victor Mature movies. He was wavy-haired and heavy-lidded and wore a dark shirt with a white tie. The collar of his leather jacket was turned up and a cigarette smoked in the corner of his mouth. Behind me I heard Hawk snort.

Leo looked at us, and back at Fay. Meg stood against the far wall by the kitchen.

"You lousy bitch. You set me up," Leo said in his mumbly voice. He was carrying a briefcase. Not the neat square attaché kind, but a big scuffed satchely one.

I said to the women, "Go get your luggage."

Meg started to speak and Fay took her arm and said, "Shhh," and they went back down the hall.

Leo looked at me. There was sweat on his upper lip. His eyes were moist and bright.

"I'm going to fry their ass," he said.

Hawk said, "No point talking."

"No," I said. I bit my back teeth hard together and shot Leo. He went back a couple of feet and fell.

Allie had his hand under his jacket when Hawk shot him. Allie fell on top of Leo, his legs sprawled toward the kitchen. I picked up the briefcase and took it to the counter and opened it. The smell of the shooting was strong in the room and the sound of it seemed to ring in the silence. I opened the briefcase. It was full of money. Hawk had taken Leo's wallet out and Allie's and was going through them.

"Leo appear to have about six different credit cards in six different names," Hawk said. "That seem dishonest to me."

Fay and Meg edged back down the hall and looked carefully out into the living room.

"I think you'll like all this better," I said, "if you don't look at the bodies."

Meg turned back at once, but Fay looked carefully past me at the two corpses. Her face had no expression. Then she looked at me.

"What about us," she said.

I took four hundred dollars from the briefcase and gave it to her. "Two days' pay," I said.

"And we can go?"

"Yes."

"You shot him for us," she said. "He'd have blamed us."

There was too much money in the briefcase to count quickly.

"Toss what you got in here," I said, "and let's roll."

Hawk put credit cards and licenses and Allie's gun and the money from the two wallets in the briefcase and I closed it.

"Got some car keys," Hawk said. "Hope he ain't driving something look like a carnival ride."

"With those clothes," I said, "no chance. Probably a BMW."

Fay was still standing in the hallway. Meg had come down the hall behind her carrying two suitcases. Fay was watching me.

"You didn't have to burn them," Fay said. "Why'd you burn them?"

"Seemed like a good idea," I said.

"Two guys you didn't even know, for two whores you didn't even know."

"Know you better than we know Leo," Hawk said.

"Good-bye," I said. "Sorry for the trouble."

Meg said, "Good-bye."

Fay simply looked after us as we went out the door and down the steps to the street.

A silver gray Volvo sedan was parked at the curb.

"You pretty close," Hawk said. "A preppy pimp. Can't count on nothing out here." He got in the driver's side. I put the briefcase on the backseat and got in beside him and we rolled out onto Mission Street.

"First we eat," Hawk said. "Then what?"

"Mill River," I said. "I want to take a gander at Jerry Costigan."

"You like buffalo stew?" Hawk said.

"Certainly. And Cleveland stew and Detroit stew . . ."

"No. Buffalo meat. There a place up on Van Ness serve buffalo stew, we slip in, eat some, slip out, and head for Mill River."

"And if the cops show up," I said, "we can circle the wagons."

We locked the briefcase in the trunk of the Volvo and went into Tommy's Joynt and ate buffalo stew. Buffalo stew tastes very much like beef stew. But there's nothing wrong with beef stew. We each had a large bowl and sourdough rolls and a side of coleslaw and three bottles of Anchor Steam Beer. No cops came. No sirens blew. Warner Anderson and Tom Tully didn't come in and put the arm on us. We finished our meal and went outside and got in Leo's Volvo and headed south again toward Mill River.

Ten minutes out of the city I made Hawk stop the car and I threw up on the side of the road.

When I got back in the car Hawk said, "You shot Leo to protect those whores."

I nodded.

"Had to be done," Hawk said.

"I know."

"You'll feel better in a while," Hawk said.

"Better than Leo," I said.

Chapter 11

WHILE HAWK DROVE I CANVASSED THE BRIEFCASE. ALLIE'S gun was a Colt .45 automatic with a full clip. That gave us four guns, but no spare ammunition. And each gun took a different load. If this took long we'd have to reorganize the arsenal. I kept my .25, put the .45 and the police .38 with one round spent into the briefcase. Then I counted the money. We were back on 101 south of the airport when I finished.

"Eleven thousand, five hundred and seventy-eight dollars," I said.

"Eight bucks?" Hawk said. "Who pays a whore eight bucks? 'Give you round-the-world for thirty-eight big ones, honey.' "

"The pocket money from Allie's wallet, probably," I said.

"He look like a guy carries eight bucks," Hawk said. I put the money back in the briefcase. Then I looked at the credit cards and licenses. There were three American Express cards, a Visa, two MasterCards, all in different names. There were licenses to match each name and a picture of Leo on each.

"You get some horn-rimmed glasses," Hawk said, "and shave off that five-day growth you might get by using those cards and licenses. You preppy like Leo."

"I'll leave the beard," I said. "They'll think I've grown a beard since the picture and it will cover up the fact that I have a strong manly jaw and Leo's is weak and unassertive."

I put the credit cards back in the briefcase.

"Remember where Mill River Boulevard is?" I said.

"Un huh."

"Jerry Costigan lives off it on something called Costigan Drive in something called The Keep."

"The Keep?" Hawk said.

"The Keep."

"The more money you honkies get," Hawk said, "the sillier you get."

"Wait a minute," I said. "Didn't you grow up in a place called The Ghetto?"

"Shit," Hawk said. "You got me."

"See, you intolerant bastard."

Hawk drove quietly for a moment and then he began to laugh. "Maybe I move to Beverly Farms," Hawk said, "buy a big house call it The Ghetto." He made *ghetto* a two-word phrase.

"The Wasps would turn lime green," I said.

"Match their pants," Hawk said.

The sun was beginning to set as we pulled off Route 101 and the slant of its decline hit the rearview mirror and Hawk had to tilt his head to keep from being blinded. We went the wrong way on Mill River Boulevard on our first try and had to U-turn and head back before we spotted Costigan Drive. Hawk pulled over to the side of the road and we sat with the motor idling and looked.

There was a redwood sign that said PRIVATE DRIVE, in gold lettering. The road curved up past it into a canyon. There were no mailboxes, no evidence that anyone else lived up the road. The hill into which the canyon cut was wooded and quiet. Not even birdsong broke the silence.

"Let's walk in," I said.

"Might be far," Hawk said.

"We got time to be careful," I said.

Hawk nodded. He got out and opened the trunk and took out the jack handle. I stuck the .25 in my hip pocket. We began to walk up the road. The butt of the big .44 stuck out of Hawk's side pocket. The weight of the guns tended to tug at our pants. They'd removed our belts at Mill River PD.

"Next stop," I said softly to Hawk across the narrow road, "we gotta get belts."

"Rescuing maidens suck if your trousers fall down," Hawk said.

"Didn't Sir Gawain say that?"

Hawk raised his hand and we froze. There was no one in sight but around the next bend of the road we could hear a radio playing: Fats Domino singing "Blueberry Hill."

"A golden oldie," Hawk murmured.

We stepped into the woods and slipped through the woods toward the sound of the music.

The music came from a gatehouse, on the left side of an ornate wrought-iron gate from which extended on either side a ten-foot fieldstone wall with razor wire swirled along the top. Beyond the gate the road curved up through some dandy-looking green lawn and out of sight again. Hawk squatted on his heels beside me. We listened to a disc jockey make a cash call to someone in Menlo Park. Through the open door of the gatehouse I could see the head of a man leaning back with his hands clasped as if he was in a swivel chair with his feet up.

"Name the amount and it's yours," the disc jockey said, his voice electric with excitement.

"I only see one," I said to Hawk.

Hawk said, "Hard to be sure, though."

"Ohhh, I'm sorry," the disc jockey said, his voice trembling at the lip of despair. "But keep on listening, will ya. You never know, we may call you back."

"Even if there's only one, he's inside and we're outside. We try to bust in he'll trip an alarm."

The radio played Lennie Welsh singing "Since I Fell for You."

Hawk and I stayed still and watched. No one came in. No one went out. The head in the door of the guardhouse moved out of sight. Some insects made a small hum in the alder and scrub cedar around us. On the radio there was a commercial for a restaurant with a famous salad bar. Then Elvis Presley sang "Love Me Tender."

"How come everybody like him," Hawk said.

"He was white," I said.

The guard appeared at the door of the gatehouse. He was wearing a straw cowboy hat, and a white shirt and chinos and cowboy boots. He had a handgun in a holster on his right hip. He looked at his watch, surveyed the road and went back inside the guardhouse.

"We need to get him out," Hawk said. "But we don't want to do it with a big ruckus 'cause we only want him."

"The tar baby," I said.

"You speaking to me," Hawk said.

"You ever read Uncle Remus?" I said.

"You gotta be shitting," Hawk said.

"Br'er Rabbit and the tar baby," I said. " 'Tar baby sit and don't say nuffin.' "

Hawk was quiet, watching the guardhouse.

"I'm going to go out and sit in the road and wait for him to come out and see what the hell I'm doing."

I took the .25 out of my pocket and palmed it. Then I moved back through the woods to the road out of sight of the gate. I walked slowly up the road directly toward the gate, and when I was about ten feet from it I sat down in the road and folded my hands in my lap with the gun out of sight and stared at the gate.

The guard came out of the guardhouse and looked at me through the gate.

"What the hell are you doing," he said.

He was a stocky man with a drooping mustache and a thick neck. When I didn't answer he looked at me carefully. I didn't move. I kept my eyes focused on the gate at about belt level.

"You hear me?" he said. "What are you doing out there?"

Tar baby sit and don't say nuffin.

"Listen, Jack, this is private property. You're on a private road. You understand? You're trespassing. You keep sitting there and you're subject to arrest."

Nuffin.

The guard took his hat off, and ran his hand over his nearly bald head. He put the hat back on and tilted it forward over his forehead. He pursed his lips and put one hand on his gunbelt and the other hand on the gate and looked at me.

"Español?" he said. Behind him the radio aired a commercial for a law firm that specialized in accident claims. "Vamoose," the guard said.

I was sitting with my legs folded like Indians sit in the movies, and I was developing a cramp. I didn't move. From the guard shack the radio played. It was the Big Bopper. "Chantilly lace, and a pretty face . . ." The guard took a big breath. "Shit," he said, and opened the gate. As he walked toward me he took a leather sap from his right-hand hip pocket.

When he got to me he said, "Okay, pal, last chance. Either you get on your feet and haul ass out of here, or I'll put a knot on your head while you sit."

I unfolded my hands and pointed the .25 straight up at him as he bent over me. "How dee doo, Br'er Bear," I said.

The guard's eyes widened and the rest of his expression went blank. He remained half bent over.

I said, "Put the sap back in your pocket, and straighten up and I'll get up and you and I will walk to the side of the road, just like I'm doing it because you told me to." I thumbed the hammer back on the automatic. "Anything goes wrong I'll shoot you in the head."

The guard did what I told him to. I kept the gun near my body and the guard between me and the gate in case someone came down and saw us. At the edge of the road I said, "Step ahead of me into the woods." Five feet into the woods Hawk was leaning against a tree. When we reached him he hit the guard across the back of the head with the jack handle. The guard grunted once and fell forward. He lay still except for his right leg, which twitched slightly.

"Br'er tire iron," Hawk said.

Chapter 12

HAWK AND I WALKED THROUGH THE OPEN GATE AND CLOSED IT behind us. The radio was playing something I'd never heard by a group I didn't recognize. In the guard shack was a desk, a swivel chair, a phone, what appeared to be a remote electronic opener for the gate.

I opened the top drawer of the desk.

"Nice to find some ammo," I said. "Too many pieces, too few bullets."

There was no ammo in the desk. I put the guard's gun in and closed the drawer.

Hawk had left the tire iron in the woods. The loop of the guard's blackjack hung from his left hip pocket. The .44 stuck out of his right-hand side pocket.

The sun was down and it was getting dark as we walked up Jerry Costigan's curving drive with his immaculate green lawn spreading silently out on either side. At the next curve there was a stand of evergreens, and past them, though still a hundred yards away, was the house. It was brightly lit with concealed spotlights.

If the folks who built Disneyland had been asked to design a home for a reclusive and unsavory billionaire, they would have built Jerry Costigan's house. Hawk and I stood in the carefully tended stand of trees and stared. The trees we stood in were obviously planned serendipity. Here and there across the infinite lawn were other groves. The house itself looked, more than anything else, like an English country house. Family descended from the Normans. There was an enormous terrace skirting the tall square fieldstone house with a mansard roof. At each corner there were small round towers with tall narrow windows in them. Good for pouring hot oil on Vikings. The drive curved around out of sight behind the house.

"Be dark in another ten, fifteen minutes," Hawk said.

I nodded. We stood quietly in the serendipitous trees. Lights were on in the house and the windows glowed with a slightly yellower warm than the white gleam that the spotlights created. Two men walked easily around on the apron terrace, pausing to talk then moving on, making a slow circle of the house. Even a hundred yards away I could smell the cigarette smoke on the soft evening air. At the two visible corners of the house television cameras were mounted under the eaves. They moved slowly in an arc, panning left and right.

"Cameras," Hawk said.

"I see them."

"Security like this," Hawk said, "they going to find the gate guard pretty quick."

"I know," I said. "I'm surprised they don't have both surveillance systems tied together."

"If they had they be shooting at us now," Hawk said.

"Dumb," I said. "Dumb to put together this kind of

security and allow it to be breached by taking out one man."

"Good to know they dumb," Hawk said.

A black Ford Bronco with a whip antenna on the rear and a 4 X 4 lettered in white on the side appeared from behind the house and drove down toward the gate. Two men sat in the front.

"They're getting smarter," I said.

I looked at the house. Nothing had changed. I looked back at the Bronco, its taillights red in the new darkness.

"Time to move," Hawk said.

"Let's get the truck," I said.

We left the trees and ran back down the curving drive after the Bronco. Hawk had taken the .44 from his pocket and held it in his left hand as he ran. Our feet, in running shoes, made very little sound on the driveway. Ahead the Bronco was parked by the guard shack, its motor idling, its doors ajar, its interior lights on. In the headlights, one man was examining the gate. The guardhouse radio made no sound.

"Take him," I said to Hawk. "I'll take the guardhouse."

The man in the guardhouse stood with his back to the door looking down at the log sheet on the desk. He had his hands flat-palmed on the desk and his weight was forward on them. He heard me behind him barely in time to stiffen and not in time to straighten up. I pressed the muzzle of the .25 into his neck under his earlobe and just behind his jaw hinge.

"Not a sound," I said.

He stayed as he was. This guard was tall and fleshy. He wore a short-sleeved white shirt and a handgun in a clip-on holster pressed against the roll of fat that pressed over his belt. Another .357. Costigan issue. I unclipped the gun, holster and all, from his belt and stuck it in my hip pocket. Hawk came into the guardhouse. He was smiling.

"Man had a world-class belt," he said. I glanced down. Hawk was wearing it. It was buckled up tight and too long for him. The end stuck out from the buckle like an anteater's tongue. The .44 was stuck in the belt in front. The blackjack strap still hung from his back pocket but now it was in the right-hand pocket.

"Put your hands back on the desk," I said to the guard, "and back away and spread your feet apart."

I patted him down and came up only with a pocket knife. A good one, a buck knife with a two-and-a-half-inch blade. I gave the knife to Hawk and he cut off the loose end of the belt. He closed it, handed it back, and I put it in my pocket.

"Neatness is important," I said.

Hawk reached over and took hold of the back of the guard's shirt collar and pulled him upright and put his face close to the guard's.

"Let's talk about the security here," he said. "Aside from how it sucks."

"I'm not talking about shit," the guard said. He had a haircut with no sideburns, and a lot of skin showing above the ears.

I hit him with my right forearm, bringing it up along his jaw. He would have fallen but Hawk held him up.

"Tell me about security," I said.

He started to shake his head and I hit him again with my forearm. He almost went limp and I could see the muscles bunch slightly in Hawk's neck as he increased the force to keep the guard upright.

"Last chance," I said. "If you don't tell me this time, I'll kill you and find out for myself."

"Twenny-five men," the guard mumbled. "Three shifts

of six on the grounds and seven for Mr. Costigan when he travels."

"What's the surveillance setup?"

Hawk still held the back of his shirt, but the guard was standing now. Hawk wasn't holding him up.

"Cameras on the perimeter. Monitors in here. Cameras on each corner of the house, monitors in the security room."

"What brought you down here?"

"Gate guard is supposed to call in every fifteen minutes."

"Somebody waiting to hear from you?"

The guard shook his head. "I'm in charge of the shift."

I put the .25 hard against the tip of his nose. "There's the gate guard, you two, and the two guys walking around the house. That makes five. You said there's six on a shift."

Hawk said, "Tell me 'fore you shoot. I don't want his brains all over me."

"Awright," the guard said, "awright. Bob's in the security room. We're supposed to report in."

"Do it," I said. "Call in and say you caught two prowlers and you're bringing them up to security. Tell him your partner is going to stay with the gate guard for a while, make sure that's all there was."

I moved the gun from his nose and Hawk let go of his collar. There was a line of sweat on his upper lip, and his face was pale except for a reddish streak along his right jawline where I'd hit him. He picked up the phone and punched out two numbers with the same hand that held the receiver. Then he put the receiver to his ear.

"Hello, Bob. It's Rocky. Yeah, it's all right. We got two prowlers. Slade's going to stay here with Mickey for a while. Make sure. I'll bring the two prowlers up. . . . Yeah. Be up in a minute. . . . Okay. Bye."

He hung up. Hawk said, "Rocky?"

I took Rocky's gun off my hip and emptied it, and put it back in its holster and clipped it back onto his belt. I put the shells on the desk. Hawk pulled his shirt out and let the shirttails hang over the .44, stuck in his belt. We went out of the guard shack and walked to the Bronco. Rocky's partner lay at the edge of the guardhouse in the shadows, his neck turned at an odd angle. He wasn't moving, and wasn't going to. There was a bench seat in the front of the Bronco, and we sat three across, Hawk and I slouching like cowed felons, Rocky driving.

"How long you figure it take us to pick off the whole twenty-five?" Hawk said.

"More time than we got," I said. "But not much. Were you guys in charge of security at Pearl Harbor?"

Rocky swung the Bronco around the house and pulled to a stop in front of the brass-studded oak door on the basement level. There were two other identical black Broncos parked in the wide turnaround, and a bright green light gleamed over the entrance.

I palmed the little .25 again.

"You take each of us by the arm," I said to Rocky, "and walk between us into the security office. You let go of either one and I'll kill you. You got that."

"Yeah."

"Let's go." I reached over and took the keys from the ignition. We got out of the car and Rocky came around and took each of us by the arm, grasping firmly just above the elbow. At the door we turned sideways and Hawk went in first, and then Rocky and then me, with Rocky holding on to each arm for dear life. A portly red-haired man wearing a western-style gun belt with a pearl-handled revolver in the holster was sitting on a high stool looking at four television monitors in a bank along the far wall. Below the monitors was a two-way radio rig, and three telephones.

Without taking his eyes off the monitors he said, "Sit them over there. Do I need to talk with them before we call Mill River PD?"

Hawk took the sap out of his pocket and hit Rocky at the base of the skull with it. Rocky's legs went limp and folded beneath him and he fell the way a building implodes from a wrecker's blast. Bob heard the thud and turned from the monitors, his hand going toward the pearl-handled gun on his hip. He stopped half turned and stared at the small unwinking eye of the .25 an inch from him. Hawk stepped across Rocky's prone position and sapped Bob. Bob lurched forward off the stool and took a staggering step and Hawk hit him again and he pitched forward, toward the monitor panels. I caught him before he hit them and guided him onto the floor.

"Twice?" I said.

"It's an unfamiliar blackjack," Hawk said. "Ain't got the feel quite right."

I looked at the monitors. There was nothing on them except the still lawn and the two guards slowly making their intersecting circles of the house, appearing on one screen then another as they moved. I looked around the security room. There were some canvas-backed director's chairs and a Formica-topped table with a Mr. Coffee machine on it and some mugs lined up on a shelf beyond it. There were newspapers scattered around and a cardboard box that donuts had come in. On the wall opposite the entrance there were two doors. The first was locked. The second opened into a full bath. On Bob's belt was a set of keys hanging from a belt loop by one of those slip-catch hooks with a ring on it. Hawk was squatting beside Bob looking at Bob's gun.

"Ruger .357 Max, single-action," Hawk said. "Man must be expecting a rhinoceros to charge in here. Got the grip customized, too."

"Keys," I said.

Hawk unsnapped them and tossed them to me.

"Better kill them," Hawk said. "You got that knife. Better cut their throats. Leaving people around like leaving a bomb ticking," Hawk said.

"We killed the pimp and his gunny."

"He'd have killed the two whores," Hawk said. "Like you said, we got them into it. We got them out."

I shrugged.

"These dudes will kill us, if they can," Hawk said.

"If they can," I said.

"If they do what happens to Susan?" Hawk said.

I shook my head and started sorting through the keys to open the second door.

"You spent your life in a mean business, babe, trying not to be mean. And so far you got away with it mostly. But there's stuff on the line that never been on the line before."

I found the right key for the last door.

"I know," I said.

"Gimme the knife," Hawk said.

"No." I turned from the door. "Letting you do it is like doing it, only worse. It's doing it and pretending I didn't."

"We after Susan," Hawk said. "That makes this your show. But I ain't along on this just 'cause I care about you."

There was no sound in the room except a faint hum from the TV monitors that only underscored the silence.

"I know," I said. "I know that. It's the way I know you're human."

"She make both of us human, babe," Hawk said. "I don't want to lose her much more than you do."

I unlocked the door. Beyond it there were stairs.

"Let's go up there," I said. "See if Costigan can help us find her."

Chapter 13

WE FOUND JERRY COSTIGAN SITTING IN A BLACK LEATHER Barcalounger by his fireplace reading a thick book by Karl Von Clausewitz. The fireplace was burning low and looked just right for roasting an ox. The room was air-conditioned. Above the fireplace were crossed broadswords and below them a family crest with lions rampant and all of that. There was a Latin inscription and the name COSTIGAN on a scroll across the bottom. The walls rose, punctuated with marble buttresses, into the darkness. The vaulted ceiling was lost in darkness. Spaced along the front wall between the leaded-glass windows that rose nearly as high as the ceiling were full-size suits of armor. On a table beside the Barcalounger was a decanter of what looked like port, a wedge of Stilton cheese and some fruit, and a silver server.

I said, "You rang, sir?"

Costigan looked at Hawk and me standing in his living room and didn't blink. Instead he picked up a leather bookmark from the table, put it in his book, and put the book on the table and said, "Well?"

I said, "I want to know where Susan Silverman is."

Costigan picked up a glass of port and sipped it. "So what?" he said.

"She is with your son," I said. "I want you to tell me where they are."

Costigan sipped a little more port.

"What will you do if you know where they are?" he said.

"Find her, take her away."

"If you can," Costigan said.

"We've gotten this far," I said.

"So I notice. I told my security people that we were vulnerable until we unified the two security systems."

"Probably installed the perimeter ones first," I said. "And when you added the house stuff you didn't think to overlap them."

"We are in the process," Costigan said.

"Where's Susan?" I said.

"Is this the gentleman who hit my son recently and was jailed for it?"

Hawk moved close to Costigan and stuck the muzzle of the big .44 against Costigan's neck at the base of the skull.

"He stalling," Hawk said. "He waiting for help."

I nodded and moved closer to Costigan. "You hit a button some way," I said.

"It's under the book, on the table," Costigan said. "If anything is placed on that spot the alarm goes off."

At the far end of the room two men appeared with Uzi submachine guns. They came into the room and stepped to either side of the door. The room was so big I wasn't sure the Uzis had the range. Four more men came in behind the first two and fanned out along the wall. All had revolvers.

"Drop the weapons," I said, "or we will blow Costigan's head off at the neck."

"No," Costigan said.

The bodyguards froze, guns leveled.

"You kill me and you'll lose the girl for sure. You'll be dead and, believe me, my son will take it out on her."

"Won't do nothing for you," Hawk murmured.

"What would Clausewitz call this," I said.

"A stalemate," Costigan said. He held his head steady against the press of Hawk's gun. "They can't shoot, because you have me. But you can't shoot because they have you."

"Is she here?" I said.

"No," Costigan said.

"We have to know," I said.

Costigan shrugged. No one else moved.

"On your feet," I said. Hawk took hold of Costigan's collar with his left hand and pulled him up out of the seat, rising behind him as he did with the muzzle of the .44 pressed up under Costigan's chin. If it is possible to look contained while you're being dragged upright with a gun pressed under your chin, Costigan did it.

"Room by room," I said. "Starting at the top." Hawk and I stood pressed close to Costigan, Hawk holding him with the gun at his chin. The six bodyguards fanned slowly around us as we moved toward the door. Three in front, the other three in back. I watched the back three. We moved, a kind of traveling ambush, into the front hall and slowly up the vast winding stairway that went two stories to the top floor.

"They shoot *Gone With the Wind* here?" Hawk said as we went up a slow step at a time.

"Probably not," I said. "Why? You still hot for Butterfly McQueen?"

"It was her, or Aunt Jemima," Hawk said. "You given any thought to how we get Susan out of here, if she here?"

"One thing at a time," I said. "First we see if she's here."

"Orderly," Hawk said.

Except for us all was silence. The three bodyguards in front of us backed up the steps a stair at a time, one Uzi and two handguns. Behind us the other three kept the circle closed with the same firepower. I was getting sick of looking at .357 magnums.

On the third floor we began to move in our peculiar minuet from room to room, turning on the lights in each. Several of the rooms were clearly housing for the bodyguards. Others were apparently for show, full of elegant furniture, gleaming with lemon oil and tree wax and devoid of human sign. As we moved slowly from room to room sweat began to form on Costigan's forehead. I understood it. There was sweat on mine, too. The strain of moving always with infinite care, always in a circle of threat, made the world beyond that circle seem insubstantial. The world within was intensely immediate.

Hawk was humming softly to himself, "Harlem Nocturne," as we moved from door to door.

"He appears to be enjoying this," Costigan said, his speech constricted slightly by the pressure of Hawk's gun.

"Paradigm of the black experience," I said.

The circle of guards moved in perfect concert to our movement. Hawk had Costigan's collar and I held on to his belt in front, keeping my back to him, facing out toward the guards. The guy with the Uzi was a thin man with a long neck and a big Adam's apple. The Adam's apple kept bobbing up and down as he swallowed. He swallowed a lot. The guard next to him had a thick blond mustache; his blond hair was razor cut and blow-dried and sprayed so firmly into place that he looked like he was wearing a helmet. He looked like he was thinking of other things. Surfboards,

maybe, or his new Neil Diamond album. The third guard
was middle-aged and gray-haired and medium-sized. He
didn't look nervous or distracted or eager or anything. He
looked like he might hum along with Hawk soon.

Of the three I could see, the blond beachboy was the
weak link. The guy with the Uzi and the Adam's apple was
the most likely to shoot when he shouldn't. Gray Hair was
the one who'd be the hardest. The other three were Hawk's
problem. I couldn't see them without looking away from
my three, so I didn't think about them.

There was no one in any room on the third floor. We
moved slowly back down the stairs to the second floor and
began the careful, agonizing, complicated business all over
again. Nine of us, moving in limited space without ever
losing sight of one another. Each door we opened was
crucial. Was there a lady in there? Or a tiger? I could feel
my shirt getting wetter and clinging to my back. Each door
we opened and closed off brought the conclusion closer
and none of us had a plan for the conclusion. Even though
the conclusion might be eternal. At the bottom of the stairs
we had to turn a sharp left. My three guards backed slowly
around the corner, I held on to Costigan's belt and slid
around after them.

"Dosey doe," I said.

Hawk had changed tunes, and mode of presentation. He
was whistling softly through his teeth now, "Autumn Sere-
nade."

"You're going to go through every room?" Costigan
said. His voice sounded strained, as if his throat had narrowed.

"Yes," I said.

"And when you're finished, and you haven't found her,"
he said. "What then?"

"We'll see," I said.

We went into a suite of rooms. They must have been the son's quarters. If The Sharper Image catalogue sold fully furnished suites for young men they would look like this.

The furniture was mostly of clear plastic, formed in one-piece curved shapes. A huge globe stood on a black lacquer coffee table. The bed had a canopy. There was a whole wall of stereo, television, tape, radio components in gleaming silver, with enormous speakers. In a living room off the bedroom was a glass and lacquer bar, fully stocked, and a small kitchen. The bathroom included a sauna and steam, there was a Jacuzzi in the tub. All of the appliances and tile were in emerald green with gold accent touches. There were fireplaces in bedroom and living room and over each hung a silver-inlaid shotgun. On the mantel in the bedroom was a picture of Susan and a man. The picture appeared to have been snapped at a party.

"Russell," Hawk said.

Susan's head was back and her mouth was wide open with laughter. Russell's head was tipped toward her and he seemed to be exhaling cigarette smoke, a wisp of which traced off to the edge of the picture. He was surprisingly ordinary-looking for a man who'd attracted Susan. He looked young, but his hair was already receding, and there was a quality of undefinedness to his face.

Russell had a lot of clothes, three walk-in closets full, hung carelessly. Some had fallen from hangers and were crumpled on the floor. His shoes were in a pile on the floor of the closet.

"Hard to get good help these days," I said, looking at the jumble of shoes and clothes on the bottom of one of the bedroom closets.

We moved on.

There was nothing else that mattered on the second floor. We'd been looking for nearly an hour. If Hawk felt the strain of holding a .44 gun up under Costigan's chin for that long he didn't show it. My left hand felt cramped from holding Costigan's belt.

The first floor had, besides Costigan's enormous living room, an enormous dining room, an enormous kitchen, a pantry, and a two-bedroom suite in a wing off the back. One bedroom was Costigan's. It was very ordinary. Efficient and comfortable, but no more personal than the best room in a Ramada Renaissance Hotel. Off the bedroom was a sitting room that was obviously used as an office. It too was sparse. There was a phone on an oak table that was used as a desk. A swivel chair, an oak file cabinet, a Xerox machine, and a tape recorder. We went back into the hall.

"My wife is in bed through the door on your right," Costigan said.

"No help for it," I said. "Got to look."

"We three will go in," Costigan said. "The rest will wait outside. Gary, you watch us through the door."

Gray Hair nodded. The others moved down the hall a few steps.

We opened the door and went in. Mrs. Costigan was in bed watching television. She had her gray hair up in rollers and some night cream on her face and looked fifteen years older than her husband. Her bulk under the satin spread was considerable.

She said, "Jerry—Jesus, Mary and Joseph . . ."

Costigan raised one hand like a traffic cop. "Just be still, Grace," he said. "This isn't as bad as it looks."

"You'll have to join us, Mrs. Costigan," I said.

"Why you want me to do that?" she said in a little-girl voice. "I'm in my pajamas."

"Get a robe," I said.

Mrs. Costigan said, "Don't look."

Hawk said, "Hunh," softly under his breath.

Mrs. Costigan dragged the spread off the bed and held it around her as she went to the closet. She managed somehow to get an aqua velour robe around her fat body before she dropped the spread. No one saw anything. Everyone was relieved.

Mrs. Costigan's room was pink with gray woodwork and floor-length pink drapes. The carpet was gray and the furniture was white. There were pink satin sheets on the bed. A huge color television with a white cabinet stood at the far wall opposite the bed. Mrs. Costigan was watching *Dallas*. There was a sitting room off her bedroom as well, with French doors that opened onto a patio. The room was gray with pink woodwork and gray drapes and a pink carpet. One wall was all glass, and before it a large makeup table sat with lighting arranged around the mirror wall and adjustable spotlighting on the table.

No one else was in the rooms and they were the last rooms. Costigan, Hawk, and I stood touching closely in the center of the dressing room. Mrs. Costigan hovered uncertainly near, and Gary watched quietly from the doorway.

"What now," Costigan said.

"Now we talk and you tell us where she is," I said.

"Where who is?" Mrs. Costigan said.

"Susan Silverman."

Costigan said, "Grace," and Mrs. Costigan said, "At the lodge," and their voices overlapped. Mrs. Costigan heard her husband and looked at him, startled.

"If that's all they want, let them have her," she said. "Would you protect her instead of me?"

Costigan said, "Grace, be quiet." He said it with the kind

of force you expect to hear in a man who built a small business into an empire.

"Tell me about the lodge," I said.

Mrs. Costigan looked uncertain. She shook her head. I raised the .25 and aimed it carefully at her. Gary in the door crouched a little and moved his gun toward me.

"Tell me about the lodge or I'll shoot you," I said.

Costigan said, "Gary, bring the rest in. If he shoots kill him even if I die too."

Gary made a waving gesture with his left hand, behind him, and the other guards moved into the bedroom. The nervous guy with the Uzi moved up beside Gary in the doorway.

"Where's the lodge," I said.

Mrs. Costigan said, "Jerry, make him stop."

"You pull that trigger," Costigan said, "and everything stops here. All of us are gone and your girl friend's on her own."

I looked at Hawk.

He said, "This is as good as it's going to get."

I nodded. And jumped for Mrs. Costigan.

Holding Costigan still by the collar, Hawk dropped his right hand, gun and all, and jammed it from behind into Costigan's crotch and heaved him at the doorway where Gary and the Uzi stood. I spun Mrs. Costigan toward me and shoved her in the same direction. Gary, Costigan, Mrs. Costigan, and the Uzi all collided and tangled in the doorway. The Uzi bubbled out a cascade of shots that stitched a line across the ceiling. Hawk was out through the French doors with me behind him, bearing left along the patio toward the driveway and the Bronco. One of the perimeter guards came around the corner of the house and Hawk shot him with the big .44. A bullet came from behind us and rang off the flagstone patio and ricocheted off the low stone wall that rimmed the terrace. We were around the corner before another shot came, and below us was the driveway and the black Bronco parked there. Hawk vaulted the low fence and landed softly on his feet beside the Bronco. I landed beside him and felt the impact jolt my stomach and then we were in the car, Hawk driving, and heading down the driveway.

"Gate's closed," Hawk said.

"Jam the Bronco up against it, take the keys and we'll jump the fence," I said.

Another bubbling cascade of fire from the Uzi sounded behind us and I felt the Bronco lurch and begin to sway.

"Tires," Hawk said.

We reached the gate and Hawk braked, slamming the Bronco into a skid and jamming it against the gate sideways. With a sharp twist he snapped the key off in the ignition and we were out of the car and up onto the hood. The gate was chest-high from the hood of the car and no razor wire. We went over it without trouble and landed again with a soft thump on the other side. In ten feet we were out of the light and hidden by the darkness, running full out for the Volvo. Behind us the two Uzis sprayed fire through the fence into the dark. We could hear bullets cut the leaves and snap twigs as we rounded the bend of the road, and the Volvo was still there. The heavier crack of the handguns sounded and above it, in the distance, the sound of sirens. We were in the Volvo and driving back along Mill River Boulevard when the first police car passed us going in the other direction.

"Figure they got the Bronco out of there yet?" Hawk said.

"Somebody probably popped the ignition," I said.

"I don't know," Hawk said. "Got to be city to know about popping ignitions. They don't look city to me."

We were heading for 101 again. I was getting used to the trip. Hawk kept the car at fifty-five and we went sedately through the quiet California night, moving briskly, going no place special.

"Got to look at this lodge," I said.

"They know we coming," Hawk said.

"Still got to look," I said.

"They'll have something set up for us," Hawk said.

"And they'll have taken Susan somewhere else," I said.

"Still got to look," Hawk said.

Chapter 14

"IT BOTHERING YOU THAT WE DON'T KNOW WHERE THIS LODGE is," Hawk said, slouched down in the Volvo.

We were in the parking lot of the Fisherman's Wharf Holiday Inn, parked in a slot near the building where a passing cop wouldn't wonder about us at 3:00 A.M.

"We'll ask Dr. Hilliard," I said.

"Susan's shrink? How's she gonna know?"

"Maybe she won't. But people talk about things with shrinks, and shrinks are used to remembering."

The seat backs in the Volvo reclined back and we lay in the dark car nearly prone.

"Been good," Hawk said, "we collected some firearms while at Costigan's."

"I know," I said. "Things just got rolling downhill."

"Things been doin' that since we got here," Hawk said.

"Readiness is all," I said.

It was very quiet. Occasionally I could hear the sound of a truck easing up through the gears along the Embarcadero. It was a little chilly in the darkness but I didn't want to turn on the heater. An idling car might attract a cop.

"We piling up some pretty good-looking list of charges," Hawk said. "We got B and E and assault for sure at Costigan's, to go along with murder one and felonious escape and assault on police officers."

"I wonder if they can make us on kidnapping?" I said.

"Holding Costigan and the missus?" Hawk said. "If they do, it a chicken shit charge."

"Of course we have two counts of murder and one count of armed robbery for Leo and his driver."

"If they make us," Hawk said.

"If they try hard," I said.

"Figure San Francisco cops won't get real hysterical somebody dusted Leo."

A light went on in one of the guest rooms in the hotel. It stayed on maybe two minutes then went off again. Susan wouldn't be there when we found the lodge. The Costigans weren't that stupid. But we had nowhere else that made any more sense to look. So we'd find it. And the Costigans would be waiting for us and maybe when that worked out there'd be more momentum rolling downhill and maybe something would come out of it. I thought of her face laughing in the picture beside Russell. I thought of Hawk's description of her with the frozen half smile and the tears in her eyes. *Things are awful, but I love you.* I thought of Leo when I shot him. Had to do that. No other way. The whores would have suffered for it and it wasn't their fault. A night watchman walked through the parking lot, his heels loud as he came. Hawk and I stayed slouched and motionless as he passed. It wasn't the whores' fault. But they didn't have to be whores. Maybe they did. I didn't like shooting Leo. But I had to find Susan.

"How the Christ did we end up here," I said.

"I the victim of sociological forces," Hawk said.

"You're a goddamned leg breaker because of racism?" I said.

"No, I a leg breaker 'cause the hours are short and the pay is good. I end up here 'cause I hanging around with a middle-aged honkie thug. You what your momma wanted?"

"Don't remember my mother," I said. "I was raised by my father and my two uncles. My mother's brothers."

"They stay with your father?"

"Yeah. They had a carpentry business. How my father met my mother."

"She split or she die?" Hawk said.

"Died."

The security guard moved back up the next line of cars. His footfall muted slightly as he moved away.

"We locate this lodge," Hawk said. "Maybe we better like get outfitted, you know. Bullets, jackets, a belt for you, that kind of thing."

"First we find out where it is," I said and shifted in my seat. I'd never slept on my back and wasn't getting any better at it.

At five thirty the sun was up. At six thirty we found a place open that sold us coffee and English muffins, and at seven thirty I called Dr. Hilliard from a pay phone on the corner of Beach Street and Taylor. Her service answered and I asked that she call me as soon as she could.

"It's about Susan Silverman," I said. "And it's life and death. Tell Dr. Hilliard that." I gave the number of the pay phone and hung up and stayed there. Two people stopped and looked at the phone and each time I picked it up and listened to the dial tone until they moved on. At seven fifty-five the phone rang.

I picked it up and said, "Hello."

"This is Dr. Hilliard."

I said, "My name is Spenser. Probably Susan Silverman has mentioned me."

"I know the name."

"She's in trouble. My kind of trouble, not yours. I need to talk with you."

"What specifically is your kind of trouble?"

"Russell Costigan is holding her against her will," I said.

"Perhaps that grew out of my kind of trouble," she said.

"Yes," I said. "But she needs my kind of help now, so she can get your kind of help soon."

"Be at my office at eight fifty," Dr. Hilliard said. "Since you knew my phone number I assume you know my address."

"Yes," I said. "I'll be there. Have you seen me on television?"

"Yes."

"Are you going to call the cops when I hang up?"

"No."

Chapter 15

HAWK WAITED OUTSIDE AND I WENT IN. DR. HILLIARD'S OF-
fice was in a big pastel mauve Victorian house on Jones
Street near Filbert. There was a walkway made of two-by-
eights that led around to the back door and a sign that said
RING BELL AND ENTER. I did both. I was in a small beige
waiting room with two chairs and a table between, with a
clean ashtray on it. The chairs and table were Danish mod-
ern. The ashtray was several-colored mosaic that looked
like it might have been someone's Cub Scout project.
There was a pole coatrack with its top spring slightly askew,
and a pole lamp with one of its three bulbs burned out. On
the table were piles of *New Yorker* magazines, some *Atlantic
Monthly*s, some *Scientific American*s. And, on the opposite
wall, a pile of intellectual magazines for children. No *Marvel
Comics*. No *Spiderman*. No *National Enquirer*. Maybe people
with plebian tastes didn't get crazy. Or didn't get cured. In
the corner of the room opposite the entry door was a wide
staircase that went to a landing six steps up then turned out
of sight. The stairway and the waiting room were carpeted

in quiet gray and a white sound machine *shush*ed on the floor in the other corner near the radiator. I sat in the chair near the radiator. In two minutes a young woman in black tweed slacks and a frilly white blouse came down the stairs and out the door without looking at me. There was the sound of movement upstairs, a door opening and closing, then another silent minute and then a woman appeared at the landing and said, "Mr. Spenser?"

I said, "Yes."

She said, "Come on."

And I went up the stairs. Dr. Hilliard was standing in an open door at the end of a short hall at the top. I walked past her into the office. She closed the door behind me, then another. Secure. No secrets will escape. *Doctor I can't stand my mother. Doctor I never achieve climax. Doctor I'm afraid.* The double doors keep it all in. So you can let it out. *Doctor I'm afraid I'm gay. Doctor I can't stand my husband.* The truth business. Behind the double doors. *Doctor I'm afraid.*

I said, "No cops."

She said, "No cops."

I sat in the chair by her desk. Behind me was a couch. For crissake there actually was a couch. Beyond the desk was a tank in which tropical fish drifted. There were diplomas on the wall and a bookcase filled with medical books, next to the double door. Dr. Hilliard sat down. She was maybe fifty-five or sixty. White hair in a French twist, good makeup well applied. A look of outdoor color to her skin. She wore a black skirt and a double-breasted black jacket with a black-and-silver-striped silk shirt, open at the neck, the collar spilling out over her lapels. There was a heavy antique gold chain around her neck from which a diamond hung. Her earrings were old gold too, with diamond chips. On her left hand was a white gold wedding band.

"What do you know about me?" I said.

"You are a detective. You and Susan have been lovers. You have suffered, what, an attenuation of your relationship recently, but that bond between you remains truly impressive. If I am to believe Susan you are, though flawed, inherently good."

The weight of Dr. Hilliard's intelligence was palpable. She reminded me a little of Rachel Wallace. In fact she reminded me some of Susan. There was in her the force and richness that Susan had.

"I bet you made up the part about 'flawed,' " I said.

Dr. Hilliard smiled. "The reality I try to deal with in here is hard enough," she said. "I don't have to make anything up."

So much for light badinage.

"Here's what I know," I said. "A year or so ago Susan went to Washington to intern. She met Russell Costigan and they began an affair. When she got her Ph.D. she moved out here and set up in Mill River, working at an outreach clinic at Costigan Hospital there. We stayed in touch and when she found she could neither give me up nor come back to me she began to seek your help. About two weeks ago she called a mutual friend, Hawk."

"The black man on the news with you," Dr. Hilliard said.

"Yes. And she said she needed help and she felt she couldn't ask me and would Hawk come out. He did. He got into a scrape with Russell Costigan and the Mill River cops. A man was killed, Hawk was arrested. Susan sent me a letter. The letter said, 'I have no time. Hawk is in jail in Mill River, California. You must get him out. I need help too. Hawk will explain. Things are awful, but I love you.' I came out and busted him out of jail and we went up to Jerry Costigan's house looking for Susan and didn't find her but heard she was at 'the lodge.' And we left and came here and I want to know, among other things, where 'the lodge' is."

Dr. Hilliard smiled. " 'Hawk will explain,' " she said. "She never doubted that you'd come or that you'd rescue him."

"Do you know where this lodge is? Has Susan ever spoken of it?"

Dr. Hilliard sat perfectly still, her hands folded in her lap. "You clearly can't go to the police with this. Though perhaps I might?"

"Which police," I said. "What jurisdiction. Logically it's Mill River. That's where she lived. But they belong to the Costigans. They were part of the setup for Hawk."

She pushed her lower lip out slightly and drew it back in. Her eyes were steady on my face.

"The lodge is in the Cascade Mountains, outside of Tacoma, Washington. Crystal Mountain. The police there, informed that there was a possible kidnapping, might be effective."

I shook my head. "We don't know whether Costigan owns them too," I said. "He's an owner. He would be inclined to influence his neighborhood. Wherever his neighborhood was."

Dr. Hilliard nodded.

"Besides," I said, "Susan won't be there. They know we will go there."

"Then why go?" Dr. Hilliard said.

"It's a place to start."

Dr. Hilliard nodded again. We were quiet. The fish drifted in their tank.

"You've not asked me about Susan," Dr. Hilliard said. "Most people would have."

"What happens in here is hers," I said.

"And when you find her. Then what?"

"Then she will be free again to come here and work with you until she can make the choices she wishes to make."

"And if you are not that choice?"

"I think I will be. But I can't control that. What I can do is see that she's free to choose."

"Control has been an issue," Dr. Hilliard said. It was neither a question nor a statement, simply a neutral utterance.

"I think it has been," I said. "I think I probably tried too much to control her. I'm trying to cut back on that."

"Have you been in therapy, Mr. Spenser?"

"No, but I think a lot."

"Yes," Dr. Hilliard said.

The fish drifted. Dr. Hilliard was motionless. I didn't want to leave. Susan had come here every week, maybe more than once a week. She had sat in this chair, or the couch? No. She would have sat in the chair, not lain on the couch. Before me was a woman who knew her. Knew her perhaps in ways that I didn't. Perhaps in ways that no one did. Knew about her relationship with me. With Russell. I was sitting with my hands clasped behind my head. Unbidden the biceps tightened in my upper arms. I saw Dr. Hilliard notice that.

"I was thinking of Susan with Russell Costigan," I said.

Dr. Hilliard nodded.

"Susan," she said, "grew up in a family of people who, out of their own phobic needs, treated her as an item, a thing useful for making them feel good, or important, or adult. She never learned to value herself as a person, only as someone else's person. As she matured and learned, she became more aware of this. It was the basis of her first marriage. She was, after all, training to be a psychologist, and her work had been in that line for years. At the time that this insight began to take shape, your need for her became more intense, and it manifested itself to her as control. She had to get away."

"And Russell rescued her," I said.

"He rescued her from you. Now you will rescue her from him," Dr. Hilliard said. "I share your view that it must be done. Her situation is hopeless if she is not free. But it would be better were she able to rescue herself from him."

Dr. Hilliard paused and looked straight at me. The pause lengthened. Finally she said, "I am torn. The confidentiality of Susan's therapy is imperatively important. But in order to save her spirit, we must first save her physical self."

I didn't say anything. I knew what I said wouldn't be what decided Dr. Hilliard.

"It is important for you to remember that she fears dependency, despite, in fact because of, its attractiveness to her. Being rescued will do nothing to dispel those fears. It will present you as more complete, more dangerous to her because she's still incomplete."

"Jesus Christ," I said.

"Exactly," Dr. Hilliard said.

The sunlight filtered in through the venetian blinds on the window above Dr. Hilliard's desk. It splashed across Dr. Hilliard's muted beige carpet.

"She'll want to be rescued," I said. "But she won't like me for it."

I sat still for a time rubbing the knuckles of my left hand along my chin. "But if I don't rescue her . . ."

"Don't misunderstand. She must be rescued. Duress is never positive. And everything I know of you suggests you are the best one to do it. I say all this only so that you will understand what may come afterward. If you succeed."

"If I don't succeed, I'll be dead," I said. "And the matter will be less pressing to me. Best plan for success."

"I think so," Dr. Hilliard said.

"I'll rescue her from Costigan and she can then rescue herself from me."

"As long as you understand that," Dr. Hilliard said.

"I do."

"And when she has rescued herself. If she chooses to be with you, do you want that?"

"Yes."

"And Costigan doesn't matter?"

"He matters," I said. "But not as much as she does. She's been doing the best she could, right from the start. He was something she had to do."

"And you'll forgive her?"

I shook my head. "Forgiveness has nothing to do with it."

"What does have something to do with it?"

"Love," I said.

"And need," Dr. Hilliard said. "I too believe in love. But you forget need only at great peril."

"Frost," I said.

Dr. Hilliard raised her eyebrows.

" 'Only where love and need are one,' " I said.

"And the next line?" she said.

" 'And the work is play for mortal stakes,' " I said.

She nodded. "Do you have eighty dollars, Mr. Spenser?"

"Yes."

"That is what I charge an hour. If you pay me for this hour, I can make a defensible argument that you are a patient and that patient-doctor transactions are privileged."

I gave her four twenties. She gave me a receipt.

"I guess that means you're not going to call the cops," I said.

"It does," she said.

"Anything else I can know?"

"Russell Costigan sounds like a man," she said, "unhampered by morality or law."

"Me too," I said.

Chapter 16

WE BOUGHT A ROAD ATLAS IN A WALDENBOOKS ON MARKET Street, and then we went to a flossy sporting goods store near the corner of O'Farrell and outfitted for our assault on the lodge.

To drive north from San Francisco you had your choice of the Golden Gate Bridge and the coast road, 101. Or the Oakland Bay Bridge and connection to Interstate 5. For people on the run toll bridges were bad places. Traffic slowed, and cops could stand there and look at you when you paid your toll. It was a favorite stakeout for cops.

"They'll stop every car with a black guy and a white guy in it," Hawk said.

"We'll go around," I said.

And we did. With me driving and Hawk reading the road atlas we went south on secondary roads all the way to Palo Alto and swung around the tip of the bay and headed north along the east side of it. We never went on a big throughway until we finally went on to Interstate 5 north of Sacramento, in a town called Arbuckle.

From Arbuckle it took us seventeen hours to get to Route 12 in Washington State, south of Centralia, and another two hours to get ourselves up into the Cascades near Crystal Mountain, northeast of Mount Rainier. Near Chinook Pass, where Route 410 makes a kind of Y fork, we found a store and snack bar. A sign out front said BREAKFAST SERVED ALL DAY. In front of the store was a gravel parking lot. It had been fenced by embedding truck tires halfway into the ground so that the lot was outlined with black half-moon shapes. An oil drum had been converted to a trash barrel and placed near the front door. As far as I could tell it hadn't ever been emptied. Styrofoam cups, sandwich wrappers, beer bottles, cigarette packages, straws, chicken bones, and a lot of stuff that was no longer recognizable spilled out of it and littered around it in a spread of maybe eight feet. The store itself was one story and looked as if it had once been a bungalow, the kind they put up in a couple of days right after the Second World War so that the returning GI's could get going on the baby boom. It had brick red asphalt shingles for both siding and roof. A front porch had been scabbed onto the front, running the entire length of the store, and it had a rustic look that may have been intentional, or may have been bad carpentry. A pair of antlers hung over the two steps that led onto the porch, and the glassy-eyed head of an elk stared down at us from over the door.

Inside the store was a lunch counter and six stools, along the left wall. The rest of the store had shelves and tables that sold canned goods and frypans and fishing gear and toilet paper and insect repellent and souvenir mugs shaped like Smokey the Bear.

Behind the counter was a fat guy with thin arms and a patch over his right eye. On both forearms were tattoos.

The one on the left said *For God and Country*. The one on the right said *Valerie* and had a wreath around it. The fat guy wore a T-shirt and a blue cap that said CAT on it. He was reading a paperback book by Barbara Cartland. We sat at the counter. No one else was in the store.

"You guys want to eat," he said.

"Breakfast," I said. "Two eggs, sunny side, ham, home fries, whole wheat toast, coffee."

"Got no whole wheat. Got white."

"No dark?" Hawk said.

The counterman looked at him sideways. "No," he said. "Just white."

"I'll have white toast," I said.

"Me too," Hawk said. "Same order as his. 'Cept over easy on the eggs."

The counterman drew us two cups of coffee and put them before us. He still didn't look directly at Hawk. Then he turned to the grill and got going on the breakfast.

"We're looking for Russell Costigan's place," I said. "Know where that is?"

"Yeah."

"Feel like telling us?" I said.

"Wait'll I get through cooking," the counterman said. "You know? One thing at a fucking time."

"Things are simpler in the country," Hawk said to me.

I drank some coffee. Hawk and I had alternated driving and trying to sleep on the drive up. My eyes felt like there was sand under the lids.

The counterman had the eggs and ham and home fries on the plate just as the four-slice toaster popped. He brushed melted butter on the toast and served us breakfast. I took a bite. The home fries had been frying for a long time.

"Now what was it you wanted to know?"

"Russ Costigan," I said. "We want to know how to get to his place."

"Yeah, well, it's easy enough. Biggest goddamned place in the mountains. Russ has got a bundle, you know? Good guy though. Acts just like folks. Just like folks, you know. No airs. Nothing fancy. Just comes in here buys his stuff and goes. Always got a pretty good story to tell, too, Russell."

"Yeah," I said. "Russ is a sketch, all right, and I'm dying to hear some good jokes. How do we get to his place?"

"Easy," he said, and told us.

"Thank you," I said. "Who thought of the nice fence idea outside?"

"The tires? Ain't that something. The wife thought of it."

"Dynamite," Hawk said.

"When you see Russ," the counterman said, "tell him it was me gave you directions."

We finished breakfast and went out to the Volvo and headed up Route 410. Towering evergreen rain forest, bright air, streams splashing vigorously downhill.

Ah wilderness.

Chapter 17

THE ROAD TO THE LODGE WAS WHERE THE COUNTERMAN HAD said it would be. A dirt road that curved up into the high evergreen forest without a sign of life. It was ten thirty on a warm fall morning. There was birdsong in the woods and the faint soft scent of Puget Sound easing in on a light breeze. I drove on past the road and parked a mile away.

"They ain't going to buy Br'er Rabbit here," Hawk said.

"I know."

We got out of the car and stepped into the woods. The trees were so tall and dense at the top that the forest floor was relatively uncluttered and dark, with only modest undergrowth.

"We'll go straight east," I said. "Keep the sun in front of us. Then in maybe half an hour we'll turn south, see if we can circle in around the lodge. If we miss it short we'll cut the road."

"We miss it long we walk to Oregon," Hawk said.

The people at the lodge would expect us. But they didn't know when to expect us. We had time. We could be patient.

We could look carefully. Susan maybe wasn't happy but she was probably safe. Put her one up on me. The ground beneath our feet was thick with the accumulated autumns of a century. The trees through which we moved reached straight up, bare-trunked and austere, until the branches thickened near the sunlight and spread out and interlaced. Sometimes we had to skirt a tree that had fallen, the barrel of the trunk maybe five feet in diameter, its branches broken by the fall, the root mass suspended and higher than my head. There were birds in the woods but no sign of anything else. At eleven o'clock we turned south, keeping the sun now to our left.

At twenty past eleven I smelled woodsmoke. I looked at Hawk. He nodded. We stopped, sniffing the air and listening. There was no human sound, only the bird sounds and the light wind moving in the woods.

"They waiting for us, they going to have people out in the area," Hawk said softly. I nodded. The smell of the smoke lingered. We began to move slowly and carefully through the woods. It was hard to locate the direction the smell came from, but it seemed vaguely ahead and right and we inched along in that direction. I had the automatic out, a shell up in the chamber, the hammer half cocked. Ahead and off to my right I saw a glint of sunlight reflected off something. I touched Hawk's arm. He nodded and we moved toward it, putting each foot carefully down on the soft floor of the woods, walking very carefully, looking before each step, straining to listen and smell and see. Watching for people with guns, watching for sticks that would snap loudly if we stepped on them. Watching for electrified wire or television cameras.

Then below us, across an open area on the opposite wall of a small hollow, was the lodge. A huge chalet with a lot of glass and a high steep roof. There was a wide fieldstone chimney rising on the north end of the building and the smoke we had smelled had drifted from it. A balcony ran the length of the building across the second floor. The railing had fancy carved risers in it, and behind the balcony the wall was of glass sliding doors that faced southwest.

Hawk murmured beside me, "The hills alive with the sound of music, babe."

In front of the lodge, on level ground on the floor of the draw, was a macadam drive with a turnaround circle. The drive was lined with a rustic fence and at intervals a street-light that was made to seem a lantern. There was a red Jeep with a white canvas top parked in the turn around beside a black Jeep Wagoneer with fake wood side molding. The only movement was the woodsmoke curling up from the chimney.

"Homey," I said.

"Y'all come," Hawk said. "Walk on in and have some mulled cider by the fire."

"No trouble expected."

"Sure do look that way," Hawk said.

"Think we ought to stroll in?" I said.

"Be easier just to shoot each other up here, save the walk."

I nodded. "Let's sit and watch for a while."

We sat among the low spread of a big evergreen with our backs against the bare trunk beneath the limbs and looked at the lodge. Nothing happened. It was a pleasant fall day in the rain forest of the Pacific Northwest and the smell of woodsmoke spiced the easy wilderness air.

"You figure they staked out around the house in the woods?" Hawk said.

"Yes," I said.

"They probably work in shifts," Hawk said.

"And if we sit quiet maybe we can watch the shift change."

"Un huh."

We could see the whole lodge area maybe a hundred yards away in its little valley. Rustic with its shining glass and carefully fitted fieldstone. The power lines ran along one side of the road and crossed over and tied into the lodge near the southwest corner of the balcony.

"Takes a lot of discipline to sit quiet for hours in the woods without any idea when someone going to show up," Hawk said.

"Too much," I said. "We'll spot them in a while."

"How long we going to sit."

"Until something happens," I said. "We got time. We'll sit and watch until we see what's going on."

"Be nice to know what we're doing," Hawk said. "Been scrambling since we came out here."

Chapter 18

THE SHIFT CHANGE CAME AROUND THREE IN THE AFTERNOON. Four men with long guns came out of the lodge and went into the woods at four points around the clearing. Four other guys came out of the woods and went to the lodge.

"Rifles," Hawk said. "Look like .30-.30's."

"Okay," I said. "We know that setup. I wonder what's in the house."

"Some guns," Hawk said. "But we don't know where or how many."

"And maybe Susan," I said.

"Doubtful," Hawk said.

"Got to know," I said.

"Yes."

There were some squirrels in the woods, looking oddly out of place away from the city. And there was bird sound. When the sun went down around five thirty it began to get colder.

"The best thing for Susan would be to save herself," I said.

"Don't look like she can right now," Hawk said. "Maybe we just get her out and away and then let her save herself."

"Yeah."

"Course we eliminate Russell and then maybe there be nothing to save herself from."

"Maybe that wouldn't be good for her."

Hawk was silent for a while. When the sun went down floodlights went on all around the lodge, lighting the entire area.

"Photoelectric switch," I said.

Hawk said, "You saying we go easy on Russell?"

"I don't know, exactly, what I'm saying. I don't know enough. I am trying to make sense out of stuff I don't understand."

"That called life, babe," Hawk said.

"Maybe she needs to be able to save herself and that may mean dealing with Russell."

"I been working on the assumption," Hawk said, "that Russell is a dead man. I owe Russell some things."

"I know," I said. "I been thinking about how we'd decide which one gets him. But maybe not."

"Ah's jess a simple darkie, bawse. Killing the mother-fucker seem like a good idea to me."

"But if it's bad for Susan?"

"Then we don't," Hawk said. "Ah ain't that simple. We not here to fuck her up. I don't need to kill Russell, I'd just like it."

"I'd like it too," I said. "Maybe more than you."

"I would guess, maybe more than anybody," Hawk said.

"At the moment I think we shouldn't unless we have to," I said.

In the light that spilled into the woods from the floodlit clearing I could see Hawk shrug.

"Delayed gratification, babe," he said.

"Yeah," I said.

Lights went on and off inside the lodge but there was nothing in the pattern that told us anything. We couldn't see enough through the windows to help. The outdoor guard shifts changed. Hawk and I put our hands into our pockets and sat and watched. We ate some granola bars and some trail mix. We dozed a little, but not much. The night went on. The lights inside the lodge went off, except for one downstairs. The outside floods stayed on. The outdoor shifts changed again. Toward morning it rained. I stood slowly in the downpour and shrugged my back and neck. I felt like a junk car.

"Russell show up now," Hawk said, "I think we over-matched."

"Have some trail mix," I said.

Hawk took a handful and chewed it without pleasure.

"I look like fucking trail mix to you?" he said. "I look like a fucking granola bar? I eggs Benedict, and mimosa, I room service, man."

"The rain is nice," I said.

"Refreshing," Hawk said.

Along with the woodsmoke I could smell coffee, from the lodge.

"If they start to fry bacon in there," I said, "I'm going to cry." We were both on our feet, stretching quietly, talking softly, trying to get warm and loose without disturbing the lodge patrol. It was raining steadily and still dark.

"We plug that chimney," I said, "and the smoke will back up into the house and drive people out."

"What if Susan in there?"

"They would bring her out too," I said. "They got no reason to want her dead. I assume Russell likes her."

"Means one of us got to get up on the roof," Hawk said.

"Yes."

We stood in the rain watching the house. There were no birds today, no squirrels. I was looking at the power and phone cable where it ran to the house.

"We need to do some stuff," I said. "We need to confuse and distract them. We need to cause a diversion."

"We good at causing diversions," Hawk said.

"Think we could shoot that power cable out?"

"From here?" Hawk said. "Not with a handgun."

"We could get a rifle," I said.

Hawk smiled. "Yes, we can. I know where there's four."

"Closest one is down there," I said. "Maybe seventy-five yards."

Hawk said, "I'll get the rifle. You circle around behind the house on the hill back of it. When I shoot out the power cables they'll all come charging over here. You get on the roof and stuff something in the chimney."

"While they're chasing you."

"While I shooting their ass with my new rifle," Hawk said.

"I like it," I said. "Give me time to get around there. I'll go for the roof when you start shooting."

"No hurry," Hawk said. "I be getting my new rifle while you circling."

I moved off through the woods, staying crouched, moving slowly through the rain. Stepping carefully in the spongy wet leaf mold on the forest floor. The sound of the rain spattering down among the evergreens deadened the sound of my movement. I took a careful slow half hour to get around behind the house. From the slope behind it I could see that the lodge was built into the side of the hill and from a tree I could jump to the roof. Maybe.

I found the best tree and crouched beside it. The rain had soaked through my jacket and some of it trickled down my neck and along my spine. I stayed in the tree, crouched among the bottom branches, for maybe another fifteen minutes. Then I heard the first shot. It was a rifle, and there was a second and a third. The third shattered the porcelain mount on the lodge where the power cables went in. All the floodlights went out. The cable fell free and sparked as it hit the wet ground. There was movement in the woods below, and from the guesthouse some of the security people appeared. The rifle sounded again and one of the security people fell. Gunfire started back toward the woods. I went up the tree in the faint gray light, got high enough and launched out onto the roof of the lodge. The roof was covered with hand-split shakes and made a decent footing, even in the rain. I scrambled up to the roof ridge and along it to the chimney opening. There were two flues in the chimney. The woodsmoke was heavy and hot close up as it rose from the open flue. I shrugged out of my jacket, jammed the ammunition into my hip pocket, and shoved the wadded-up jacket into the flue. It made a sodden solid mass and no more smoke escaped. Below, the gunfire increased. Most of it aimed into the woods, and I was peripherally aware of movement in the open yard. I slid along the wet shakes down the front slope of the roof and landed on the cross balcony, and flattened out on the floor with the automatic in my hand. I could hear footsteps moving in the house and men's voices. There was yelling. The outside security people were firing at random into the woods. Smoke began to seep out from the glass doors. I heard doors open below and more voices and the sounds of confusion. I edged along the floor of the balcony and peered down into the yard. Four men came out of the house with handguns. One carried a flashlight. Two more men came out behind them.

A voice came up out of the hubbub, "What the fuck happened?" Humanity's cry.

"Must be something blown in the wiring, the lights went out and there's a fire somewhere."

"How many shooting?"

"I don't know."

Rifle fire came from a different part of the woods.

"Jesus, they're shooting at the vehicles."

The flash trained on the Jeep Wagoneer and I saw it cant slightly as the air went out of a tire.

"Everybody out of the house?"

"I think so. How many of us were there?"

Another rifle shot from the woods and the flashlight spun and skittered along the ground.

"Jesus, they got Gino."

"Fan out, God damn it, fan out."

I turned and snake-walked across the deck on my stomach and slid open one of the glass doors. Smoke billowed out. I stayed on the floor and slithered along into the house. Close to the floor there was still breathable air. And I had an advantage on everyone else. I knew the house wasn't on fire.

There were four bedrooms on the top floor of the lodge, organized in a square around an interior balcony that opened onto a cathedral-ceilinged first-floor space that ran the length of the lodge. I moved as fast as I could on my stomach. My eyes were stinging and watering. It was hard to breathe. There was no one in any of the bedrooms. In the dawn half-light, muddled by the smoke, it was hard to see much more than that. I took a deep breath at floor level after the last bedroom proved empty. Then I stood and went down the stairs into the main room. There was no one there. I went to the fireplace that covered one wall at the far end, and raked the burning logs out onto the floor with a hooked poker. The carpet began to smolder. I was fighting to hold my breath. I moved the length of the room and dropped to the floor and breathed as shallow as I could. There was no one in the main hall. I hadn't thought there would be, but the disappointment that she wasn't here felt like something heavy in my chest. The back side of the lodge was set into the hillside so there were no windows on the first-floor back wall. Holding my breath I went back up to the second floor and out a back window. It was barely a five-foot drop into the woods on the hill. Behind me the floor of the lodge had caught and I could see the tips of the flames shimmering against the second-floor windows.

The rain was pelting down now. I had shipped to Korea out of Fort Lewis some time back and I remembered how often it rained in Washington. I was moving through the woods in a crouch, circling back toward the road and the place where we'd parked the car. The rain was cold, and without my jacket it soaked through my black turtleneck sweater. Behind me I heard a large *huff* as the flames burst out of the second-floor windows of the lodge. We hadn't found Susan yet, but we were certainly annoying the Costigans. Better than nothing.

Chapter 19

HAWK WAS SITTING IN THE VOLVO WITH THE MOTOR RUNNING as I sloshed out of the woods. He'd have the heater on. I got slapped one last time across the face with a wet branch and then the woods relinquished me and I stepped out onto the road about ten feet behind the Volvo.

When I did about ten guys with guns stepped out with me. From my side, from the other side, in front of the Volvo. One of them was the fat guy with skinny arms who had been working the counter where we'd had breakfast yesterday. He was pointing a double-barreled shotgun at me.

"Who's minding the store," I said.

"It's Mr. Costigan's store," he said.

"I imagine so," I said.

The Volvo engine suddenly snarled and its tires whined as they spun on the wet pavement. The guys in front of it had time to put one shot through the windshield before they dove out of the way and the Volvo screeched off uphill and around the curve in the road.

"Son of a bitch," the counterman said.

"Greedy," I said. "You wanted to wait and make sure of us both."

"Got you," the counterman said. He grinned at me over the gun. "Your buddy hauled ass and left you," he said. "Most niggers'll skedaddle like that."

I shrugged. The Volvo was out of hearing already. The group gathered around me. The gunny who fired at Hawk said, "I mighta winged him, Warren."

The counterman nodded. Even when the Volvo had bolted and the shooting had followed he'd never wavered. He'd kept looking straight at me down the long twin barrels of the shotgun. "Bobby, you and Raymond go get the cars. Soon's I kill this boy we'll get after the nigger," he said.

Everyone was quiet as the two men walked down the highway. I could hear the hiss of the rain and the beat when it landed and the slower syncopated plop of the droplets that fell from the leaves and branches. The counterman stepped closer, so that the shotgun barrels were six inches from my face.

"I figure both barrels at once will blow most of your head off completely," he said.

"Unless you miss," I said.

He giggled. "Miss," he said and giggled some more. "You dumb fucker. How can I miss with a shotgun from six inches." His shoulders shook with the giggle.

"Come on, Warren," one of the gunnies said. "Shoot him and let's get after the nigger. Mr. Costigan's gonna be pissed."

Warren nodded. "Okay, stand away less you want to get blood and brains all over you." Then the smile vanished and his eyes narrowed slightly. He took in a slow breath, and while he was taking it in, his head jerked, a round red hole appeared in the middle of his forehead, and a gunshot sounded from the woods to the right. Warren staggered back a step and the shotgun sagged and then fell from his hands and he keeled over backward. Everything froze in that posture and I turned and plunged back into the woods. The rifle shots continued fast, at about the rate it would take to lever a shell into the chamber of a .30-.30 rifle.

I headed for the place the shots were coming from, my gun out now, forcing through the wet woods as hard as I could go. Running in a crouch, with my left forearm bent in front of me to keep from being blinded by a branch. Gunfire from the road cut leaves and branches around me as I ran, but most of it seemed aimed at where the rifle fire came from.

In front of me, Hawk said, "Spenser," and I saw him standing behind a tree in a small clearing, feeding shells into the magazine of a Winchester. The gunfire from the road was nearly continuous. I scuttled on all fours across the clearing and behind Hawk's tree. A bullet thudded into it at eye level.

"Dumb to shoot so high," Hawk said.

The clearing was maybe thirty feet higher than the road, and below me I could see three bodies sprawled in the angular repose of death. The rest of the gunnies were crouched off the shoulder of the road opposite, firing toward us.

"Road does almost a hairpin," Hawk said. "Car's about ten yards that way." He jerked his head behind us. "With the motor running."

"Let's get out of here before they bring the cars up," I said.

Hawk nodded. There was a cut under one eye, and blood ran in a neat trickle down his cheek, diffused pink by the rain before it dripped onto his shirt. He fired six shots down at the enemy as fast as he could work the lever on the Winchester. Then he dropped it behind the tree and we ran for the Volvo. They returned fire, but you tend to shoot high uphill and in five strides we were on the down side of the hill and the bullets hummed and whined harmlessly above us. We half slid, half scrambled the last ten yards as the muddy hill turned into a steep slick banking and then we were sprawling into the road beside the Volvo and, soaking and smeared with mud, we were in the Volvo and spinning rubber away from the hill with me driving. Fifty yards up the road, I jammed the car into a screeching U-turn and headed back down toward the bad guys with the accelerator pressed to the floor. We roared by them and the two cars, which had just pulled up, heading in the other direction and were around the next curve with only three more shots at the car. One shot went through the back window, the other two missed.

I kept the accelerator hard down and drove a lot too fast for the wet curving road. The first crossroad I came to I turned right and at the next I turned left and at a third I turned right again. There was no one behind us. I slowed to sixty.

I looked at Hawk. He had a wad of cloth pressed against the cut on his cheek. "Glass?" I said.

"Yeah, when the dude shot through the windshield."

"Counterman worked for Costigan," I said.

"Sort of a forward observer," Hawk said.

I nodded. "And they covered the way out once they knew

we'd gone in. So just in case the ambush didn't work at the lodge . . ."

"Thorough bastards," Hawk said.

"Be good to remember it," I said. "There's Band-Aids in the glove compartment."

Chapter 20

We were heading north on 410. "anything in the house?" Hawk said.

I shook my head.

"We knew there wouldn't be," Hawk said.

"Yeah."

Hawk reached the road atlas from the backseat and opened it in his lap. "We can pick up a major highway in Seattle and head east," I said.

"Shit," Hawk said.

"We knew she wouldn't be there," I said.

"Yeah."

Hawk was dripping on the road map. The rain came steady and the windshield wipers beat their metronomic half-circle swipes.

Hawk had removed his jacket and thrown it on the backseat floor. But his shirt was wet and his jeans, like mine, were soaked through.

"What route we looking for?" Hawk said.

"Ninety," I said. "Runs east all the way to Boston."

"We going home?"

"I don't know where we're going."

"Might make sense to get dry, maybe get breakfast, sorta regroup."

"Soon," I said. "Don't want to show up too close to the lodge looking like a couple of guys spent the night in the woods."

"We get the other side of Seattle," Hawk said, "we stop and change in the car."

I nodded. The wipers wiped. The wheels turned. The rain didn't let up. In the parking lot of a Holiday Inn off Route 90 in Issaquah we got our extra clothes out of the trunk and changed awkwardly in the car, putting the wet clothes in a sodden heap in the trunk. Then we headed east again across the Cascade Mountains, through the unvarying rain.

"Costigan has more money than Yoko Ono," I said. "He and Susan could be anywhere in the world."

Hawk nodded.

"We haven't got a clue," I said.

Hawk nodded again.

"If she tried to reach us she couldn't," I said. "She doesn't know where we are either."

Hawk nodded.

"We need help," I said. "We need to get someplace where if she has a chance to reach us she can. We have to find a way to know what we're doing. We should go home."

"Long ride," Hawk said.

"Spokane," I said. "There's an airport in Spokane. We'll fly out of there. We'll use Leo's credit card and when we get to Boston we'll hole up and get organized."

"You ever been to the Spokane airport?" Hawk said.

"Yeah."

"They got food there?"

"Sort of."

"Good. I ain't had anything since breakfast yesterday except that goddamned weasel food you bought."

"Weasels don't eat granola," I said. "Weasels are carnivores."

"So am I," Hawk said. "And I don't want to eat no more fucking seeds and dates."

"Nuts too," I said. "Hazel nuts."

"Let Hazel worry 'bout them," Hawk said. "I'm getting me a mess of good boondock airport food."

"Probably get a meal on the plane too," I said.

"Lawzy me," Hawk said, "I done died and gone to heaven."

"But," I said, "you know what it's like trying to get off the West Coast after noontime?"

"No harm we stop by and ask," Hawk said. "Maybe pick up some grub. I yearning for some stuff ain't good for me, you know. Something with a lotta cholesterol, maybe too much salt. Some additives."

"Can always get that at an airport," I said.

"Good to be able to count on things," Hawk said.

When we got to Spokane Airport we bought four hamburgers and two coffees and ate them and sat all night in the Volvo. In the morning we went and washed up in the airport and had some more coffee and were first in line to board United Airlines 338 to Boston via Chicago.

At six forty-nine that evening we stumbled off the plane at Logan Airport full of booze and airline food and feeling like the last day of Pompeii.

"My car's parked in the Central Garage," I said.

"And you think the cops ain't spotted it?"

"Yes," I said, "and I also think that you can trust what the President says on television."

We took the shuttle bus to the airport subway station and took the subway into Park Street Station.

"Got a friend," Hawk said, "lives on Chestnut Street, on the flat of the Hill, near the river. She be glad to put us up."

We walked across the Common in the pleasant fall evening. Ahead of us a middle-aged man walked, holding hands with a middle-aged woman. She wore a plaid skirt and a tweed jacket with the collar turned up and a long maroon scarf hanging loose around her neck. We went through the little archway at the Charles and Beacon streets corner of the Common and walked along Charles to Chestnut. Halfway down the flat of Chestnut Street, with Beacon Hill rising in a dignified jumble behind us, we stopped and Hawk rang the bell at a glass door framed in white. There was no answer.

"She a stewardess," Hawk said. "She travel a lot."

"Cabin attendant," I said. "Have you no sensitivity to minority nomenclature, you dumb jigaboo?"

Hawk grinned and rang the bell again. No answer. Beside the door was a small evergreen in a large pot. Hawk reached in among the dense lower branches and came out with a small plastic case. Hawk took a key from the case and opened the door.

"Second floor," Hawk said.

We went up some stairs along the left wall. The stairs were walnut, the walls were raised panels painted white. The balcony was white too with elaborate turned risers. At the top Hawk took another key from the case and opened the apartment door. There was a living room that ran at right angles to the door and looked out onto Chestnut

Street. Off the left wall was a kitchenette and beside it a door that opened into the bedroom. The living room walls were white. There was a pink couch, a gray Art Deco streamlined coffee table, two wing chairs, one pink, one gray. The brick fireplace had been painted white, and a Japanese fan served to screen the firebox. The fan was pink with a gray pattern.

"Au courant," I said.

"Yeah, Yvonne trendy," Hawk said.

"She got a shower?" I said.

Hawk nodded and walked to the kitchen. He opened the refrigerator.

"She got 'bout fifteen bottles of Steinlager beer, too, honey."

"Lawzy me," I said. "I've died and gone to heaven."

"Done died," Hawk said. "Ah done died and gone to heaven. Haven't you ever watched any Mantan Moreland movies?"

"Give me a beer," I said. "I'll drink it in the shower."

Chapter 21

AT EIGHT FIFTEEN THE NEXT MORNING HAWK AND I WERE eating fried egg sandwiches on whole wheat toast and drinking pot-brewed coffee in Yvonne's sun-splashed living room.

"No way to know what Susan knows," I said. "She will assume I got her letter and came out to California. After that she may not know anything."

"She'll know you won't stop looking for her," Hawk said.

We were both naked, our clothes churning through Yvonne's washer-dryer. A double treat for Yvonne if she came home suddenly.

"Okay," I said. "So she won't expect me to be at home or at the office."

Hawk nodded.

"So she'd try Paul," I said.

"She figure you'll stay in touch with him."

"Yes. It's a good time to call him. He'll be asleep for sure. Once he's up you can never get him."

I called Sarah Lawrence and got the switchboard and

asked for Paul's dorm. After eight rings a kid answered. I asked for Paul. The kid went away and I could hear him holler in the background. Then he came back and said, "He's asleep."

"Wake him up," I said. "It's very important."

The kid said, "Okay," in a tone that implied nothing could be so important as to wake Paul Giacomin up at eight twenty-five in the morning. There was more hollering and a long pause and then Paul said, "Hello," in a voice thick with sleep.

I said, "Do you know who this is?"

He said, "My God, yes."

I said, "Okay. Is it safe to talk?"

"Sure. What's happening?"

"A lot. But first, have you heard from Susan?"

"No. But Lieutenant Quirk wants you to call him."

"Quirk?"

"Yes. He called me up and left a message I should call him, so I did and he says if I hear from you that you should call him."

"Okay," I said. "I'm with Hawk at . . . what's the street address?"

Hawk told me and I relayed it to Paul. I also read him the number off the phone. "You and you alone are to know where I am. You understand. Except Susan, and her, only directly. No one calling for her, or anything. You understand?"

"Sure. What's going on?"

I told him, as briefly as I could.

"Jesus Christ," he said when I was through.

"That will wake you up in the morning, won't it?"

"Clears up the old sinuses," he said. "Want me to come home?"

"No," I said. "There's not enough room here as it is and if Yvonne shows . . . No, you stay put."

"You'll get her back," Paul said.

"Yes," I said. "We will."

"Kid's okay?" Hawk said when I hung up.

"Yes," I said. "Quirk wants me to call him."

Hawk raised his eyebrows. "God damn," he said. "Give you a chance to surrender?"

"I doubt it."

"I doubt it too. But one thing about Quirk. He won't cross your ass. He ask you to call him, he won't have a trace on the line."

"I know."

The dryer clunked to a stop in the kitchenette and I went and got my clothes out and put them on still warm from the machine. Hawk dressed too.

"Let's see what he wants," I said and called police head-quarters and asked for Homicide, and when I got it I asked for Quirk and in about ten seconds he came on the line.

"Spenser," I said.

"I know that name," Quirk said. "You are, I believe, wanted for violating the entire California penal code. You and your fucking soulmate appear to have pissed off every law enforcement agency west of the Rockies."

"It was nothing," I said. "Hawk gets a lot of the credit."

"I want to talk," Quirk said. "Be on a corner of your choice and I'll pick you up. Both of you."

"Charles and Chestnut," I said.

"I'll be there at nine," Quirk said and hung up.

At 9:02 a tan Chevrolet sedan pulled up at the corner of Charles and Chestnut. Belson was driving. Quirk sat beside him. Hawk and I got in the backseat and Belson eased the car back into traffic, heading toward the Common. Quirk half turned, rested his left arm on the back of the seat and looked at Hawk and me. His shirt was radiantly white, and brisk with starch. His camel's hair jacket was fresh from the cleaners and fitted across his thick back without a wrinkle. His brown knit tie was knotted precisely the right size to highlight the small roll in his collar. His thick black hair was cut short and newly barbered. I'd never seen it when it wasn't.

"You guys look like you shipped back here in a crate," Quirk said.

"Clothes are fresh from the dryer," I said. "Just need a little ironing."

"So does your life," Belson said. He turned at Beacon Street.

Hawk leaned back in the seat and folded his arms and lapsed into stillness. The Public Garden was on our left with its ornate wrought-iron fence. The foot of Beacon Hill was on our right with its high-windowed apartments. Belson was thinner than Quirk, with graying hair, and the blue shadow of a heavy beard, an hour after he shaved. He was chewing on a dead cigar.

Quirk said, "Tell me your side of things."

"What do you know?" I said.

"I know Hawk's wanted for murder, and you for accessory after. I know you're both wanted for jailbreak, assault on a police officer, two counts for you, more than I can remember for Hawk. I know you're wanted for breaking and entering, assault—Christ, maybe a dozen counts—violation of the California hostage statutes, destruction of property, suspicion of arson, theft of a rental car, theft of two handguns . . . other stuff. I don't have the warrants."

"They missed some of the good stuff," Hawk said.

"You," Quirk said, looking at Hawk, "would do all of that

stuff for any simple reason. Like someone paid you to. Spenser's reasons would be more complicated. I want to hear his reasons."

I looked at Hawk. "Anything you want left out?"

He shook his head, his face blank and peaceful.

"Okay," I said. "Susan is in trouble."

"Her too," Belson said as if talking to himself. We were driving along Beacon Street outbound.

"She has taken up with a guy named Russell Costigan. She called Hawk and said she wanted to leave Costigan but couldn't. Hawk went out to help her. Got set up, probably not by Susan, the cops and Costigan were in on an assault frame, but they underrated Hawk and one of Costigan's people got killed. Hawk was jailed in Mill River, California, which is a company town with company cops and Costigan's old man is the company."

"Jerry Costigan," Quirk said.

"Uh huh. So Susan got a letter to me telling me Hawk's in jail. I go out and bust him out and we start looking for Susan. We had to roust some people at Costigan's house . . ."

"Including Jerry," Quirk said.

"Yes. But she wasn't there and we had to look for her at the Costigan lodge in Washington State."

"Which you burned down."

"I didn't know that," Hawk murmured. "On purpose?"

"Yeah."

"I like it," Hawk said.

"But she wasn't there either," Quirk said.

"No. So we headed home to regroup."

Belson stopped the Chevy at a red light where Mass Avenue crosses Beacon. Then he turned right and started across the bridge toward Cambridge. Quirk rested his chin on his forearm. On the Cambridge side, Belson made an illegal left turn and headed out along the river on Memorial Drive.

"There's a couple of federal guys want to talk with you," Quirk said.

"FBI?" I said.

"One of them."

"What do they want to talk about?"

Quirk shifted in his seat so that he was faced back around front, talking without looking at me, staring out the front window while he spoke.

"They want to talk about helping you with the California authorities."

"Mighty white of them," Hawk said.

"Yeah," I said. "Isn't that nice."

"And then maybe you can help them with something," Quirk said.

"Ah yes," I said.

"They want you to take Costigan out," Quirk said.

Belson took his dead cigar out of his mouth and threw it out the window. He took a thin cheap cigar from the breast pocket of his corduroy sport coat. He stripped the cellophane from it and stuck it in his mouth and lit it with a wooden match that he snapped into flame with his thumbnail. We passed the Hyatt Regency and went up the little hill and over the underpass where the BU bridge comes in.

"Jerry?" I said.

"Un huh."

"How about Russell?"

"Your option, I think," Quirk said. "They'll give you details."

"Be an honor," Hawk said, "help our government in time of need."

"An honor," I said.

Without looking back Quirk said, "And maybe we can give you a little help finding Susan."

"How about if the deal with the feds falls through?"

Quirk turned again and looked at me.

"I'm a cop," he said. "I been a cop for thirty-one years. I'm serious about it. You understand. I wasn't serious about it, I'd have done something else for thirty-one years. You're wanted for murder, I got to arrest you. And I'm not claiming it would break my heart. You are a world-class pain in the balls. And the goddamned phantom beside you is a lot worse. But if I don't have to arrest you, I won't. And I might feel okay about that too. Either way, I'll help you with Susan. I like her."

"Thank you," I said.

"You're welcome," Quirk said.

We picked up Mt. Auburn Street, past the hospital. Belson's cigar smelled like a burning shoe.

"Phantom?" Hawk said.

"The ghost who walks," I said.

"Oh shut the fuck up," Quirk said.

Chapter 22

BELSON PULLED THE CHEVY IN BY THE CURB OF A YELLOW diner in Watertown. Quirk and Hawk and I got out. Belson sat in the car with the motor idling.

"You want me to bring coffee out?" Quirk said.

"Yeah," Belson said. "Black."

The three of us went into the diner. There was a long counter opposite the door and along the right wall four booths. In the back booth two men sat with thick white china mugs in front of them. The wall behind the counter was mirrored and two large coffee urns loomed at each end. On the counter there were slices of pie in glass cases, and muffins, and plates of donuts. We went to the back booth and slipped in opposite the two men. I knew one of them slightly, McKinnon, an FBI agent. Both of them wore gaberdine raincoats although it was sunny and not very cold. A very fat middle-aged woman with dark skin and a mole on her chin came to take our order. I ordered black coffee. Quirk ordered two black, one to go. Hawk ordered hot chocolate and a double order of French toast. The two feds accepted a refill on the coffee. The waitress brought everything except Hawk's French toast. Quirk took the black coffee to go out to the car and gave it to Belson, then he came back in. Nobody said anything while he was gone. He came back in and sat down and picked up his mug and sipped the coffee. He looked at Hawk.

"French fucking toast?" he said.

"I give you a bite when it comes," Hawk said.

McKinnon said, "McKinnon, FBI. This is Ives."

Ives looked like a salt cod. He was lean and weathered and gray-haired. His raincoat was open and under it I could see a green bow tie with little pink pigs on it.

"I'm with the three-letter agency," he said.

"You with the Tennessee Valley Authority," I said. "Well damn, I always wanted to meet someone like you. TVA is my favorite."

"Not TVA," Ives said.

"He's with the fucking CIA," Quirk said.

When Quirk said the sacred letters Ives looked uncomfortable, like he was fighting the impulse to turn his coat collar up.

He said, "Let's not broadcast it, Lieutenant."

Hawk said in a full voice, "Broadcast what?" and Quirk looked away trying not to smile.

McKinnon said, "Come on, we know you're both funnier than a case of the clap. You've proved it, now let's move on."

"We are trying to pursue this informally," Ives said. "We don't need to. I can have Lieutenant Quirk place you under arrest and the discussion can be held more formally."

Quirk looked carefully at Ives and spoke very distinctly. "You can't have Lieutenant Quirk do anything at all, Ives. The closest you can come is to ask."

"Aw, Jesus Christ, Marty," McKinnon said. "Come on. Let's see if we can't just talk business here and stop fucking around."

The fat waitress appeared with a huge platter of French toast and a pitcher of syrup.

"Who gets the toast," she said.

"Here," Hawk said.

The waitress put the food down and went away.

"Be hard," I said, "for anyone to distinguish you from the rest of us."

"Yeah," Hawk said. "Me and four honkies, how could she remember?"

"That's real progress, I should think," Ives said.

"That someone confuse me with you?" Hawk said.

Ives cleared his throat. "Let's begin again," he said. "We may be in a position to trade marbles."

I nodded. Hawk cut a square off one of the pieces of French toast and held it across the table toward Quirk. Quirk lipped it off the fork and ate it.

"Costigan has chips on a lot of squares," Ives said. "One is selling armaments. He is licensed and in and of itself there is nothing illegal about being an arms dealer, as I'm sure you people know. But Costigan deals covertly with proscribed nations."

"Heavens," I said.

"There's nothing frivolous about this," Ives said. "It translates into a lot of human suffering. Moreover, Costigan or his representatives not infrequently act as agents provocateurs, burning the oil on troubled waters in sensitive parts of the world. It enhances their marketing posture."

Hawk finished his second piece of French toast. The waitress came over and asked if we wanted anything else.

McKinnon said, "No."

The waitress slapped a check down in front of him and went away.

"We, that is the government, have penetrated Costigan's schoolyard several times. Each time the agent has disappeared. We have had the organization under surveillance for five years. Nothing. For God's sake, we do better infiltrating a foreign national organization. That's where most of our information comes from, the buying end of Costigan's business. But no paper. No records. No bills of lading. No invoices. No checks. No letters of credit. Everything appears to be cash and numbered bank accounts. Over the years we have had two eyewitnesses. Both of them were killed."

The waitress came back and looked at the check still lying facedown in front of Ives. She took a deep breath, let it out slowly, and went away again.

"Now we have information which suggests that he may begin dealing nuclear weapons. Not the big bang, but tactical weapons, and tacs are plenty bad enough. You might wish to pause and think about the implications of atomic weaponry in the hands of, say, Idi Amin."

"I thought he was out of business," McKinnon said.

"He is," Ives said. "I chose to use him as a hypothetical example for just that reason. But we all know that there are leaders in the Middle East and Africa and other suburbs of civilization who are just as irrational and savage. You can understand our concern."

Hawk gestured toward the waitress. She came over, looking at the check. "I'll have another hot chocolate, please," Hawk said.

The waitress looked as if she was going to say something. Hawk smiled pleasantly at her. She paused, then she picked up the check and huffed away. Ives was silent while she went for the hot chocolate, and silent when she came back and put it down and slapped the revised check down beside it and cleared Hawk's dish and cutlery away.

When she had gone again he said, "We had decided to recruit someone to de-effectuate Costigan. All of this is, of course, off the record."

"Deep background," I said.

"When, fortuitously . . ." Ives said.

"He mean lucky," Hawk said to McKinnon.

Ives sounded a little impatient. "Fortuitously, perhaps, for *all* of us, it was brought to our attention that you two were already involved in a pissing contest with Costigan."

"How did that come to your attention?" I said.

"McKinnon."

"How did it come to your attention?" I said.

McKinnon nodded at Quirk.

"You knew about Costigan?" I said to Quirk.

Quirk shrugged and tipped his cup so as to drain the last of his coffee without lifting his elbow from the table.

McKinnon said, "He won't tell you, so I will. He didn't know Costigan except as a famous name any more than you did. When the arrest warrants for you two started flowing in from California, he came in to see me. See if we could do anything to get your ass out of the crack, you know? I'd been talking with other people"—he nodded at Ives—"about their problem with Costigan and I got hold of them, and here we are."

Hawk looked at Quirk and raised his eyebrows. "I knowed that, I give you two bites of my toast."

Quirk said to Ives, "Let's hear the rest."

"So, when your situation came to our attention, we

looked into you both. What we found about you tells us that you are just the people to twist Costigan's tail for us."

"And if we do?" I said.

"You'll be doing your country a service. Your country will wish to repay you."

"We kill Costigan," Hawk said, "and you kill the charges on us."

Ives nodded.

"Just Jerry Costigan?" I said.

"Cut off the head and the snake dies," Ives said.

"How about Russell?" I said.

Ives shrugged. "If Russell takes over his father's business the world can rest easier," he said. "Russell will have all the gears jammed in six months. On the other hand, my information is that you might have your own reasons to want to drop the hammer on him. If you do we don't object."

"And the charges?" Quirk said.

"The charges will quite simply be deep-sixed," Ives said. "It's a fabric we know how to weave."

Quirk said, "You are probably going to have to kill him anyway."

I nodded.

"He's got a contract out on both of you," Quirk said.

"Figures."

It was late morning by now. The diner was starting to fill with people for lunch. The waitress glared at us as she passed, but she was too busy now to stop and stare at the check.

I looked at Hawk.

Hawk said to Ives, "I don't give a fuck about the emerging nations, or the needs of my government. I don't give a fuck whether Jerry Costigan dies or he doesn't or gets rich or pays his back taxes. I am interested in getting Susan

Silverman away from him and his kid. You help with that and I'm happy to put the state of California away for you, if you want."

Quirk said, "What happened to the superfly accent?"

Hawk grinned. "Sometimes ah forgets."

Ives looked at me. "You agree with your friend?"

"He said it very well."

"We help you chercher la femme, and you dispense Costigan."

"Yes," I said.

"And you fix the arrest warrants," Quirk said.

McKinnon said, "Whose fucking side you on in this, Marty?"

"It's a fabric they know how to weave," Quirk said.

"No problem with the charges," Ives said. "What will you need to find the girl."

"Woman," I said. "She's a grown woman."

Ives laughed briefly and shook his head quickly. "Whatever. What do you see us doing for you?"

"Guns," I said. "Money, access to my apartment. Intelligence."

"What kind of intelligence," Ives said.

"Whatever you have. Addresses, locations, phone numbers, habits, acquaintances, favorite color. Everything you have."

"Most of that is a walk in the spring rain," Ives said.

"We will need a place," I said. "In case Susan tries to reach me. We need a place to stay with a phone where Paul can reach me."

"You think she might escape on her own?" Ives said.

"I'm not sure she's exactly a captive," I said.

"Well, what the hell is she," Ives said.

"We'll see," I said.

"She walks out of the woods on her own," Ives said, "you've still got the murder raps and all that other garnish."

"We say we'll do it, we'll do it," I said.

Ives looked at Quirk. Quirk nodded.

"Roger," Ives said. "We'll set you up with a safe house, a phone, currency and weapons. It'll take a day or so. Once we've set it up, I can have some people come by and brief you. Meanwhile, where can I reach you?"

"Quirk will know," I said.

Ives was silent for a moment, then he shrugged. "Right," he said. "I need you I'll give Lieutenant Quirk a jingle." He reached inside his coat and came out with a business card. "You need me, call me." The card said simply Elliot Ives, and a Cambridge phone number. I put it in my wallet.

Ives picked up the check, looked at it, put four ones down on top of it, and took a small notebook out of his coat pocket. He entered the amount in his notebook.

"We'll be in touch before the weekend," Ives said. "I think we're going to be very happy together." He stood up and put the notebook in his coat pocket. "But remember one thing. I am not your wife. Don't try to fuck me."

"You sweet-talking bastard," Hawk said, and we went out of the diner.

Chapter 23

THEY PUT US IN AN APARTMENT ON MAIN STREET IN CHARLES-town, just out of City Square. It was on the second floor of a recycled brick building. There was a living room and kitchen across the front and two bedrooms and a bath across the back. If you looked out the front window you could see the Charlestown down ramp from the Mystic River Bridge. The kitchen was stocked with food. There was beer in the refrigerator and fresh linen on the beds. There were new toothbrushes in the bathroom. Hawk and I stayed there for two days drinking beer, doing push-ups and watching cable television before Ives came with an-other guy to brief us. The other guy looked like Buddy Holly.

"As I'm sure you are aware," Buddy Holly said, "our agency has no authorization for internal matters, so this briefing is entirely informal and off the record." His heavy horn-rimmed glasses slipped down his thin nose a little and he pushed them back up with his left forefinger. He had a three-ring binder on the table in front of him.

Hawk and I didn't say anything. We were sitting at the dining table at the end of the living room next to the kitchen. Buddy Holly sat opposite us and Ives sat on the couch with his legs stretched out and his arms resting on the back of the couch. Today's bow tie appeared to have a maroon dolphin motif. A big leather suitcase lay on the floor in the middle of the living room. There was a duffel bag beside it.

"Perhaps we should open the gifts, first," Ives said. He was running his eyes over the contours of the room as he spoke.

"Right," Buddy Holly said. He stood and went to the suitcases. "First," he said, "clothes." He opened the suitcase and began to lay the contents out in two piles.

"Underwear," he said. "Jeans, socks, polo shirts."

"I'm not wearing no shirt with a reptile on it," Hawk said.

"These seem to have small foxes on them," Buddy Holly said.

He continued to unpack. "Sweaters, a watch cap for each of you, a belt for each of you. Two new pair of Puma running shoes, one size nine, one size nine and a half. Six handkerchiefs apiece." He looked up at us and smiled.

"Handkerchiefs?" I said.

"Well, yes. You don't use handkerchiefs?"

"Only to tuck in my suitcoat pocket," I said.

"I'm afraid these aren't that kind."

I shrugged. "Don't seem to have a suit anyway."

Buddy Holly smiled. "No. We felt you would have no need for dressing up on this mission. But if it becomes a necessary expense I'm sure the agency will approve it."

"Enough of the software," Ives said from the couch. "Give them a gander in the duffel."

The duffel bag contained: two folding knives, with stainless steel handles and four-inch blades; two Smith & Wesson Model 13 .357 magnum revolvers with three-inch barrels in a bluesteel finish, still in their nice blue boxes; a Winchester .30-.30 rifle with lever action, and a walnut stock; a Mossberg 12-gauge shotgun with pump action; two boxes of .357 cartridges, one box of .30-.30, and a box of 12-gauge shotgun shells. There were shoulder rigs for the revolvers and belt-threaded ammo pouches. There were two Westwind warm-up jackets with quilted linings. There was a pair of binoculars, and two black leather saps. Buddy Holly set each of these items out with a brief description of its value and potential use to us. When he was through Ives said, "If you think you'll need anything else, let me know. If you need more ammunition say so."

"We use up all this," I said, "either we won't need more, or more won't help us."

"We can provide automatic weapons if you think you'll need them," Buddy Holly said.

I shook my head. "This will be fine," I said.

Buddy Holly glanced at Ives. He did that every few minutes. Then he said, "Good, well, let's get to the paper work."

He came back to the table, and sat down across from Hawk and me and opened his three-ring binder, and turned it so that Hawk and I could look at it as he spoke of its contents and pointed at it upside down, the way an insurance agent does when he points out the advantages of a Mod 5–10 in case you should, sir, God forbid, step out of the picture.

"Here's a picture of Jerry Costigan," he said, pointing with the eraser end of a pencil at the 8 1/2-by-11 glossy in its clear plastic envelope. "And this is Russell." He pointed at another 8 1/2-by-11 glossy on the facing page.

Russell still had ordinary features in a smallish face. The features seemed a little close to one another, as if his face were cluster zoned. His hair looked artfully tousled. Hawk leaned slightly forward, looking at the picture. I was leaning forward too.

"That Russell," he said.

"Recent?" I said to Hawk.

Hawk shrugged. "Still look like that," he said.

We both looked at the still glossy of Russell.

Finally Buddy Holly said, "Ah, now, is that enough? Will you remember his face?"

Hawk nodded. I said, "Yes."

"Good," Buddy Holly said. "Now, the pictures I'm going to show you are those of some of the men with whom the Costigans deal." He turned the page. There was a dark man with a large mustache wearing an ornate uniform.

"No," I said.

"No?"

"No. I don't care who Costigan deals with. What I need is information as to where Susan Silverman might be."

Buddy Holly glanced sideways at Ives. "Susan Silverman," Buddy Holly said.

"This too hard for you?" I said.

He looked at Ives again.

"The maiden in the tower," Ives said. "She's part of the deal."

Hawk's head lifted and he glanced at me. I turned slowly toward Ives. "She is the deal," I said.

"Absolutely," Ives said. "No question about it."

Buddy Holly looked confused. "Then they don't get the whole briefing?" he said to Ives.

Ives shrugged. "It's not stamped on their dog tags that they have to," he said.

"We need to know where Susan might be," I said. "Homes, apartments, resorts, hotels Russell often stays in, places he often goes. If you have anybody on his tail it would be good if you knew where he was now."

"We're not allowed to do domestic surveillance," Buddy Holly said.

Hawk got up and went into the kitchen, which was separated from the living room by a low counter. He looked over the wine bottles on the counter, took a Napa Valley Pinot Noir, uncorked it, poured some in a big wineglass, and came back in carrying the bottle and the glass. He gestured with the bottle at Ives.

"Too early in the day for me," Ives said.

"Probably always will be," Hawk said. He took a sip of wine and walked over to the front window and stood looking out at the off ramp.

"What have you got on the domestic habits of Russell Costigan?" I said.

"He lives with his parents," Buddy Holly said, "on Costigan Drive in Mill Valley, California."

Hawk turned slowly from the window. He was smiling widely, his eyes bright with pleasure. "Mill Valley?" he said.

Buddy Holly said, "Yes." He glanced at some notes in his folder. "Costigan Drive, it's on Mill River Avenue in Mill Valley. Mill Valley is north of San Francisco, I believe."

Hawk smiled some more. He looked at me.

"Good to know they're keeping the Russians at bay," I said.

"It's Mill River," I said. "Mill River is south of San Francisco."

"And it Mill River Boulevard," Hawk said. "Not avenue."

Buddy Holly studied his folder some more.

"I have here Mill Valley," he said. "And they maintained

a hunting lodge in the state of Washington. The lodge was recently destroyed by a fire of suspicious origin."

Hawk turned back toward the window. He poured some more wine from the bottle to the glass, and sipped some more as he looked out. "You folks get a chance, you want to send in some champagne?" he said. "French? Moët and Chandon, Taittinger, Dom Perignon, something like that?"

I got up from the table and walked to the kitchen and rested my hands on the kitchen sink and looked out the kitchen window.

"Good spot to hide us out," I said. "Hawk'll blend in perfect with all the other blacks in Charlestown."

"Maybe I use a disguise," Hawk said. "Faith and begorra, motherfucker."

"Listen," Ives said. "We don't keep these furnished nurseries everywhere. This is the best we had."

Buddy Holly said, "I really don't have too much else in domestic terms."

"Most of the domestic bird-dogging is done by our cousins in the Bureau," Ives said. "Perhaps Brother McKinnon can help you."

"Where'd you get this stuff?" I said, pointing with my chin toward Buddy Holly and his folder.

"The FBI supplies us with most of our domestic intelligence," Buddy Holly said.

"Sure," I said. A red Ford Bronco like Susan used to have came down the ramp from the bridge and turned left onto Main Street heading toward City Square. "We'll get them to help us."

Ives stood. "Punch in with us now and anon," he said. "We'll keep our nose right on the ground and feed you anything we catch."

I nodded. I could hear the click as Hawk poured himself

some more wine. Buddy Holly closed his folder and slipped it into his briefcase and stood.

Ives opened the door. "Happy trails," he said. He went out.

Buddy Holly followed. "Glad to be able to help," he said. "Good luck."

"Sure," I said. "And it's a damned shame about you and the Big Bopper."

Chapter 24

HAWK WAS DOING HANDSTAND PUSH-UPS AGAINST THE FAR wall of the living room when Rachel Wallace arrived. I introduced them and Hawk said hello upside down, and kept doing push-ups.

"We haven't had much chance to work out," I said. "And we're both getting feverish."

Rachel Wallace smiled and put her face up and kissed me. She looked good. Her dark hair was nicely brushed back from her pleasant face. Her makeup was careful and quiet. She wore gray slacks and a white blouse open at the throat. She had on a black velvet blazer and black boots with considerable heels. She took my hand when she kissed me and held it a moment after the kiss, as she stepped back and looked at me. Her nails gleamed with clear polish. On a chain around her neck were black-rimmed half glasses.

"How are you," she said.

"Functional," I said. "Perhaps even efficient. Thank you for coming up."

"Easy," she said. "And since my publisher is in Boston I can deduct the costs as business travel. Before I go back I'll have lunch with John Ticknor and make it all legitimate. Do you remember John?"

"Yes," I said. "But I'm a licensed investigator and I'm afraid I'll have to turn you in on the tax rap."

"I understand," she said. "But first can we make some martinis?"

I shook my head. "We're subsisting on government issue," I said. "There is a bottle of Scotch, blended, but after a couple you barely notice. And it gets the stains off your teeth."

Hawk rolled out of his hundredth or so push-up and into some sit-ups. I poured Rachel Wallace some Scotch over ice. And one for me, straight up.

"No beer?" she said.

"Scotch is quicker," I said.

"Yes it is," she said. "Are you drinking much?"

"Not as much as I want to," I said.

"Why not?"

"Need to be sober," I said. "I'm working."

Rachel Wallace nodded, touched my glass with hers, and drank about an ounce of the Scotch. We were leaning our hips against the kitchen counter.

"You want to talk about your feelings a little?" Rachel Wallace said.

I shook my head. "No, not now."

She looked at Hawk. "Would you like to go somewhere else and talk?"

"No," I said. "I have a lot of feelings. And I'm not embarrassed to talk in front of Hawk. It's just that the feelings won't help me now. Now I have other stuff I have to do. When it's done, maybe."

"I understand," she said. She took another whack of her

Scotch. "Well, let's get to work. How are we going to do this?"

"I'm not sure," I said. "But I know how we're not. We're not going to ask the feds to help us. The people I've talked with would have trouble finding Rin Tin Tin at a cat show."

Hawk came into the kitchen. He had his shirt off and a faint gloss of sweat covered his torso, head, and face. His breathing was easy and peaceful. He took a bottle of Moët and Chandon White Star champagne from the refrigerator and opened it. The bottle made a soft sigh as the cork came out. Hawk poured champagne into a large wineglass and shook his head.

"No wonder the country is going to hell," he said. "God-damned government don't even know enough to stock champagne glasses."

I nodded. "You'd figure a Republican administration would at least get that right."

We went into the living room and Rachel Wallace sat on the couch and put her boots on the coffee table and took a small note pad out of her purse. I sat at the kitchen table and nursed my Scotch. Hawk leaned against the doorframe that led to the kitchen. He held his glass in his left hand and the bottle in his right. He was looking at Rachel Wallace. She looked up at him and smiled. Hawk smiled back. There was nothing in Hawk's smile. Neither warmth nor insincerity. Hawk only communicated when he wished to.

"Why are you looking at me?" Rachel Wallace said. There was no hostility in her voice. Only curiosity.

"You a nice-looking woman," Hawk said.

"Thank you," she said. Hawk continued to look at her, and Rachel looked amused and turned to me.

"Hawk cannot believe," I said, "that any woman who is not ugly can fail to feel lust for him."

Rachel Wallace's smile widened and she nodded her head.

"Of course," she said. She looked back at Hawk. "It is difficult even for me," she said.

Hawk nodded and poured champagne. "That's heartening," he said in a North Shore twang. "I hate feeling insecure."

"I imagine so," Rachel Wallace said. "I'm sure you're not used to it."

"You want some more Scotch," Hawk said.

"Yes," Rachel Wallace said.

Hawk went and got the bottle and poured her another shot, over the ice that remained in her glass.

"You really a lesbian," Hawk said.

"I really am," Rachel Wallace said.

"Well," Hawk said, "save money on diaphragms I guess."

Rachel Wallace, halfway into a sip of Scotch, burst into laughter and nearly spilled all of her drink. Hawk grinned. This time there was warmth. I patted Rachel Wallace on the back until she stopped choking on the half-swallowed whiskey.

"Hawk has that special insight into minority situations," I said. "You have anything new on Costigan?"

Rachel Wallace took a deep breath. "Yes," she said. "Specifically I have the address of his wife."

"Not ex-wife," I said.

"As far as I can find out they are not divorced," Rachel Wallace said.

"Where's she live?"

"Chicago, Lake Shore Drive." She gave me the address, tearing the page from her notebook.

"What else?" I said.

"About the wife? Nothing else. I've already told you her name, Tyler Smithson. The two children live with her. She doesn't seem to work, though I'm not sure. Microfilm can take you only so far."

"What else do you have on any of the Costigans?"

"Transpan had labor problems at one time. There was a matter before the NLRB stemming from problems at a manufacturing site in Connecticut. I have only a second-hand reference to it yet, but I'll track it down. Once it gets into the government process it's just a matter of time."

I sipped a little more Scotch. The glass was empty. Hawk poured a little Scotch into my glass and took Rachel Wallace's glass and got more ice and poured Scotch into it and brought it back. She smiled at him.

"Thank you," she said. She was looking at him almost as he had looked at her. Then she looked at me and back at Hawk.

"He commands loyalty," she said, "doesn't he?"

"Spenser?" Hawk said.

"Yes," Rachel Wallace said. "Here you are, and here I am." She drank some of her Scotch. "Remarkable," she said.

Hawk poured some champagne into his glass and drank half of it. He didn't sip champagne, he drank it as if he was thirsty.

"I in jail in California, he come and got me out," Hawk said. "Turn it around, I do the same thing. But that ain't it. You see a black guy and a white guy working on something, you think the black guy helping the white guy. Lawzy me, Marse Spenser, let me lie down in front of dis heah truck fo' ya'll."

Rachel Wallace was still, looking very intently at Hawk.

"He dead," Hawk said, "and I be doing exactly the same thing. Susan need help, I help her."

Rachel Wallace looked down into her Scotch for a moment, then back up at Hawk, and her gaze was steady.

"I'm sorry," she said. "I treated you as his sidekick."

"That's right."

"I can't undo it," she said, "but I won't do it again."

"That's progress."

Rachel Wallace drank the rest of her Scotch. She reached for the bottle and Hawk beat her to it.

"Allow me," he said.

"Chicago in the morning?" I said to Hawk.

"First thing," he said.

"That leaves the rest of the day open," Rachel Wallace said. "Shall we get drunk?"

"We'd be fools not to," I said.

Chapter 25

Tyler Smithson's apartment was on the lake front near the point where W. Goethe Street joins the Drive. The march of high Gold Coast apartment buildings along the water was splendid to look at in the late summer sunshine, standing at the near north edge of Chicago. In other times Susan and I had come here and walked through Lincoln Park and hung around the zoo, holding hands and looking at the lions. We'd have dinner at Le Perroquet and go back to the Park Hyatt and make love in an elegant room with dark green walls.

The doorman called up to Tyler Smithson from the lobby phone.

"Gentleman named Spenser," he said into the phone. "Says it is in reference to Russell Costigan."

He nodded his head at me and hung up the phone. He was wearing a black uniform with red trim, his round pale face was freshly shaved, and he smelled of cologne.

"Penthouse," he said. "Elevator is straight back."

The elevator was lined with beige leather. It went up

silently and I stepped out into a small foyer. The walls were papered with something that looked like red velvet and might have been. There was a skylight above and a thick gray carpet below and straight ahead a raised panel door painted ivory and gilded around the perimeter of each panel. I rang the bell and smiled winningly at the peephole in the door. Just a friendly guy, come to visit, cut up a few touches about old Russell, easygoing, charming, welcome everywhere. The door opened. I widened my smile. It deepened the dimples in my cheeks and drove women wild.

"Hello," I said.

"Mr. Spenser?"

"Yes." Tyler Smithson Costigan was tall and slender with pale skin and blond hair cut in a Dutch-boy. She was wearing a pink shirt with a round collar, open at the neck, and a green plaid skirt with a pin in it.

"What is it about Russell Costigan?" she said.

"May I come in?"

"Yes, certainly. Sit down. Would you care for coffee, tea? Something to drink?"

"Coffee would be good," I said. "Black."

A middle-aged black woman appeared in the archway that apparently led to the kitchen.

"Two coffees, please, Eunice," Tyler Costigan said.

The black woman smiled and turned away and disappeared. I sat in a pink armchair. It was part of a collection of pink furniture that sat elegantly around on a gray rug like the one in the foyer. The walls were white on three sides of the room, and the fourth side was floor-to-ceiling glass that let you look across Lake Michigan. The view was startling and the light in the room was flood level. Tyler sat across from me on a pink couch and crossed her ankles. Her shoes were pink fabric, with flat heels and no arch. The pink matched her shirt, which matched her furniture. She smiled faintly at me.

"What is it about Russell Costigan, Mr. Spenser?"

"I can't think of a slick way to say this, Mrs. Costigan. Russell is somewhere with a woman I love. I wish to find them. I'm not convinced that she's with him by choice."

Tyler Costigan's smile disappeared.

"Susan? Whore."

I nodded my head slightly. "Can you help me find them?"

"My husband and his newest whore," Tyler Costigan said. It was hard keeping my dimples in place.

"You are separated from your husband, Mrs. Costigan?"

"Yes. His priorities seem muddled."

"What are his priorities," I said. Eunice came in with the coffee in a silver pot on a silver tray with silver cream pitcher and sugar bowl and silver spoons and two china cups with gilding on the rim and two china saucers with gilding around the edge. She put the tray on the white coffee table in front of Tyler Costigan, smiled at neither of us, and went out again. Tyler Costigan leaned forward and poured the coffee and handed it across the table to me. I took it and holding the saucer in my left hand took a sip from the cup. It was very good coffee and it had a slight vanilla edge to it. Tyler Costigan sat back without pouring any coffee for herself. She tucked her legs up under her on the couch, smoothing her skirt down over them.

"Russell Costigan's priorities are cocaine, whores, and whiskey, I believe in that order."

"By whores you mean women in his life, not necessarily always, ah, professional prostitutes."

"Decent women do not break up marriages," Tyler Costigan said. "Decent women do not fuck married men. Men with children and family. Men with homes. I call them whores."

The inelegant four-letter word was startling when she used it. I'd heard it almost hourly since I was a little boy, but from her it sounded dirty.

"Well, we have a common goal here, I think," I said. "We'd like to terminate this affair."

"How?"

"As I say, I think Susan is not with Russell entirely by choice. If I can find them, I'll help her to leave."

"They are always there by choice, Spenser. They love him. He's funny, and loose, and richer than you can imagine. He takes them places they've never been, he has them doing things they once blushed to think about. And after a while, he gets tired of them. Tired of fucking them, tired of feeding them dope and booze and teaching them things, and he kicks them loose and comes home."

"And you welcome him?"

"He makes himself welcome. The Costigans are very rich. Do you remember what somebody said about rich people? That they are different?"

"Fitzgerald," I said.

She shrugged. "The Costigans own everything they want. They have power. They'll know you were here, for instance. I'm always watched."

"That thought occurred to me," I said.

"If you persist, they will kill you," Tyler Costigan said.

"Russell is that potent?"

"His father is," she said. "Russell's potency is more narrowly specific."

"Is that why you welcome him back each time," I said. She shook her head.

"You love him?"

"Yes," she said, "but I could learn not to. It's . . ." She stopped talking and turned her head away toward the bright window wall where the light poured in. I was quiet. Way out on the lake a boat moved by itself. There was nothing else in sight on the surface of the lake, which stretched away to the horizon.

Tyler Costigan turned her face back toward me. "They let me keep the children," she said.

I nodded. Tyler Costigan leaned forward without untucking her legs and poured more coffee into my cup. I drank some.

"If you help me," I said, "I'll try not to hurt him."

She made a small laugh. "I would be better off if you killed him," she said. "But there's not much danger of that. The Costigans don't get killed, or hurt. Though I'm afraid you very well might."

"Where do you think he and Susan might be?" I said.

"Where have you looked?" she said.

"The Costigan house in Mill River. The lodge in Washington."

Tyler Costigan widened her eyes. "Do the Costigans know?"

"Yes," I said. "Jerry was in the house when we went in. We talked."

"You forced your way in?"

I nodded.

"You must have," she said, as I nodded. "Well, you are an interesting man."

"My friend helped me," I said.

"Your friend? My God. I'd have said the Marine Corps couldn't force their way into The Keep."

I drank some coffee.

"And the lodge?"

"We burned it down," I said. "Susan wasn't there."

Tyler Costigan opened her mouth and closed it and opened it again and didn't speak. The boat was almost to the left edge of the picture window, moving away at an angle.

Finally she said, "You must be as good as you look."

"Better," I said.

"Russell must love it," she said. "He loves to see his father lose."

I waited. The boat went out of sight.

"And, he must be having a wonderful time playing hide-and-seek with you."

"There's no allie-in-free," I said.

"He doesn't care. If it gets too bad his daddy will bail him out."

"How bad is bad?"

"If he starts to lose," she said. "Then he'll call his fat little momma and she'll speak to Jerry, and Jerry will send some people out to fix it. And"—she looked at me hard—"they will."

"If they can," I said.

"They always can," she said.

"We'll see," I said. "Where do you think they might be now?"

"You really believe you can win this, don't you?"

"Yes. I'm highly motivated."

"You want her back."

"Yes."

"And you think if you can get her away from Russell, she'll come back?"

"I'll get her away from Russell because she doesn't want to be with him. Once that's done we'll see about us."

"But you'd have her back."

"Yes."

"Because you love her?"

"Yes."

Tyler Costigan laughed. There was no pleasure in the sound and no humor. "I understand that perfectly," she said. She turned again to stare out into the bright afternoon. "I got Russell," she said without turning from the window. "She got you."

"The ways of the Lord are often dark," I said. "But never pleasant."

Chapter 26

THE BOAT WAS GONE NOW, AND THE LIGHT HAD SHIFTED SO that it slanted in from the west edge of the picture window. I had drunk six cups of coffee and felt as if maybe my skin would jump off and dance along the baseboard.

"The rich really are very different," Tyler Costigan was saying. "Especially if they are also unscrupulous."

"One of the ways they got rich," I said.

She nodded, but she wasn't paying me much attention. "They have always gotten what they wished, and after a while they think they are supposed to. If they have a problem they hire someone to solve it. And they become ever more contemptuous of people who cannot. They even become contemptuous of people who have problems. And eventually they are contemptuous of everyone and care only about what they want."

"Maybe that's true only of the Costigans," I said.

She looked at me as if I'd startled her from a reverie. "I believe it's true in general," she said.

"Okay," I said. "But I don't care about in general. I only

care about Russell Costigan. And, in truth, at the moment, I don't even care about him, only about where he is."

"If I had to guess," she said, "I'd guess he's in Connecticut."

I nodded.

"They have an arms manufacturing facility there, which includes a testing and training site. And it is very secure. Russell loves hide-and-seek, if his hiding place is safe."

"Where in Connecticut," I said.

"West of Hartford, near a town called Pequod."

"What's the name of the company?"

She shook her head. "I don't know," she said. "I don't know if it goes under Transpan, or they have a subsidiary name."

"Did they have labor trouble a few years back?"

She shook her head again, impatiently. "I don't know. I paid as little attention to the family business as I could. Russell didn't have that much to do with it either. He did some lobbying in Washington for a time. Or that's what he called it. It was mostly having parties and going to other parties and having lunch at Sans Souci. I think his father sent him there to keep him occupied. His mother loved it. 'Rusty deals with the government,' she'd say."

"Rusty?"

"Grace calls him that. Have you seen her?"

"Yes."

"She's incredible," Tyler Costigan said. "She is a fat little dumb woman. She must be sixty-five and still talks baby talk, and she jerks those two men around any way she wants."

"No other kids?"

Tyler Costigan smiled. "Just Rusty," she said, making the *R* sound almost like a *W*.

"Probably an adorable baby," I said.

"In many ways he's an adorable man," she said. "Except
. . ." She leaned her head back, thinking of how to say it.
"Except he hasn't got any . . ." She took a breath and
made an aimless gesture. "He hasn't got any realness. He's
funny and fun and warm and loving, but if anything gets too
hard he moves on. He's never loved a great love. Unless it
was Grace, whom he now hates."

The sun must have moved behind something, off window
left, and the room was much dimmer.

"Maybe that's why the whores. They don't require what
he doesn't have, or doesn't know how to offer. If any of the
whores start to want it he can move on."

"Russell is probably Susan's first affair," I said. "She's
not a whore."

She smoothed her skirt again although there wasn't a
wrinkle in it. "I know," she said. "I'm sorry. It's a way for
me to dehumanize them."

"I understand that," I said.

"But if I were a man," she said, "I imagine you wouldn't
let me say it."

"No," I said. "If I didn't need your help, I wouldn't let
you say it."

She sat a little straighter and leaned slightly back as if to
look at me better. She smoothed her skirt again over her
thighs, her legs still curled beneath her.

"You're very clear, aren't you, on what you want."

"Yes," I said.

We were silent. "Life is surely difficult," she said.

I didn't say anything.

"Why must it be so hard," she said. She wasn't looking at
me. She was watching the afternoon gather into evening
out over Lake Michigan. I looked at it too. "Why must love

be so hard?'' she said. She turned her head from the window and looked quite sharply at me. She leaned forward slightly over her smoothed skirt, her hands still resting on her thighs. "Do you know why?" she said.

"Original sin," I said.

As I came out of Tyler Costigan's building a maroon four-door Pontiac slid up along the curb beside me. The doors, front and back, opened on the sidewalk side and a guy got out of each of them. The one who came from the front wore a gray glen plaid suit and a black shirt open at the neck with the collar points spread out over the lapels of his jacket. He was taller than I am and had his slick black hair combed straight back in even waves. The guy from the backseat wore designer jeans and stack-heeled boots and a shiny brown leather jacket with a short mandarin collar. There was a strap on the collar in case a typhoon hit. He had a brown beard trimmed very short, and short brown curly hair. A block up the street a gray Plymouth swung around the corner onto the drive and idled by the curb.

The man in the suit said, "Get in the car, we want to talk with you." His partner with the curly hair stood to my left. His jacket was unzipped.

"You from Costigan?" I said.

The guy in the suit said, "Mm hm," and jerked his head at the open back door of the Pontiac.

"What do you want to talk with me about?" I said.

"We want to talk with you about fucking around where you got no business fucking around."

"Oh," I said. "You want to talk with me about that too."

"Come on, come on," he said and flashed his coat open to show me the gun on his belt.

"Show me that again," I said.

He opened his coat again and I hit him a gorgeous left

hand in the V under his ribs where the sternum ends. It paralyzed his diaphragm and he gasped and doubled over and then pitched forward onto the sidewalk. Curly's hand went inside the jacket toward his left armpit and the driver of the Pontiac threw open the door on his side and came out of the car. I looped my right fist overhand in a movement that developed out of the left to the stomach and hit Curly square on the nose. Blood came at once. He had the gun half out of the holster, his hand still under the jacket, when I grabbed his wrist with my left hand and held his gun hand against his chest, the gun caught under the jacket, and I hit him twice more with my right, square in the nose. He sagged and I shoved him away, ducking as I did so, feeling the driver more than seeing him. He had his gun out and brought it to rest on the roof of the car, his door swinging wide into the street, when the gray Plymouth swung in beside the Pontiac and picked the driver off and the open door and scattered them onto Lake Shore Drive. I ducked around the Pontiac and jumped in on the passenger side of the Plymouth.

"You want to run over the other two," Hawk said.

I shook my head and Hawk pulled the Plymouth away and we headed down the Drive.

I said, "Did you take the insurance option when you rented this thing?"

"Sure," Hawk said, "but since I used a fake ID and a phony credit card, I don't guess it make a big difference."

"There's that," I said.

Hawk pulled onto North Michigan Avenue.

"Those folks from Costigan?" he said.

"Yes. Said they were going to talk with me about fucking around where I have no business fucking around."

"You explain that your profession?" Hawk said.

"I was going to," I said, "but he kept showing me his gun and frightening me."

Hawk turned right onto Ontario Street heading for the Kennedy Expressway.

"Find out anything from the broad?" Hawk said. "You in there long enough."

"It took her a while," I said. "Something I learned that I didn't expect to, she loves the son of a bitch. She hates him too, but she loves him."

"Don't care about who loves him and who don't," Hawk said. We pulled up onto the Kennedy heading for O'Hare Airport. "She got any idea where he might be?"

"Yeah," I said and told him, in sequence, just what Tyler Costigan had told me. Telling him that way helped me sort through and see if there was anything that I hadn't noticed first time through. Hawk listened silently, driving with the barest movement of his hands, his eyes steady on the road.

"Connecticut," he said when I was through. "Christ. We should have enrolled in one of those frequent flyer programs when this started. Get ourselves a free trip to Dallas or something."

"Second prize is two free trips to Dallas," I said.

Chapter 27

PEQUOD STANDS ON THE FARMINGTON RIVER, TWENTY MILES west of Hartford in a green hilly section of Connecticut. There was a small bend in the river and as you came around a curve in the road that hugged the river, there it was. A three-story brick building with a cupola on the roof, a restaurant on the first floor with some hanging plants in the window. There was also a Sunoco station, a Cumberland Farms convenience store made as rustic as a Cumberland Farms was likely to get, with texture 1-11 plywood siding stained gray. Across from the restaurant was another three-story brick building. No cupola this time, but across the second story an open balcony ran the length of the building. There were two or three white Victorian-vintage houses with wide verandas that sat on the small slope that ran up from the road, and then you were through Pequod, and the hills and the river were all there was again.

"Look like a dynamite liberty port," Hawk said.

"Throbbing," I said.

"Only thing they don't seem to have is a . . ." Hawk

flipped open the manila folder on his lap and read from Rachel Wallace's notes. "Diversified Weapons Fabrication and Testing Facility."

"A subsidiary of Transpan International," I said.

Five miles past Pequod we turned left at a sign that said DEVILS KINGDOM, with an arrow, and crossed the river on a small bridge. Instead of paving, the roadbed of the bridge was made of crisscrossed steel bars, rather like a grating, so that if you looked straight down out the side window you could see the river moving below.

Coming off the bridge the road forked, the main macadam two-lane highway stretching straight north toward Massachusetts, a smaller road veering left along the river and disappearing in a copse of sugar maples. We went along the small road. Past the trees a plain stretched out north from the river and on it stood a long cinderblock building, a small frame building, and perhaps six Quonset huts painted gray. A chain link fence stood ten feet high, topped with razor wire, around the buildings. At each corner was a watchtower.

"Look like a prison," Hawk said.

"Transpan International," I said. "Unless Rachel Wallace is badly confused."

"I bet she ain't," Hawk said.

We drove slowly past. There was a large gate with a guard shack beside it. Beyond the fenced area there was a firing range and past that something that looked like it might be an obstacle course that led into the woods. There was no one on the range but there was movement on the obstacle course; people in camouflage fatigues ran and jumped among the trees, hard to see through the foliage at a distance.

Hawk watched silently as we drove past.

"Fire on the range," he said, "run the obstacle course, that get you a twenty-four-hour pass to Pequod."

"Makes you want to re-up," I said.

"But whose army?" Hawk said. "Who these guys in the dappled threads?"

A hundred yards up the road I stopped the car and we sat looking back at the complex.

"What Rachel say they have government trouble about?" Hawk said.

The big metal roll-up door at one end of the nearer cinderblock building opened and a forklift truck bearing several stacked crates beetled from the door and across the open mill yard and into the next building.

"Federated Munitions Workers tried to organize the place. Transpan did a lockout. Federated sued, the NLRB got involved in mediation. Transpan brought in non-union workers. There was some violence. The thing's been in the courts since 1981."

"Security look excellent," Hawk said. "See the dogs."

"Yes." Inside the perimeter of the chain link fence a guard in mottled fatigues walked with a German shepherd on a short leash. The guard had an automatic weapon slung on his shoulder.

"There's three more," I said.

"Yep, walking so that one is always along each side of the square."

"And the watchtowers on the corners," I said.

"And you want to bet they got the fence wired," Hawk said. "Rachel say what they doing in there?"

"No. Arms manufacturing. But what arms, and what the assorted doughboys are for, she doesn't say."

"What you want to do," Hawk said.

"Figure there's no place else around here. If these guys are going to drink they'll have to come into Pequod. Maybe we can hang around the bar there and see what we can learn. Unless you want to shoot our way in."

Hawk grinned. "Not yet," he said.

A dark blue Jeep came out of the front gate and drove up the road toward us. Hawk slid his handgun out from under his warm-up jacket and held it down beside his right leg between the seat and the door.

The Jeep stopped beside us and two men in blue coveralls and blue baseball hats got out and walked over to the car. One stood behind our car, the other came around to the driver's side. Both wore army-style flapped holsters on web belts. A patch on the sleeve of the jump suit said TRANSPAN SECURITY. The guard leaned down and looked in the car window. He wore reflecting sunglasses and a dark beard and very little of his face showed under the down-pulled bill of his hat.

"Excuse me," the guard said, "may I ask why you gentlemen are parked here?"

"Gee," I said, "we didn't mean any harm. We were just wondering what this place was. Is it an army base?"

"I'm sorry," the guard said, "but this is a restricted area and I'll have to ask you to move on."

"This area? I didn't know. I thought it was a regular public road."

The guard shook his head. "I'll have to ask you to drive on."

"Sure, officer," I said. "We're from out of state. Is there anyplace good around here to get a steak and a few beers?"

"Pequod House," he said. "Go down here, cross the bridge, and about five miles east you'll find it."

"You go there?" I said. "Is it good?"

He grinned, his teeth suddenly bright in his beard. "Good, bad, doesn't matter. It's the only place in fifty miles."

"Oh," I said, "I gotcha. Okay, thanks. We'll go there then. You guys Army?"

"No, private operation. Turn it around now and move out."

"Yes, sir," I said. "Thanks for the tip."

I U-turned and we drove slowly back down the way we'd come. The Jeep followed us, past the Transpan complex and all the way to the bridge.

Across the bridge Hawk slid the magnum back under his coat.

"You kept your dignity," Hawk said. "You didn't jump out and kiss his ass."

"Humble but proud," I said. "And we know where the guards hang out off duty."

Chapter 28

HAWK AND I GOT A ROOM ON THE SECOND FLOOR OF THE Pequod House, dumped our luggage in it, and went down to the bar.

It was a big square room with a bar along one wall and tables filling the rest. There were three men at the bar and one middle-aged couple at the far end of the room sitting at a table having early supper. The waitress had stiff blond hair and bright pink lipstick. She was thin and her brown waitress uniform was too big for her. She put two mimeographed menus down in front of us.

"Specials tonight are chicken pot pie and calves' liver with bacon," she said.

"You have steak," Hawk said.

"Yes, sir," she said, "best in the Valley."

"I believe that," Hawk said. "I'll have one, medium rare. And a double vodka martini on the rocks with a twist."

"You want that before the meal, sir?"

"Un huh."

I ordered the same thing. And the waitress went briskly to the bar.

"You gonna ask her, she seen Susan Silverman," Hawk said.

"Not yet."

The waitress came back with the martinis.

"Go good with dinner," Hawk said. "But I thought they'd serve it in a jelly glass with a straw."

I drank a little of the martini.

"I think I know your plan," Hawk said. "You figure we sit here till Russell and Susan decide to go out to dinner and catch them when they come here."

"Hell, I don't have a plan that good," I said.

"You know what you doing?"

"No."

Hawk drank some martini. "Not bad," he said.

"Even bad martinis aren't bad," I said.

We drank again. "Didn't want to order champagne," Hawk said. "This the kind of place you order champagne they bring you Cold Duck in a styrofoam cup."

I finished mine and waved at the waitress and put up two fingers. She came over.

"Did you wish something, sir?"

"Two more," I said.

"Two more drinks?"

I smiled attractively. "Yes," I said.

"What kind, sir?"

I smiled harder. "Two more martinis," I said. "On the rocks, with a twist. Actually with two twists, one in each martini."

"Yes, sir."

She raced off toward the bar.

"Probably hurrying so she won't forget 'fore she get there," Hawk said.

"No wasted motion," I said.

The waitress came hurrying back, carrying a tray. She put steak and french fries down in front of us. She put out two small dishes of canned carrots, and a basket of rolls. There were squares of foil-wrapped butter in the basket with the rolls.

"I'll get your drinks right away," she said.

Hawk looked at his plate and then at me. The steaks were wide and flat, covering nearly the whole plate, and about a half-inch thick at best. There was a large bone in each steak.

"Better wait and drink the second martini," I said.

"What kind of steak you figure this is," Hawk said.

"Camel."

Hawk nodded. "Well, we didn't actually say *beef* steak, did we."

The waitress brought the second martinis. Hawk and I each drank some.

"Gin," we said simultaneously.

"We could send them back," Hawk said.

"Yeah, but the next one might be made with Kool-Aid," I said.

"You right," Hawk said and drank some more.

The steak looked better than it tasted. The french fries were not edible. The carrots had been cooked for maybe an hour and a half. The rolls tasted like sugarless marshmallows.

"Wow, you boys must have been hungry," the waitress said when she cleared the plates.

The place was filling up, some diners and a lot of drinkers. I paid the check and we moved to the bar. We each ordered beer.

"What do people do for a living around here," I said to the bartender.

"Transpan mostly," he said. "Half the people in here tonight work out at the facility."

"What's Transpan," Hawk said.

"They make guns," the bartender said. He had on a white shirt and a black string tie. His gray hair was short. "They got a big factory about five miles from here. There's a range and a test course. Big facility."

"They hiring?" I said.

"Hard to get hired," the bartender said. "Need specialist skills, you know? Gunsmith, heavy-weapons specialist, that kind of stuff. I never heard of them hiring anyone local."

"We know a little about weapons," I said. "And we're not local. Who do we talk to?"

The bartender shrugged. "Got me," he said. "Guys at the big round table work there. Maybe they can help. Was me I'd go down to the state employment office in Hartford."

He moved away.

I turned away and leaned my elbows on the bar and sipped the draft beer and looked at the big round table. They were drinking Pabst Blue Ribbon beer from long-necked bottles and a number of them had collected on the table. They had placed a ring of lit cigarettes on the table and were arm wrestling inside the ring, the loser getting his knuckles burned. The winner of the first two matches was a fat guy with crew-cut red hair and a full beard. He had on a denim shirt with the sleeves cut off and his arms were bright pink and thick as country hams.

I said to Hawk, "Let's get in on this?"

"Which of us?"

"Whichever one sees the chance," I said.

"Should we win or lose?"

"See how it goes," I said.

We went with our beers in hand and stood near the group watching the contests. The fat man won another, slowly overpowering a lean black man and pressing his knuckles briefly against the cigarette. The rest of the table whooped.

The fat man looked around the table. There was another black, a squat man with long arms, wearing a baseball cap backward.

"You want to hold up the honor of the spooks, Chico?"

The black man shrugged and moved over beside the fat man. He set his elbow on the table and they locked hands.

"Anytime," the fat man said. Chico turned his wrist sharply, trying to catch the fat man unready, and he almost made it. The fat man's arm went maybe forty-five degrees down before he began to hunch his shoulder and steadily press Chico's arm back and down toward the cigarettes. Chico held for a moment six inches from the tabletop, then his arm gave way and the back of his hand pressed against the burning cigarettes. The fat man held it there.

"Got to yell, Chico. Got to say ow."

Chico said, "Ow."

The fat man grinned. "Goddamned near got me, Cheeks. Goddamned near made it. Be a son of a bitch if I lost my first time to a goddamned spook."

Chico grinned and put the back of his hand to his mouth.

Hawk said, "How about me?"

The fat man looked up. "Hell yes," he said. "How about a little money on it. With friends I do it for fun. But strangers . . ." Hawk took a twenty out and tossed it on the table.

He said to Chico, " 'Scuse me, bro," and sat in the chair.

"Name's Red," the fat man said. He was looking at Hawk carefully.

Hawk nodded.

"You got a name," Red said.

"Black," Hawk said.

"Well, you're hot shit, ain't you," Red said.

Hawk sat opposite Red and placed his elbow on the table. He and Red locked hands. Next to Red, Hawk looked nearly slender.

"Anytime," Red said.

Hawk nodded and said, "You say."

Red said, "Now," and lunged his forearm against Hawk's. Slowly Hawk's forearm bent backward toward the tabletop. Red's teeth showed through his beard. Hawk had no expression. He looked at me. Four inches from the tabletop Hawk's arm stopped moving down. Red grunted with effort. Hawk kept looking at me. I nodded and mouthed the word *win*. With no change in expression Hawk began to lift Red's arm back up the way it had come. It was a steady, apparently effortless movement, except that the muscles in Hawk's arm swelled so that the hem on the sleeve of his polo shirt split. He pressed Red's hand firmly against the lit cigarette.

Red said, "Ow," and Hawk released his hand, picked up the two twenties and folded them neatly lengthwise in half, running his thumb and forefinger along the crease to smooth it. Red stared at him with the back of his right hand pressed against his mouth. No one spoke.

Hawk gestured at the waitress. "Bring us a round," he said, and handed her one of the folded twenties.

"You got me when I was tired," Red said. "My right arm was tired."

Hawk nodded pleasantly.

"Double or nothing, left-handed," Red said.

Hawk nodded toward me. "Try him," Hawk said.

Red looked at me. "You left-handed?" he said.

"No."

"Double or nothing?" Red said to Hawk.

Hawk nodded. He stood and I took his seat. Red and I locked left hands.

"I'll call it," Red said.

"Sure."

Red said, "Go," and I slammed his hand down onto the lit cigarette. The force scattered the cigarettes.

"Wait a minute," he said. "Wait a minute. I wasn't ready."

"Okay," I said. "We'll do it again. You call."

We locked hands again. Red took in a couple of deep breaths.

"All right," Red said. "When I say go."

"Sure."

"Go."

Red's grip tightened and he tried to turn my wrist.

"You ready?" I said.

Red nodded, straining against my wrist.

"You sure?"

"Ya."

"Okay," I said and slammed his hand against the table.

The waitress arrived with a tray of beer bottles and there was silence while she distributed them and picked up the empties. She went away.

"Where the fuck did you guys come from," Red said. "You guys got to be from another fucking planet."

"It's because our hearts are pure," I said.

"I ain't got the forty," Red said. "I gotta owe it to you."

"When do I get it," I said.

"Tomorrow, you gonna be around. I get paid tomorrow."

"Sure," I said. "We'll be around tomorrow."

"I'm good for it," Red said. "Ask any of these guys. I pay what I owe."

"I believe you," Hawk said. "But where you work, case we have to come find you, case you forget."

"Transpan," Red said, "but I won't forget. Man, ask anyone. I owe you money, it's like you got it in the bank. Tell him, Chico. He's a brother, he'll believe you."

Chico nodded.

I ordered another round. "Winner buys," I said.

Red licked the back of his right hand where the cigarette burn was reddening.

"Another goddamned planet," Red said. Hawk snagged a chair from another table and sat at the round one.

"You guys all work at Transpan?" I said.

"Yeah," Chico said. "Sort of."

The waitress brought the beer.

"What do you mean, sort of?" I said.

"Contract work," Red said. "We signed on to do training and weapons testing. Working on a two-year contract. After two years we can sign on again or get out."

"Like the army," I said.

Red looked at me for a moment.

"Yeah," he said. "It's like that."

Chapter 29

THE NEXT NIGHT RED SHOWED UP AS PROMISED. HAWK AND I had hung around Pequod all day, topping off the excitement with a five-mile run along the highway, and we were just sipping the first beer of the day when Red came in.

"Who gets the forty," he said.

I put out a hand and Red put two tens and a twenty in it.

"Winner buys," I said. "What will you drink?"

"Beer."

I gestured at the bartender. He gave Red a beer, and a glass. Red ignored the glass and drank half the bottle from the neck.

"We're looking for a place to live," I said. "Got any ideas?"

Red shrugged. "Not much around," he said. "I live out at the facility."

He finished the beer. I ordered him another. "Want a shot with that," I said. "Get a good foundation for the evening."

"Sure," Red said. "CC," he said to the bartender. "Straight up."

"Everyone live there?"

"Yeah, all of us." He popped the shot and washed it with a swallow of beer. Hawk gestured at the bartender to bring another. "Us guys, the workers, security people. Nice facility."

"How 'bout the bosses," Hawk said.

"Sure, them too. Got an executive house. Fucking mansion." Red drank half of his second Canadian Club. "Nice lawn, right on the river. Can't see it from the road, it's in the trees."

"Outside the complex?"

"Un uh. Everything's inside the complex, except the training range."

We had another round of beers. Red turned and leaned his elbows on the bar and surveyed the room.

"Thing about this job is you're stuck out here in the fucking sticks, you know," he said. "Pussy is scarcer than balls on a heifer."

"No broads at the complex?" I said.

"Couple old ugly fat-assed secretaries," Red said. "Some executive quiff over at the mansion. But nothing for the blue-collar stiffs like you and me, you know."

"No wives?"

"Naw, they don't hire married guys."

"Except the executives."

Red finished his Canadian Club. Hawk got him another.

"Not even them. Except for the kid."

Red drank a little of the Canadian Club, sipping it carefully as if it were a fine cognac.

"There a kid there?" Hawk said.

Red laughed. "Naw, the kid. Guy owns the whole Transpan thing is a guy named Costigan. I never seen him but his kid comes around once in a while, like to inspect, you know.

Kid's about thirty, thirty-five. Comes in like the regimental commander—you guys been in the service?" We both nodded. "Kid comes in, lives at the mansion, comes around watches us train, shit like that. Sometimes he brings a broad." Red grinned. "Usually ain't the same one."

"Must be a pain in the ass," I said, "having him around."

"Naw, not really. Most of the time him and the broad are just at the mansion. They got a pool over there and a game room, place is like a fucking resort, you know. Shit, they been here about two weeks, now. We ain't seen him for ten minutes."

"Big bucks, huh?"

"Biggest. You ever hear of the old man? Jerry Costigan? He's worth more than Saudi Arabia, for crissake. Kid goes everywhere with about eight bodyguards." Red continued to survey the room. "Damn," he said, "sure would be nice to see a little pussy."

"How long you been here," I said.

"Eight months. If it wasn't for that skinny waitress we'd all be dating Mary Palm and her five daughters. Like fucking a bundle of kindling, but it's better than nothing."

The blond waitress in question hurried intently past us carrying a plate of gray pork chops toward a table in the front.

"Queen of the Transpan Forces," Red said. "Any of us get the clap, we all get the clap." He laughed and drank the rest of his whiskey. "Just pass it back and forth through Doreen."

We got another round.

"Where'd you work before?" Hawk said.

"Angola, Zambia. Put in some time in Rhodesia."

"The old country," Hawk murmured.

"Construction?" I said.

"Shit, no, man. Soldiering."

"Mercenary?" Hawk said.

Red drank some whiskey. "Bet your ass, mercenary. Soldier of fucking Fortune, Jim. All of us are."

"Done a little of that," Hawk said.

"Yeah? Where'd you soldier?"

"Did a little Foreign Legion," Hawk said.

"No shit? The Frenchies?" Red laughed with pleasure. "C'est la fucking guerre, monsieur. Huh?" He put his hand out palm up and Hawk slapped it.

"Oui," Hawk said.

"You in Indochina?" Red said.

"Un huh."

"Missed that," Red said. "But I done some shit in Malaya. God damn, I love it. A fire fight. Jesus. A fire fight's better than fucking, you know. That's got to be the most fun in the world. You like that shit?"

"Fucking ain't bad," Hawk said.

"Ain't that the truth," Red said. "How 'bout you, pal. Where'd you soldier?"

"Korea," I said.

"He got medals," Hawk said.

"And seventy-eight bucks a month," I said.

"Mercenary's better," Red said. "Get the same fun and a lot more bread."

We finished the round and had another. "You quit soldiering after Korea?" Red said.

"Yes."

"Don't like the life?"

"Don't like the chain of command."

Red nodded. "Yeah, that's a pain in the ass. The chicken shit. That's why I like this. I don't like the chicken shit, I quit. Move on. Fuck it." He drank his whiskey. "And the guys, man. I love soldiering with the guys, you know?"

I nodded. "I know," I said.

"So what do you do for a living," Red said.

I shrugged. "Little of this, little of that."

"Mostly we scuffle," Hawk said.

Red tipped his head. "Scuffle?"

"Yeah," I said. "We're good with guns, we got quick hands."

"Shit," Red said, "that ain't bad. You working now?"

"No. We're sort of looking."

Red turned toward the bartender and gestured. "Man die of fucking thirst around here," he said.

"What kind of soldiering you do around here," I said.

"We're training right now."

"Giving or receiving," I said.

Red frowned. "Huh?"

"Are you training people or being trained."

"Being trained," Red said. "Counterinsurgency."

"Figured you might already know that," Hawk said.

"Oh man, shit," Red said. "Course I know that. I been an insurgent and a counterinsurgent and an imperialist fucking warmonger and fifty-three other things. But they pay me and they want to train me and I get trained."

"How come a weapons manufacturer is training troops?" I said.

Red shrugged. "Supposed to familiarize us with some new-generation weapons. So's we can go train customers. But I know counterinsurgency training when I take it."

"We were out past there yesterday," I said. "Just cruising around and the security people told us to screw."

"Yeah. Security's real tight."

"Don't want people slipping in and scooping samples," I said.

Red grinned. "Ain't people slipping in," he said. "They don't want people slipping out." His face had reddened and for the first time his speech began to slur a little. If I'd had that many boilermakers they could iron clothes on me.

"You're out," I said.

"Sure, they don't worry about us. They worry about the workers."

"The workers don't get out?"

Red shook his head. He drank. Looked around the room. His eyes picked up the thin waitress and followed her across the room. "Getting drunk," Red said. "Always tell when Doreen starts looking better."

"How come the workers don't get out?" I said.

"Got me," Red said, his eyes still on Doreen. "Probably paying them shit and afraid one of them will complain to somebody. Most of them are foreign, probably illegal."

"Complain about pay and get deported," I said.

Red shrugged. "Company gets its ass burned too, though."

Doreen hurried past, frowning with concentration. Red patted her backside as she passed. She neither slowed nor looked at him.

"They hiring out there," I said to Red.

"Don't think so. You guys know weapons?"

"Up to mortars," I said. "For sure. After that, maybe."

Red nodded. "Anything else? Sometimes they need instructors."

"Hand-to-hand," Hawk said. "PT. Arm wrestling."

Red grinned, "Yeah, too bad we ain't looking for arm wrestlers. We got a PT and unarmed combat guy. Big old buck name of Elson."

"Billy Elson?" I said.

"Naw, Lionel Elson from Hamtramck, Michigan."

"Don't know him," I said. "How about PT?"

Red laughed. "I look like a guy does a lot of PT. Lionel does the PT but most of us don't pay much attention. Him and Teddy Bright."

"Well, ask around, will you? We're looking for work and we'd rather work in some out-of-the-way place, you know?"

"Where there ain't a lot of cops," Red said.

"Where it's quiet," Hawk said.

Red winked and finished his drink. "I can dig it, babe. Lot of us got places we better not go back to."

Hawk smiled pleasantly.

Red rocked slightly against the bar. "I'll ask the cadre chief," he said. "You never know."

"Hardly ever," I said.

Chapter 30

"MAN GOT HIMSELF A PRIVATE ARMY," HAWK SAID. "LIKE A Chinese warlord."

I nodded. We were driving toward Hartford, east, directly into the morning sun. The road was curvy and not wide.

"We could kick the shit out of Lionel and Teddy," Hawk said. "Maybe persuade folks we could do their job better."

"That's always an option," I said. "Let's try this way first."

Hawk shrugged. "Hate getting tied in to those government assholes," Hawk said. "They could fuck up a square knot."

We found a diner in West Hartford with an outside pay phone. Hawk went to order breakfast and I called Ives on the number he'd said was always manned. He'd misstated slightly. This morning it was womaned. She said a noncommittal hello. I said I wanted to talk with Ives and she said could he call me back. I gave her the pay phone number and hung up and waited.

Ives called back in five minutes. "Good to see you early-birding it," he said. "Caught any worms yet?"

"Not yet," I said. "Here's what we need. We need two guys that work at the Transpan weapons facility in Pequod, Connecticut, to disappear."

"Permanently?" Ives said.

"A month ought to be plenty," I said.

"What are their names?"

"Lionel Elson and Teddy Bright."

"Teddy Bright?"

"Would I make it up," I said.

"What else can you tell me?"

"They are instructors in hand-to-hand combat and physical training at the Transpan test range."

"Why does a manufacturer have a hand-to-hand combat instructor?"

"We'll find that out," I said. "After you scoop Lionel and Teddy."

"Do you care how we do it?"

"No. We're angling to get hired in their place and so it shouldn't look rigged and it shouldn't connect us."

"Hurry?"

Behind me a big ten-wheeler ground past, down-shifting as it slowed for a stoplight in the next block.

"Ives," I said. "You need to remember why I'm in this?"

"Ah yes, the maiden in the tower."

"After this is over, Ives, you and I may have to discuss your tone. But right now I want her out of that tower," I said. "And every day she's not out of it is a long and wearing day."

"We'll move with judicious speed, young Lochinvar. Sit tight."

"Do it in the evening when Hawk and I are sitting around the bar in the Pequod House."

"We know our business," Ives said. "We don't need too much advice."

"Didn't you guys engineer the Bay of Pigs."

"Before my time, laddie buck. I'll call you at the Pequod House when it's done and tell you your order has been delayed."

I hung up and went into the diner. Hawk was on a stool eating steak and eggs. There was a teen-age girl behind the counter wearing cutoff jeans and rubber shower clogs. She looked at me when I sat down.

"Coffee," I said. "Cream and sugar."

She brought it black in a thick diner mug and pushed the cream pitcher and the sugar shaker at me.

"Ives gonna do it?" Hawk said.

"Yeah."

"He gonna fuck it up?"

"Maybe not," I said.

"Folk at Transpan might think it funny that these guys disappear right when we come on the scene."

"Maybe, but if they do what have we lost. We're outside looking in now."

"They get suspicious," Hawk said, "maybe they decide to clip us."

"They'll decide to try that sooner or later," I said. "I still don't see us being any worse off for trying."

Hawk wiped up some egg yolk with his toast. He put the piece of toast in his mouth and wiped his fingers on a napkin.

"And it might work," he said.

"We never lost money yet," I said, "underestimating the intelligence of the Costigans."

Hawk put the last piece of steak in his mouth and chewed carefully. He wiped his mouth with the napkin. "Good point," he said.

Chapter 31

HAWK AND I HUNG AROUND PEQUOD, CONNECTICUT, FOR THE next twelve days. During that time I ran about seventy-five miles, did more than a thousand push-ups, the same number of sit-ups, ate badly, drank thirty-four long-neck bottles of Pabst Blue Ribbon beer, read *The March of Folly* and *One Writer's Beginnings*, reread *The Road Less Traveled*, studied 203 box scores in *The Hartford Courant*, and discussed with Hawk whether there was a difference between good sex and bad.

On the thirteenth day, Hawk said, "I think I in love with Doreen."

"Don't blame you," I said.

"How you feel about interracial marriage," Hawk said.

"Against the law of God," I said.

"You sure?" Hawk said.

"Says right in the Bible," I said. "Thou shalt not marry a spook."

"Shit," Hawk said, "you right. I remember that part. How 'bout I just fuck her?"

"Far as I know that's okay," I said.

We were at the bar. Red came in wearing fatigue clothes

and a John Deere hat. The shirt hung out over his belt and he looked like an ambulatory mess tent coming toward us.

"Might have a job for you guys," Red said. "Cadre chief wants to see you."

"Let's go," I said.

We went in a Transpan Jeep driven by one of the security people in blue coveralls. At the gate the driver said something to the gate man and we went on through and into the compound. To the right was a square-frame one-story building. We stopped in front of it and got out. The Jeep pulled away. A black lettered sign over the door said ADMIN-ISTRATION.

"You guys wait here," Red said and went into the building. The frame building was central to the layout of the place. The metal Quonsets ranged along the far line of fence, and the manufacturing plant itself loomed directly behind the administration building. Past the factory and to the right of it was a white colonial house, partially concealed by trees. A white picket fence separated it from the rest of the compound.

Red came out of the administration building. With him was Chico, with his hat on backward, and a tall angular man wearing starched fatigues and gleaming engineer's boots.

"This here's Mr. Plante," Red said. "He's the cadre chief."

Plante nodded. "Red tells me you gentlemen are hand-to-hand combat experts."

I said, "Un huh."

"We have an opening for two men, to instruct in that area. Are you interested."

"Sure," I said.

"Very well," Plante said. He nodded at Chico and Chico produced a hunting knife with a six-inch blade from behind his back. He held it with the flat of the blade parallel to the ground and the cutting edge turned in. "Take the knife away from Chico."

Chico grinned a little and crouched slightly and I kicked him in the groin. Chico gasped, doubled up, fell forward on the ground, the knife dropped from his limp hand, and I leaned over and picked it up by the blade. I handed it to Plante.

"We get the job?" I said.

Chico was moaning on the ground. Plante looked a little startled.

"He wasn't ready," said Plante.

"It's mostly being ready," Hawk said.

"You want to give him another chance," I said. "You want another go, Cheeks?"

"No mas," Chico gasped.

I said to Plante, "You want to trot out another one, or do we get the job?"

"What about him," Plante said, nodding at Hawk.

"You got the knife," I said. "Give him a try."

Hawk grinned a friendly neutral grin. Plante leaned back slightly, caught himself, frowned and dropped the knife beside Chico on the ground.

"No need," he said. "If he can't cut it we'll know soon enough."

"I told you they'd be good, Mr. Plante," Red said.

"Maybe you were right," Plante said. "Get Chico squared away." He looked at us. "You men come this way, we'll sign you on." We followed him into the administration building.

We gave Plante phony names, and when he asked for ID we smiled enigmatically and he nodded. We signed contracts including the pledge never to discuss the operations of Transpan. Plante walked over to one of the near barracks with us and showed us our quarters. Then a driver took us back to town where we picked up our stuff and checked out of the Pequod House. By ten that night we were in the employ of Jerry Costigan, and, if we were right, I was about two hundred yards from Susan.

Chapter 32

THE WORK WAS EASY. WE DID FOUR TRAINING SESSIONS A DAY, two hours in the morning, two hours in the afternoon. We wore our Transpan fatigues. We ate lunch in the cadre dining room in the administration building where the help was Filipino men in white mess jackets.

Most of the training force were mercenaries like Red who already knew all they wanted to learn about hand-to-hand combat, and walked through the practice routines in good-natured boredom. Some of the kids were a pain in the ass. There was a straw-blond kid from Georgia who went at the training with the single-minded intensity of a Hindu peni-tent. His goal in life was to beat one of the instructors. Each time he failed only increased his determination in the next exercise. He volunteered for every demonstration.

"Tate," I said to him on our third day in camp, "there's a time to quit."

"Quitters never win," he said. "And winners never quit."

I shook my head. "Life's going to be hard for you," I said. There was also a squat moon-faced kid from Brooklyn named Russo who was so intent on proving how bad he was that Hawk finally broke his arm on the fourth day of training.

It had a calming effect on Tate.

Each evening after supper we strolled the grounds, circling past the big white colonial with its screen of forsythia and lilacs. On the second night we heard sounds of splashing from the pool. Security people in blue jump suits patrolled the picket fence, and nearer the house occasionally we could see men in civilian clothes strolling about wearing side arms.

The workers' compound was next to the factory. There were six Quonset huts, three on each side of a dirt strip that in the army would have been called the company street. At the head of the street was a seventh Quonset with a sign over the door that said COMMISSARY. Past that a common latrine made of unpainted pine boards. There were tarpaulins stretched between the Quonsets, and shelter tops made of plywood. Small cook fires flickered at all hours of day or night. Most of the workers were Vietnamese, and when they weren't on shift they squatted flatfooted beside the cook fires and played cards for cigarettes and whiskey. A small contingent of Latin workers kept an area near the last Quonset and intermingled not at all with the Asians. In the Hispanic section someone had fashioned a weight bench out of two-by-fours, and several men worked out regularly with an old set of barbells and cast-iron plates.

There were no fences around the workers' compound but it was separated from the rest of the facility as if by measureless oceans of space.

Each shift went to work under the leadership of a blue security type, and a couple of security people were always visible at the perimeter of the compound.

"Stay out of there," Red told me. "Motherfuckers will cut your throat for a pack of Luckies."

"Have much trouble with them?" I said.

"Naw. Security keeps them under control. Plus there's all of us. Long as you don't go in there alone at night, they can't do you much harm."

"Doesn't look like a step on the executive ladder," I said.

Red laughed. "Shit no," he said. "It's goddamned slave labor, what it amounts to. They buy stuff at the commissary on credit. It gets deducted from their wages and each month they're farther behind."

"I owe my soul to the company store," I said.

"Sure. And they bitch, they get turned in as illegal aliens."

"On the other hand," I said, "if they do get turned in and they start discussing this situation with somebody from the Justice Department . . ."

"Course," Red said. "But these assholes don't know that. They figure all of us round-eyes are on one side and they're on the other. They don't even speak English, you know."

It was evening. Hawk walked into the compound and squatted on his haunches beside one of the cook fires and began talking to one of the Vietnamese.

"Get him out of there," Red said. "I'm telling you it's dangerous in there. Even for him."

"He'll be all right," I said.

"It's against the rules, too," Red said.

"No fraternization?"

"Hell no," Red said. "Bastards start talking to people they may find out they're being fucked."

Hawk strolled back.

"What'd they say?" Red said.

"Said they're bored," Hawk said.

"You speak the language?"

"Some, and some French, some pidgin," Hawk said. "I spent time there."

"With the Frenchies," Red said.

"Uh huh."

"I hear the women were something," Red said.

"Even better than Doreen," Hawk said.

At lunch at the end of our first week, I said to Plante, "Where do these guys go from here?"

"The forces? They go on permanent station at Transpan installations around the globe."

"Security?"

"Security, training, and demonstration," Plante said.

"How 'bout that mansion over in the corner by the river," Hawk said.

"Executive house," Plante said. "Mr. Costigan and his son stay there when they are in the area."

"Costigan owns all this?" I said.

"This and much more," Plante said.

"He there now?"

"His son," Plante said. "Why?"

"Saw all the security over there," I said. "Kind of like to get a look at Costigan. Man's a legend."

Plante nodded. "In an age of collectivism," he said, "Jerry Costigan is the most powerful sole proprietor in the world."

"That anything like Soul Brother," Hawk said.

Plante shook his head without smiling. "It's no joke," he said. "Mr. Costigan has never yielded an inch. He is an individual swimming strong in a sea of conformity."

Hawk nodded and drank some lemonade. I said solemnly, "Man's a legend."

"When the government came in here and told us we had

to let them unionize the work force Mr. Costigan said no, and meant it," Plante said. "We locked the bastards out and imported workers from the foreign labor pool. Workers, by the way, grateful for the chance. They need discipline. They're not used to American hustle and stick-to-it. But with guidance they do the job without a lot of pus-gut shop stewards grieving everything you try to do."

One of the men attendants cleared away dishes and poured coffee.

"Mr. Costigan's way is clean. There's no bloat in his operation. He doesn't subcontract. He doesn't depend on anyone. He's stood by the things that got us where we are. Everywhere collectivism, committeeism, collaborationism is oozing over us. Trying to creep in at every fissure. Foreign goods, foreign ideas, decision by committee, by regulatory agency, by boards and unions and . . ." Plante guzzled some coffee. ". . . damned community action groups and class action groups and affirmative action groups. Want us to be run by a bunch of fat-ass pansies from Harvard."

Hawk leaned forward, his face open and interested, his hands folded quietly on the edge of the table. Now and then he nodded. If he wanted to, Hawk could look interested in the *Playboy* philosophy.

"But Mr. Costigan." Plante gulped more coffee. A mess steward filled his cup. Plante shook his head rapturously. "Mr. Costigan, he won't budge. He does it his way. With his own workers, his own forces. He owns it all and he runs it all."

"And the forces help him," I said.

"Absolutely." There was a faint gloss of sweat on Plante's upper lip. "Absolutely. Transpan is self-contained. Self-contained. When the collapse comes, we'll be ready."

He paused, looked at his watch, and raised his eyebrows. "God, I'm running late," he said. He stood, rapidly drank a cup of coffee, and hurried out.

The mess steward cleared away his dishes impassively.

Chapter 33

HAWK SPENT A LOT OF TIME AMONG THE VIETNAMESE WORK-
ers. The fact that it was against the rules meant as much to
him as the fact that it was dangerous. Which is to say it
meant nothing at all. Someday I would figure out exactly
what did matter to Hawk. I did. Susan did. He mattered to
himself. Beyond that I hadn't got. And since I'd known him
for thirty years it said something about his containment. Or
my powers of perception. Or maybe that's all there was that
mattered to him. . . . On the other hand, how come he
spent so much time squatting on his haunches around the
Vietnamese cook fires at night.

I asked him one evening in the bar at the Pequod House.

"Forging alliances," he said.

"And fomenting rebellion?" I said.

"Case we need one," he said.

I nodded. Doreen rushed past us bearing drinks, frowning slightly.

"It'll get a lot of them killed," I said.

Hawk nodded.

"But if we do it right we'll have our shot at Susan," I said. Hawk nodded.

I drank some beer from the bottle.

"What becomes of them," I said.

Hawk shrugged.

"What is becoming of them now," I said.

Hawk shrugged again.

I shook my head. "No, let's look straight at it. I don't care what happens to them if it gets Susan out."

Hawk nodded.

Doreen hurried by in the other direction carrying empties on her tray. She wore the same frown of concentration. Hawk watched her.

"You in their place," Hawk said, still looking at Doreen as she ordered drinks from the service section at the end of the bar, "you rather do what they doing now, or take a shot at fighting your way out."

The bartender put six long-necked bottles of Pabst Blue Ribbon on Doreen's tray, rang up the bill, put that on the tray, and Doreen charged back past us toward the big round table in the corner. The tip of her tongue showed in the corner of her mouth.

"Okay," I said. I drank a little more beer, letting the bottle rest against my lower lip and then tilting it slowly down. "We gotta give them a chance, though. If it's over too quick there won't be a chance to get at Susan. We need a real battle. We need some real and extended chaos."

"Or we need to win," Hawk said.

I had the beer bottle halfway to my lips. I stopped and slowly put it back down. I looked at Hawk. He grinned and I felt my own face begin to broaden. We looked at each other, the smiles getting wider.

"They can take over the facility," I said.

"Uh huh."

"Transpan has the firepower," I said.

"But the gooks got us," Hawk said.

"We got the bastards cornered," I said.

"Okay, boss," Hawk said. "I sketch out the big picture. You fill in the details. How we going to do it."

Doreen passed again, a faint sheen of perspiration giving tone to her forehead.

"By God," I said, "you're right. She is lovely."

Hawk gestured toward the bartender for two more beers.

"And getting lovelier," he said. "But that don't answer my question."

"Okay," I said. "Are they ready to go?"

"Yes," Hawk said. "Fact I having trouble holding them down."

"They got a leader?"

"Ky," Hawk said.

"Can he control them?"

"Yes."

"Can you control him?"

"For a while."

"Can I talk with him?" I said.

"Sure."

"We don't really have to sweat the forces too much. They may have some personal weapons, switchblades, hideout guns; but the company weapons are in the armory every night."

"So we secure that," Hawk said.

"And all we have to sweat is security."

"And the gooks outnumber security."

"So if we get them some weapons, and secure the armory . . ."

"They might win," Hawk said.

"And you and I will deal with Costigan's bodyguards," I said.

"And Costigan."

I took a five-dollar bill from my pocket and left it on the bar.

"I gotta walk," I said. "I think better walking."

"I'll join you," Hawk said. "Nothing like an evening stroll on a summer night."

"In Pequod, Connecticut," I said, "there's nothing else."

"Except Doreen," Hawk said.

"True," I said.

Chapter 34

KY LOOKED SORT OF LIKE A PLEASANT SNAKE. HE WAS SLENDER and easy in his movements, and his thin face was smooth and without lines. He smiled often, but there was about him a sense of contained deadliness. He wore only a pair of black loose-fitting pants as he squatted beside the fire under the tarp, and as he moved, the skeletal muscles moved languidly, but strong, under his skin. His black hair was long, nearly to his shoulders, and he had a drooping black mustache. Around us there were twenty or thirty Vietnamese men gathered, many of them in shadow at the edge of the firelight, squatting motionless. Ky spoke to Hawk in a clutter of French, Vietnamese, and pidgin. Hawk nodded and answered him in the same.

The summer night was warm, but the fire was kept up. There was a cookpot set at the edge of the ashes. The smell of the workers' compound was not an American smell. It was a smell of different herbs and different food eaten in a different land. It was a smell of foreignness and difference. I wondered if the rest of the installation smelled that way to them.

"He say they recruited out of refugee camps in Thailand. Say if they make trouble they get shipped back to Vietnam."

"Tell him that's not so," I said.

"Told him that," Hawk said. "He doesn't think I know."

"And he thinks I do?"

"You white."

"Ahh," I said.

"Says he knows chocolate soldiers got no power. Wants to hear it from you."

"What would happen if they did get shipped back to Vietnam?"

"Ky was working with us in counterinsurgency," Hawk said. "Special task force. Root out the Commie vipers and kill 'em. All of a sudden the Commie vipers in charge, and we fighting each other for a spot in the helicopters. Say the Commie vipers be inclined to kill him with bamboo slivers. Says most of the workers got that kind of problem."

I nodded. "What color was the guy that signed him up to counterinsurgency?"

Hawk grinned. He spoke to Ky. Ky answered and looked at me and nodded and grinned.

Hawk said, "Some honkie major signed him up. Said it would be to his advantage once us Yanks had rooted them Commie vipers out. Said he could count on us Yanks."

I nodded. "So much for trusting honkies," I said.

Hawk relayed it. Ky replied.

"It lose a little in the translation," Hawk said, "but he say he got the idea."

"He's got to trust me and you, or not trust me and you. There's no way we can assure him that we won't bolt, and leave him holding the ass end of a tiger. In fact we will."

Hawk nodded. "Good point," he said.

He talked some more with Ky. Ky nodded and made a

short reply and Hawk spoke some more and Ky still nodded and then sat quietly and looked at me. No one else around us said a word. Nobody moved. All of them smoked cigarettes.

"I told him what we're up to," Hawk said. "I told him that we had some influence with the feds. I told him that we wanted them to tear this place up as a diversion so we could get at Susan."

"What did he say?"

"He say the Vietnamese equivalent of un huh."

I looked around the bright circle that the fire made, at the semi-shadowed faces of these distant foreign men. Uprooted for decades, used in the service of other people's goals. One of the things I noticed was that the way they sat shielded us from the sight of the Transpan security types.

"Here's what I think," I said, talking directly to Ky. Every few sentences I paused and Hawk translated for me. "I think that you are probably illegal aliens and run the risk of being deported if you get caught, as you are likely to if you leave here. But I think the deportation, if it happens, will be back to the refugee camp. I don't think there's any danger of getting deported to Vietnam." I was getting very cramped squatting on my haunches. "We will speak to Ives about you, and he will assure us that you won't be deported, and he might mean it or he might not. And if he does mean it, he might be able to deliver, or he might not."

I waited while Hawk spoke.

"But," I said, "what I would almost guarantee, is that when Transpan no longer needs you, you're going to get worse than we're offering."

When Hawk spoke again, Ky nodded and looked at me steadily. Then he spoke.

"He wants to know what about you," Hawk said.

"I'm going to try and get Susan away, and if I succeed I'll split," I said. "Hawk too." I was looking directly back at Ky. "You'll be on your own."

Hawk spoke it to him. Ky nodded some more. And was quiet, looking at me, smoking his cigarette in slow deep drags, holding the smoke in his lungs a long time before he exhaled slowly through his nose. Then he spoke.

"He wants to know how come you going to all this trouble. Whyn't you just call up the immigration people and report a bunch of illegal aliens."

"Because I need chaos. Immigration comes down, it will be legal and orderly and Russell will be long gone with Susan."

Hawk translated, Ky nodded.

"I can try to get some kind of contact set up for them," I said. "I can talk to Ives and see if there's some Vietnamese underground they could disappear into."

Hawk told him. Ky shrugged.

"But I can't promise," I said. "And I can't trust what Ives will say."

Hawk translated. Ky nodded and smiled.

Hawk said "He like that, you don't trust anyone, and he don't trust you."

"Calls for a lot of negative capability," I said.

"They used to it," Hawk said.

Ky said something to the men around us. There were murmurs, and one fast staccato of Vietnamese. I looked at Hawk. He shrugged.

"Too fast for me," he said. "I don't know what they saying."

Ky turned back to me and looked at me while he dug a package of Camels out of the waistband of his pants and lit one from the butt of the old one and dragged in a lot of smoke and held it. And held it. And looked at me. And then the smoke slowly trickled out through his nostrils.

He made a sharp nod of his head. "Yes," he said in English.

"Good," I said. "We'll need some planning."

"We done some of that," Hawk said, "already."

"We get the arms room for them," I said.

"Yeah. And they got some gasoline. Been stealing it a quart at a time and storing it."

"This isn't a new idea for them," I said.

"Nope."

My legs got a lot more cramped before we were through, Ky talking, Hawk translating, me replying. But before dawn we knew what we were going to do. And when.

Chapter 35

THE NIGHT MAN AT THE TRANSPAN ARMORY WAS A BLOND GUY named Schlenker who spoke English with a German accent. He wore rimless glasses when he read, and he was reading a copy of something in German with his feet up on the counter when I hit him behind the ear with the government issue sap that Ives had given us. He slid sideways out of the chair and his glasses fell off as he hit the floor.

I squatted beside him and fished the keys out of his right-hand pants pocket. I opened the door to the gun room and the sound of a siren exploded into the quiet night.

Behind me Hawk said something in Vietnamese.

A single line of Vietnamese men filed into the gun room. Each grabbed an M16 rifle and a clip of ammunition and moved back out of the armory. Every fourth man took an ammunition box.

Ky stood beside Hawk speaking softly to the men in Vietnamese. Hawk said something to him in French. Ky nodded.

The siren screamed and a series of spotlights glared suddenly throughout the compound. I went out the side window headfirst and landed and rolled and got up running. Behind me I heard the first chatter of automatic fire. Then more of it. I was behind the nearest Quonset now, and behind me I heard soft footfalls. I turned with my gun out and it was Hawk.

"So there was an alarm," I said.

"Don't matter," Hawk said. "They got the guns."

I nodded toward the far side of the compound and we headed for it on the run. No one was worried about us. They still thought we were on their side and, like the rest of the forces, were running around wondering what the hell happened.

Behind us there was a sudden great *whoosh,* a giant thud, and the armory burst into a mass of immediate flame.

"Gasoline do work nice, don't it," Hawk said. We paused in shadow along the perimeter fence. "Lead free," he said. The fire modified the harsh white glow of the spotlights and gave a bronze cast to everything and the men running across the open space became shadowed and distorted as the flames surged and wavered. The automatic fire echoed in short rippling bursts and then the ammunition left in the armory began to explode in festival bursts.

We edged our way along the fence toward Costigan's compound. Something big went off in the armory and sent a volcanic spurt a hundred feet in the air. The gunfire had spread and came from everywhere, or seemed to. Someone had set off a fire alarm and the bell clanged steadily in counterpoint to the siren.

"Lucky they're ringing that bell," I said. "Never know otherwise there was a fire."

"Alert," Hawk said.

At the edge of the fire's roar and the siren's shriek and

the bell's clang and the gunfire and exploding ammunition I could hear small sounds of human yells, but only bare wisps of sound, almost illusory, the cries of the men overwhelmed by pyrotechnics. Only when I saw the black shadowy distorted elongated forms flit briefly in front of the flames were the cries audible, as if it required the sight of near human form to connect sound with source. Around the mercenary barracks there was no sign of activity. Most of them had been in combat and most of them knew when to stay low and when to fight. When they had guns and you didn't was the time to stay low.

Chapter 36

WE REACHED THE COMPOUND AND CROUCHED ON OUR HEELS behind a low hedge. The picket fence was no problem. It was merely ornamental. Beyond the picket fence a big gussied-up Ford van was parked, with its motor running and its lights on. The van had been customized with porthole windows in back and a big chrome roof rack, and a lot of fancy custom paintwork in the form of swooshes and stripes. The back doors of the van were open and two men carried luggage from the house and stowed it away. Around the van, near the back doors, there were four men with Uzi machine guns and flack jackets. There was a light on upstairs in the house. The men carrying the luggage put the last of it in the van and closed the back doors. They both had Uzis slung over their shoulders. One of them got in the driver's seat of the van, the other opened the side door nearest the house.

"They bailing out," Hawk whispered.

"I figured they would," I said. "I was hoping we could get them while they did."

Russell Costigan came out of the back door of the house, and Susan came behind him. She wore a black leather jacket and pants. Her face in the reflected light from the car headlights looked serious but not scared. The fire across the company area made everything look reddish and a little satanic.

The guards closed around them as they stepped to the van.

"No chance," I whispered.

Hawk said, "Um."

Susan got in first, Russell behind her. Then the bodyguards got in, the doors closed, and the car lurched slightly as the driver put it in gear.

"The roof rack," I said. And Hawk and I stood and sprinted for the van. It began to move slowly across the darkened compound. I caught it from behind and put one foot on the bumper, jumped slightly, caught the rear bar of the roof rack and slithered up onto the roof of the van. The van picked up speed, I felt it rock slightly and Hawk was beside me. Both of us sprawled out flat, side by side on the van roof, holding the front bar of the roof rack as the van moved faster but not yet fast through the flame-tinged darkness.

There was no one at the facility gate, and as we pulled through it the sound of gunfire behind us became desultory, as if the fight was nearly over. Outside the facility the van picked up speed and Hawk and I held hard as the wind began to rush past us.

"We stowed away," Hawk said. "Now what?"

"Hope the road's not bumpy," I said.

Chapter 37

THE ROAD WAS SMOOTH ENOUGH, IF YOU WERE RIDING ON A springy upholstered car seat. If you were lying on your stomach on the metal roof of a van on top of steel rack ridges, you tended to wish for smoother. The van drove east through the uninterrupted night, following the tunnel of its headlights. We jolted along atop it, holding on to the roof rack, keeping our faces turned away from the rush of air that boiled up over the hood and windshield of the van. There was no other sound. We could hear nothing from the van beneath us.

"Susan wasn't there we could start shooting down through the roof," Hawk said. "Ain't but a thin piece of sheet metal."

He had his mouth close to my ear.

I answered him the same way. "Don't want to hit the driver, either," I said. "Having him roll this thing over would not be in our long-term interests."

"They got to stop sometime," Hawk said.

"And there's six bodyguards, plus Costigan," I said.

"Good idea," Hawk said. "Getting up here. We no better off than we was if we tried to take them back there."

"But it gives me time to think," I said.

"Oh good," Hawk said.

Now and then a car would come the other way, heading west in the dark, and its headlights would sweep over us. But if they saw two guys riding on top of a van they were by before they could react. And what was there to do in the way of reaction?

"How fast you think we're going," I said to Hawk.

"Hard to tell. Nothing to compare it to."

"Probably fifty-five," I said. "No reason to go faster. No one's chasing them. No point getting nabbed for speeding and all the aggravation that might ensue," I said.

"Ensue," Hawk said. "We riding on top of a fucking speeding truck with six armed guys in it in the fucking dark and you talking about ensue."

"I'm going to shoot out a tire," I said.

"They'll think the gunshot is just the tire blowing."

"I hope so," I said. "And I figure the guy's a good driver or they wouldn't have him driving Russell."

"So he won't panic and roll the van," Hawk said. The conversation was slow as we took turns talking into each other's ear.

"And when he slows down we jump off and get out of sight, and when they all get out to change the tire we make our move."

"Which is what," Hawk said.

"We'll see," I said. "Hang on to me."

Hawk held the rack bar with one hand. With his other he took hold of my belt. I twisted out over the edge of the moving van and looked down at the black road rippling by below me. With my left hand I clutched the roof rack, with my right I edged my gun out. I arched myself farther out away from the van, halfway off the roof, held by my grip on the rack and Hawk's grip on my belt. I struggled to be steady, the muscles in my lower back were cramping. The position was nearly impossible. I tightened up my stomach and strained all the muscles in my body to hold steady and aimed and shot out the rear tire on the driver's side. Almost at once the van began to swerve, the decompressed tire thumped loudly and the van heeled over toward the driver's side as it lost its level. Brakes squealed. I was concentrating all I had at not dropping my gun. I could feel myself slide a little farther out as the van swerved again and then the brakes caught and it slowed, still swerving, and bumped off the road onto the shoulder. Hawk let go of my belt and I fell headfirst off the van and hit the ground and held on to the gun and rolled twenty feet down the road shoulder, into the ditch that ran beside it. Hawk landed silently and in two steps was beside me. We scuttled along the ditch, on all fours as the van careened to a halt, on the shoulder. There were weeds in the ditch.

We were ten feet down the ditch from them in the dark when the driver's door opened and the driver got out. He walked back and looked at the blown tire, then he walked back to the door.

"It's blown, Russell. The jack and the spare are in the back under the luggage."

Someone in the van said something we couldn't hear. Then the side door of the van opened and Russell got out. He went back and looked at the tire.

"Only flat on one side," he said. He walked back to the open door. "Okay," he said, "everybody out. Got to jack up the truck and change a tire."

Susan leaned out, took Russell's hand, and stepped onto the highway.

"Leave the guns in the van," Russell said. "Don't want some state cop to come by to help us and see six guys with machine guns."

The bodyguards piled out of the van and stood along the highway looking at the van.

The driver went back to the rear door and opened it.

"Somebody gonna help me?" he said.

"Curley," Russell said, "you help him. Rest of us will check out the heavens."

He stood beside Susan. "Like those stars, baby? Romantic, huh?"

Susan didn't say anything. She stood quietly beside him. The four bodyguards stood near them at the front of the van, while Curley and the driver unloaded the luggage.

I touched Hawk's arm and pointed toward the two unloaders. He nodded and moved back down the ditch soundlessly. I edged in the other direction so that I was ahead of the van. When they finished with the luggage, the driver deployed the jack and the spare, while Curley squatted with the lug wrench and loosened the flat. The driver jacked up the van and then squatted beside Curley while both of them removed the bad tire. As they were in the midst of this Hawk came silently out of the ditch. He hit Curley across the base of the skull with the barrel of his gun and kicked the driver in the face. Curley's shout of pain turned everyone toward him and I scrambled out of the ditch behind the others and put my forearm under Russell's chin and my gun hard into his ear. From the back of the van Hawk, in a half crouch, aimed his gun at the remaining guards.

"Susan," I said, "step away from the group."

"My God," Susan said.

I said it harder. "Step away."

She did.

"You four," I said. "Facedown, on the ground, hands locked behind your head."

The four bodyguards looked at me without moving, Hawk shot the one closest to Russell. The bullet hit him and spun him half around and he bumped into the van and slid to the ground leaving a smear of blood on the side of the van.

"On the goddamned ground," I said and the three guards still standing dropped to the ground, facedown, and put their hands behind their heads.

"Spenser," Russell said. It wasn't a question.

"You finish the tire," I said to the driver.

"I'm hurt," he said. He was sitting on the ground with his face in his hands.

"Change it," Hawk said softly and the driver squirmed around and got to his knees and started on the tire. Curley was on his face with his hands pressed over his ears as if he had a headache that any sound would pierce. He rocked slightly as he lay there.

No one spoke while the driver changed the tire. I could feel Russell's breathing, steady as we pressed together. And the pulse in his neck was fast against my forearm.

The driver finished.

I said to Hawk, "Check the lugs."

Holding the lug wrench in one hand, and keeping the gun leveled with the other, Hawk squatted on his haunches and tested each of the lugs.

"They tight," he said.

"Okay," I said to Russell, "down, hands behind the head. Like the guards."

"No," he said. "I won't lie down for you."

He was wearing a gun tucked back of his right hipbone. I could feel it as I pressed against him. I moved my left arm from under his chin and reached around and unsnapped the holster and took the gun. It was a .32 Smith & Wesson Chiefs Special. With my gun still screwed in his ear, I pitched the .32 backhand into the darkness behind me.

"Susan, get in the van."

She didn't move.

"Suze," I said.

She went to the van. And got in.

"Okay," I said. "I'm going to drive, and Hawk's going to lean out the side door and stare at you with one of the Uzis and if you move while we're in sight he'll kill you."

I stepped away from Russell. And got into the driver's seat of the van. Russell stared at me and I looked back and our eyes locked. And held. It was a look of hatred and knowledge and it held unwavering while Hawk got in the backseat and picked up an Uzi. He held it level out the door while I put the van in drive by feel, still with my eyes locked on Russell, and took the emergency brake off and the van began to roll. And then I tromped on the accelerator and the van surged back up onto the pavement and we were gone.

The silence as we drove east on Route 44 was as strange as I can remember. Hawk and Susan were in back and I drove. Hawk seemed to be resting, his head back, his eyes closed, his arms folded over his chest. Susan sat erect, her hands in her lap, looking straight ahead.

At Avon I turned north on Route 202 toward Springfield and at the intersection of Route 309 in a town called Simsbury I pulled over to the side. It was three fifteen in the morning. Routes 202 and 309 are the kind that are marked with very thin lines on the road map. Simsbury was rural

Connecticut, close enough to Hartford for commuters, but far enough out for horses if you wished.

I glanced back at Susan. She was leaning forward with her face in her hands. She rocked very slightly. I looked back at the road and then adjusted the rearview mirror so I could see her. In the mirror I saw Hawk lean forward and put his hands on each of Susan's shoulders and pull her up and over toward him.

"You all right," he said. "You be all right in a while."

She put her face, still pressed into her hands, against Hawk's chest and didn't move. Hawk put his left arm around her and patted her shoulder with his left hand.

"Be all right," he said. "Be all right."

My hands on the wheel were wet with sweat.

Chapter 38

FOR SOMEONE WHO HADN'T SLEPT ALL NIGHT, SUSAN LOOKED good. Her hair was tangled and she had no makeup on. But her eyes were clear and her skin looked smooth and healthy. She broke the end off her croissant and ate it.

"Whole wheat," I said. "You can get them at the Bread and Circus in Cambridge."

"I'll bet you fit right in, shopping there."

"Like a moose at a butterfly convention," I said. "But the Shamrock Tavern in Southie doesn't carry them."

Susan nodded and broke off another small piece.

"Not many people your size in Bread and Circus, I suppose."

"Only one," I said, "and she's nowhere near as cute."

I poured more coffee from the percolator into my cup and a little more into Susan's. It was early and the light coming in the window was still tinged with the color of sunrise. Hawk was asleep. Susan and I sat at the table in the safe house in Charlestown feeling the strangeness and the uncertainty, wary of pain, slowly circling the conversation.

"You got my letter," Susan said. She was holding the coffee cup with both hands and looking over the rim of it at me.

"About Hawk? Yes."

"And you got him out of jail."

"Un huh."

"And you both came looking for me."

"Un huh."

"I knew that security intensified. Russ always traveled with bodyguards, but a little while after I wrote you, everything got much more *serious*."

"Where were you when it got *serious*," I said.

"At a lodge Russ has in Washington State."

"Had," I said.

"Had?"

"We burned it down."

"My God," Susan said. "We were there to fish for trout, but one day Russ said we had to go to Connecticut. He said we could fish the Farmington River instead."

"They were setting an ambush for us."

"Which didn't work."

"No."

Susan drank her coffee, and kept looking at me over the rim.

"Start from the beginning," she said. "And tell me everything that happened up to last night."

My eyes felt scratchy and I was jittery with coffee and raw from sleeplessness. I finished my croissant and got up and put another one in the oven to warm. I took an orange from the bowl on the counter and began to peel it.

"I had a leg cast made with a gun in the foot. Then I got myself arrested in Mill River and when they put me in jail I produced the gun and Hawk and I left."

The smell of the orange peel brightened the room. It was a domestic smell, a smell of Sunday morning mingling with the smell of coffee and warming bread.

" 'Death is the mother of Beauty,' " I said.

Susan raised her eyebrows, like she did when something puzzled her.

"Poem by Wallace Stevens," I said. "The possibility of loss is what makes things valuable."

Susan smiled. "Tell me what happened," she said over the rim of the cup.

I did, chronologically. I paused occasionally to eat a segment of orange and then, when it was heated, to eat a second croissant. Susan poured more coffee for me when the cup was empty.

"And here we are," I said when I finished.

"What did you think of Dr. Hilliard," Susan said.

"I didn't spend enough time with her to think much," I said. "She's smart. She can decide things and act on what she's decided. She seems to care about you."

Susan nodded.

"Now you have me and you haven't done anything about Jerry," she said. "What about that."

"We'll still have to do something about Jerry," I said. "We have a lot of things we can be arrested for and unless we get the feds to bury them, we'll have to be on the dodge for the rest of our lives."

"And you couldn't be acquitted if you gave yourselves up and went to court?"

"Susan, we did the things we're accused of. We're guilty. Hawk did kill a guy. I did bust him out of jail. And all the rest."

Susan had put her cup down. Most of the coffee was still

in it. It had the little iridescent swirls on the surface that cold coffee gets.

"You have to kill Jerry Costigan or go to jail."

"Yes."

"What kind of a government is that? To give you that kind of choice?"

"The usual kind," I said.

"They've required you to be simply a paid assassin."

"They helped me find you," I said.

She nodded. There was a small rounded end of croissant on her plate. She rolled it between her fingers, looking at it and not seeing it.

"And," I said, "we have annoyed the daylights out of Jerry Costigan. We have burned down his lodge, trashed his factory, invaded his home, taken his son's girl friend, killed some of his people."

"Yes," Susan said.

"You think he'll shrug and put another record on the Gramophone?"

"No," she said. "He'll hunt you down and have you killed." Her voice was quiet and clear, but flat, the way it had been in the car last night.

"Or vice versa," I said.

Susan stood and began to clear the table of the cups and plates. She rinsed them under the running water and put them on the drainboard. Without turning from the sink she said, "What about Russ?"

"My question exactly," I said.

She rinsed the second cup and put it on the drainboard and shut off the faucet and turned toward me. She leaned her hips against the sink. She shook her head. "I don't know how . . ." she said.

I waited.

She took a deep breath. She picked up a pink sponge from the sink and wet it and wrung it out and wiped off the table and put the sponge back. She walked into the living room and looked out the window. Then she walked over to the couch and sat on it and put her feet on the coffee table. I turned in my chair at the table and looked at her.

"First, you understand. I love you," she said.

I nodded. She took her feet off the coffee table and stood and walked to the window again. There was a pencil on the window ledge. She picked it up and carried it back to the sofa and sat again and put her feet back on the coffee table. She turned the pencil between the thumb and forefinger of each hand.

"My relationship with Russ is a real relationship," she said.

She turned the pencil between her hands.

"It didn't start out that way. It started to be a gesture of freedom and maturity."

She paused and looked at the pencil in her hands and tapped her left thumb with the pencil and sucked on her lower lip. I was quiet.

Susan nodded. "It's hard," she said. "The work with Dr. Hilliard."

"I imagine," I said. "I imagine it takes will and courage and intelligence."

Susan nodded again. The pencil turned slowly in her hands.

"You have those things in great number," I said.

Susan stood again and walked to the window.

"Growing up . . ." She was looking out the window again as she spoke. "You don't have any siblings, do you?"

"No."

"I was the youngest," she said. She walked from the

window to the kitchen and picked up the bowl of oranges and brought them into the living room and put them on the table. Then she sat on the sofa again. "When you came back from California and asked more from me, needed me to help you recover from failure, needed the support of a whole person, there wasn't enough of me for the job."

I sat without moving in the imitation leather armchair across from her.

She stood again and went to the kitchen and got a glass of water and drank a third of it and put the partly full glass on the counter. She came to the entry between the kitchen and the living room and leaned against the entry wall and folded her arms.

"You did help," I said.

"No. I was the thing you used to help yourself. You projected your strength and love onto me and used it to feel better. In a sense I never knew if you loved me or merely loved the projection of yourself, an idealized . . ." She shrugged and shook her head.

"So you found someone who didn't idealize you."

She unfolded her arms and picked up the pencil again and began to turn it. Her throat moved as she swallowed. She put her feet up on the coffee table and crossed her ankles.

"You can't have us both," I said. "I'd be pleased to spend the rest of my life working on this relationship. That includes the damage your childhood did you, the damage I did you. But it doesn't include Russell. He goes or I do."

"You'll leave me?" Susan said.

"Yes," I said.

"If I don't give up Russell?"

"Absolutely."

"You could have killed him in Connecticut."

I shook my head. "I don't know as much as you know, about civilization and its discontents. But I know if you are going to be whole, you've got to resolve this with Russell, and if he dies before you do, you'll be robbed of that chance."

Susan leaned forward on the couch, her feet still on the coffee table, like someone doing a sit-up. She held the pencil still between her hands.

"You do love me," she said.

"I do, I always have."

She leaned back on the couch. She swallowed visibly again, and began to tap her chin with the eraser end of the pencil.

"I cannot imagine a life without you," she said.

"Don't fool yourself," I said. "If Russell's in your life I won't be."

"I know," she said. "I can't give him up either."

"I can't force you to," I said. "But I can force you to give me up. And I will."

Susan shifted on the couch.

She said, "I'll have to give him up."

"If t'were be done, t'were well it be done quickly," I said.

She shook her head and folded her arms and hugged herself, the pencil still in her right hand.

"What are you waiting for," I said.

"The strength," she said.

Chapter 39

"YOU'RE MAKING PROGRESS," IVES SAID. "BUT DON'T THINK because you have the maiden back that you don't have to slay the dragon."

Hawk and I were walking on either side of Ives along the waterfront down Atlantic Avenue. Everywhere the mobility was upward.

"We'll kill Costigan," I said.

"You have abandoned considerable government property along the way so far," Ives said. The trousers of his seersucker suit were cuffed at least two inches above the tops of his wing-tipped cordovans.

"Really fuck up the GNP," Hawk said.

"Not the point," Ives said. "The car, the weapons, they have to be accounted for."

"We could skip killing Costigan," I said, "and concentrate on recovering the stuff we left in Pequod."

"Not funny, McGee," Ives said.

We turned into the waterfront park near the new Marriott and walked to the edge and looked at the water.

"What is your plan," Ives said.

"We were thinking about stopping in here at Tia's and having some fried squid and a couple of beers," I said.

Ives frowned and looked at me hard. "You work too hard at being a wise guy, Lochinvar."

"It's worth the effort," I said.

"Man ain't lazy," Hawk said.

"Listen, both of you. You think you're a couple of hard cases. I know. I've seen a lot of hard cases. Well, you two hard cases have your balls in a squeeze, you understand. You are in hock to us and we're calling in the chit. You want to learn about how hard a case someone can be you keep fucking around with us. You'll find yourself hanging out to dry in a slow wind."

"Eek," I said.

"Keep it up," Ives said. "You've got Costigan on one side, and us on the other. You don't know what pressure is if we start squeezing."

"Here," Hawk said. "Why don't you just give this a gentle squeeze to show you're serious."

Ives's face flushed and small dimples formed near the corners of his thin mouth. He breathed in a large lungful of salt air and let it out, turning to lean on one of the capstan posts that lined the edge of the harbor.

"You know Costigan will be after you," Ives said in a voice tight with the obvious effort of control. "He's got a contract out on both of you now, and he has an organization that can find you anywhere in the world."

"We'll kill Costigan," I said.

"If you have any doubts remember that he'll kill you if you don't, and without us to back you up, you won't."

"With or without," Hawk said.

"And what do I tell my people when they ask me your plan?"

"Tell them you don't know," I said.

"And how do I look telling them that? I'm supposed to be running you."

"They think so," Hawk said, "you think so, but we don't think so."

"And," I said, "we don't have a plan. Yet."

"Well, you weren't signed aboard this cruise to sit around and soak up per diem. Every unproductive day is another expense I have to justify to the shoo flies. They want some cost efficiency here."

"We artists," Hawk said. "We ain't cost efficient."

"Jesus Christ," Ives said.

"We know something," I said, "we'll tell you. But if it helps, we will do it. Not only because it's him or us, but because we said we would. We'll kill him."

"Well, it better be quick, or by God there's going to be some accounting called for."

"First we have to find him," I said.

"He's not at Mill River," Ives said. "We can tell you that."

"And he's not here in Waterfront Park," I said. "So that's already two places we don't have to look."

"Gonna be easy," Hawk said.

"I know it's not much, but it's all we've got so far," Ives said. "We get more we'll let you know. But you've got to check in."

I nodded.

"You people did pretty good in Pequod with the two instructors," I said.

"We have our moments," Ives said. "You guys didn't do so bad either. The Transpan facility is a shambles. Connecticut State arson people are climbing all over it. Federal Immigration people are chasing illegal aliens all over Connecticut . . . hell, all over the Northeast. They will have many questions to ask Transpan."

"What about the aliens," Hawk said.

"You sound like Steven Spielberg," Ives said and laughed.

Hawk didn't say anything.

"We'll do what we can," Ives said. "Remember, we made no promises beyond doing what we could."

Hawk nodded.

A cycle cart selling chocolate chip ice-cream sandwiches cruised by us, turned in by the Marriott and set up shop near the railing along the water. A fat old woman with short hair was selling helium-filled balloons at the crosswalk on Atlantic Avenue. Ives was leaning on the capstan gazing at the cabin cruisers moored in the slip.

"How do you expect to find Costigan," he said.

"We have a private intelligence service," I said.

"Well, be sure that we coordinate," Ives said. "We don't want a lot of people churning around in the mud obliterating the footprints."

"We'll be careful," I said.

Ives nodded, straightened, and turned toward Quincy Market.

"Tally ho the fox," he said.

I nodded. Hawk nodded. Ives left, crossing Atlantic Avenue toward the market.

"You think the Russians maybe winning," Hawk said.

"Maybe their people are worse," I said.

"Hard to picture," Hawk said.

Chapter 40

Susan had set up residence in my bedroom and I had moved in with Hawk. The safe house had twin beds in both bedrooms so nobody had to sleep with anybody. Even if somebody wanted to. Which they didn't.

"I assume this is not because you prefer me," Hawk said.

I was getting a clean shirt from the top drawer of the other bureau—a squat thing with a warping mahogany veneer and ugly glass knobs.

"There's a book by a guy named Leslie Fiedler," I said. "Claims guys like us are really repressing homoerotic impulses."

"Doing a hell of a job of it too," Hawk said. He was lying on the bed wearing a Sony Walkman with the earphones on.

"Who you listening to," I said. I had the shirt on and was buttoning down the collar. Not easy with a lot of starch in the shirt.

"Mongo Santamaria," he said.

"God bless the earphones," I said and went out into the living room. Susan was on the couch reading *Psychoanalysis:*

232

The Impossible Profession. I tucked my shirt in and sat on the couch beside her.

"Coffee?" I said. "Juice? A twelve-course breakfast elegantly prepared by me and gracefully served by me also?"

She dog-eared the page to mark her place and smiled at me.

"I've started water boiling," she said. "Why don't I make you breakfast?"

"Certainly," I said. "Mind if I sit on the stool and gaze at you across the pass-through?"

"My pleasure," she said.

In the kitchen she put coffee in the filter and poured boiling water over it. While it dripped she squeezed some orange juice and poured three glasses.

"Is Hawk decent," she said.

"He's dressed," I said.

She took him a glass of juice and when she came back the coffee had dripped so she poured three cups and brought one to Hawk. She wore white linen shorts and a pink sleeveless shirt with a big collar. Her legs and arms were tan. She turned on the oven.

I drank my juice and took a sip of coffee. Susan got out cornmeal and eggs and milk. "No corn flour," she said.

"I didn't do the shopping," I said. "This stuff is all government issue."

She took out a bag of whole wheat flour. "We'll make do," she said. She put dry ingredients in a bowl, added milk and eggs, and began to stir it with a wire whisk. I drank some more coffee.

"I know I haven't explained very much to you," Susan said. She was stirring the batter briskly as she talked. Her back was to me.

"Plenty of time," I said.

"Dr. Hilliard has impressed upon me that I can't keep talking about everything, that I need to set some boundaries on myself, do you understand that?"

"No," I said. "But I don't need to."

She lifted the whisk from the batter and watched carefully as the batter dripped back into the bowl. Then she shook her head and began to whisk it some more.

"When you came to San Francisco last year, I began to draw away from Russell."

She held up the whisk again and watched and made a small nod and waited while the batter drained off it into the bowl.

"I couldn't leave him but I tried to distance the relationship as a start."

I got up and came around the counter and got some more coffee.

"And Russell knew at once what I was doing and he . . . he hung on tighter. He put a wiretap on my phone. He had some people watch me. He wouldn't let me come to New York last winter to watch Paul perform."

"How'd he stop you," I said.

Susan greased the inside of a loaf pan, using one of those spray cans. She shook her head as she sprayed it. Then she put the can down and the loaf pan and turned and leaned her hips against the counter with her hands resting palm down on it. Her lower lip was very full. Her eyes were very blue and large.

"He said no," she said.

The connection between us was palpable. It seemed almost to seal away the rest of the world, as if we were talking inside one of those sterile rooms that immune deficient children grow up in.

"That simple," she said. "I couldn't do something he told me not to."

"What if you had?"

"Gone away? Even though he'd said no?"

"Yes. Would he or his people have prevented you?"

I could see Susan's top teeth, white against her tan, as she worried her lower lip. I drank some of my coffee.

"No," she said.

She stirred her batter once and then poured it into her loaf pan, scraping the sides of the bowl to get it all.

"That's when I went back to Dr. Hilliard," she said.

"Back?"

"Yes. I started seeing her not long after I left Boston. But Russell didn't like it. He doesn't approve of psychotherapy. So I stopped."

Susan held the loaf pan as she talked, as if she'd forgotten it.

"But when I couldn't go to New York, and I realized I couldn't leave him and I couldn't move in with Russell, and I knew that I couldn't give you up, I went back to her."

She looked down at the loaf pan and stared at it for a moment, and then opened the oven and put the pan in and closed the door.

"And Russell?" I said.

"He was angry when he found out."

"And?"

Susan shrugged. "Russell loves me. Whatever he may be elsewhere he has always been loving to me. I know you have other opinions of him, but . . ."

"Both our opinions are rooted in our experience," I said. "Both of them are true, it's just that we've had different experiences."

She smiled at me again. "It can't be pleasant for you to hear me tell you that he's loving," she said.

"I can hear what is," I said. "All of what is. Whatever it is."

Susan took a Cranshaw melon from the counter and began cutting it into crescents.

"Dr. Hilliard has shown me that what I feel for Russell, and what he feels for me, is not simply affection. When I met him he appealed to me most because he was so entirely in love with me. Anything I wanted, anything I said. He was like a child. He just loved me to death."

"Sort of dangerous child," I said.

"Yes," Susan said. "It was part of his appeal."

"The kind of love you deserved?"

Susan nodded.

"You found a way to both leave me," I said, "and punish yourself for leaving me."

Susan scraped melon seeds from the fresh-cut crescents into the sink.

"And Russell," I said.

"I'm older than he is," Susan said.

I nodded. Susan rinsed the seeds into the disposal with the spray attachment.

"And I belonged, for lack of a better word, to another man," she said.

"Me," I said.

"Un huh."

"So what," I said.

"What other woman in his life would that describe?"

I thought of Tyler Costigan sitting in her elegant Lake Front penthouse talking of Russell's "fat little momma."

I drank a little more of my coffee. "Hello Jocasta," I said.

Susan nodded.

"Dr. Hilliard convinced me that I needed to be alone, to experience myself, to stay away from you and to stay away from Russell."

"But you couldn't quite manage on your own, so you called Hawk," I said.

"I was afraid," Susan said. "I wasn't sure Russell would let me. I think if I had told him I was going away he'd have done nothing to prevent me. But he wasn't going to let anyone help me do it."

"So Hawk came," I said.

"And you know the rest," Susan said. She placed each crescent on the chopping block and carefully cut the rind away.

"Well, some of the rest," I said.

Susan nodded. She found some green seedless grapes in the refrigerator and rinsed them under the faucet in the sink and put them in a colander to drip dry.

"I don't understand it all yet either," Susan said. "I need to get back to San Francisco and see Dr. Hilliard."

"Someone around here wouldn't do it?" I said.

"We'd have to start over," Susan said. "No. I'm too far along with Dr. Hilliard to leave her now."

Susan took a wedge of Muenster cheese out of the refrigerator and began to slice it thin with a big-bladed carving knife.

"Can you sit tight until we get this thing settled with Jerry Costigan?"

"I won't sit tight," Susan said. "I will help you settle it."

I nodded. "Yes," I said. "That would be good."

I could smell the corn bread beginning to bake. Susan arranged her slices of cheese alternately on a large plate with her crescents of Cranshaw melon. She left the middle open.

"I don't know when I'll be able to sleep with you," she said.

"Champagne's as sweet," I said, "whenever you drink it."

Susan put the green grapes in the center of the plate. Hawk came from the bedroom still wearing his Walkman, poured some more coffee in his cup, looked at each of us and went back in the bedroom. Susan poured the rest of the pot into my cup and made some more.

"How are you going to find him?" she said.

"Rachel Wallace is coming up later and we're going to talk about that. She's been doing research for me. It's how we found him the first time."

"He's an absolutely awful man," Susan said. She opened the oven door and looked in carefully, studied the corn bread and then closed the door and straightened up.

"And his wife is worse," she said.

"Russell's wife said somewhat the same thing," I said.

"You've seen her?"

"Yes," I said. "She said Mrs. Costigan senior jerked her husband and son around any way she wanted."

Susan nodded. "I have never met Tyler. She must hate me."

"Yes," I said.

"When Rachel Wallace comes," Susan said, "I'll sit in. Perhaps I can help by comparing notes with her."

"Okay," I said.

Susan checked the oven. This time she took the corn bread out and sat it on a rack. She set out three plates and knives and forks and white paper napkins. She put a hot plate out on the counter too, and put the second pot of coffee on it. Then using potholders she inverted the loaf pan and gently eased the corn bread onto a platter and put it on the counter next to the coffee.

"You're willing to help me kill Russell's father?" I said.

"Yes," she said.

"You understand why?" I said.

"Partly," Susan said. She walked to the door of the bedroom. "Breakfast," she said to Hawk.

He appeared in the door minus his Walkman.

"Could y'all put it on a tray, missy, and bring it in to me?" he said.

Susan smiled with all her warmth and force.

"No," she said.

Chapter 41

Rachel wallace arrived by cab at ten twenty in the morning carrying a big briefcase. She put her arms around Susan and kissed her on the cheek.

"It is lovely to see you again," she said.

Susan nodded.

"How are you," Rachel Wallace said.

"Better than I was," Susan said.

Rachel Wallace turned to me and said, "I have spent the entire summer studying Jerry Costigan. I suspect there is no one anywhere, including Mrs. Costigan, who knows him as I do."

"It's for damn sure you're ahead of our crack government intelligence team," I said.

"Government intelligence is an oxymoron," Rachel Wallace said. "Have you coffee?"

"Yes."

"I'll need several cups, black. Quite strong." She patted Susan's arm. "It *is* good to see you here."

Susan smiled and nodded again. Rachel Wallace turned

to Hawk and gave him both her hands. "You too," she said. "It is good to see you here." She gave him a sisterly kiss on the mouth.

Hawk grinned. "You holding back," he said.

The phone rang and Hawk answered. I was pouring coffee into the filter.

Hawk said, "Un huh?"

Then said, "You got a place we can call you back?"

I stopped measuring out coffee and turned toward him.

"Okay," he said. "You call back in ten minutes. Got to talk with my man here."

Rachel and Susan turned to look at him and we all stood in that suspended way that people do waiting for someone to get off the phone.

Hawk said, "Un huh," again and hung up the phone.

"So much for the safe house," Hawk said.

I waited.

"Man say if we want to know something real important about finding Jerry Costigan we should meet with him," Hawk said.

"Have to talk with Ives about the security of his operation," I said. "Where we supposed to meet him?"

"Man didn't say. Says he'll call back in ten minutes," Hawk said.

I walked to the window and looked out. Without saying anything Susan got up and finished making the coffee. Below me Charlestown was going on undifferentiated.

"There's no reason anyone should think we would care about where Jerry Costigan is," I said.

"Less Ives's people let it out," Hawk said.

"Must have," I said. "Guy knew we were here, had the phone number, knew we were looking for Costigan. Had to be from Ives's people."

"They could fuck up a beach party," Hawk said. He looked at Rachel Wallace and made a slight apologetic head motion. She smiled and shook her head, it-doesn't-matter.

"It's a trap," Susan said from the kitchen.

"Probably," I said.

"Question is," Hawk said, "who going to trap whom?"

"Whom?" I said.

"Whom," Hawk said.

"We'll meet him," I said.

"Is that wise," Rachel Wallace said.

"Might as well get it over with," I said. "We're compromised here. And the people setting the trap, assuming it's a trap, might still be able to tell us something really important about finding Jerry Costigan."

"If they don't kill you," Susan said. She was putting coffee cups, fresh from the dishwasher, onto a tray.

"Always with that caveat," I said. "But they haven't yet, and good people have tried."

"I know," Susan said. "But in this case it would be my fault."

"Susan," Hawk said, "we let somebody kill us, it our fault."

"You know what I mean," Susan said.

Rachel Wallace said, "It's the way they live. If it weren't your situation, it would be someone else's. A few years ago it was mine."

Susan nodded without speaking. But there was something in her face. I walked from the window, around the counter, and put my arms around her. She pressed her face into my neck and neither of us said anything.

The phone rang. Hawk picked it up and listened.

I murmured to Susan, "Sure we're in this particular thing

because of things that you did. But that's not why you did them."

On the phone Hawk said, "Sure."

"You did what you had to do," I said. "The year before you left wasn't good. So you did something to change it."

Hawk said, "We be there."

"I did nothing," I said. "You took the step. Maybe not the best step. But a better step than I took. You do the best you can and you deal with the consequences. It's all there is."

Hawk said, "Un huh," and put the phone back in the cradle.

Susan rubbed her face against my neck.

"Fish pier at noon," Hawk said.

I let Susan go and walked back into the living room.

"This place is no good anymore," I said. I looked at Susan. "Would Russell try to take you back?"

"He'd want me back. He may think you've taken me."

"Would he force you?"

"No. But his father would."

"So it could be to juke us away from you so they can take you back."

Hawk said, "Yes."

"What does Russell think you want," I said.

"Time to be with myself and become someone who can decide for herself."

"He understand that?"

"No, I don't think so."

"Me either," I said.

"Now not the time," Hawk said.

I nodded and went to the phone and dialed Martin Quirk.

"I need to put two women in a safe place," I said. "One of them is Susan."

"Congratulations," Quirk said. "What about the government safe house in Charlestown?"

"Not safe anymore. Some of Ives's people appear to have talked. Maybe Ives himself, for all I know."

"Tsk, tsk," Quirk said. "How quick."

"Next half hour," I said.

"Belson will come by in a car in about ten minutes."

"Where will he take them?"

"He and I will figure that out after he picks them up," Quirk said.

"Okay," I said. "Thanks."

"Oh shit," Quirk said. "No need for thanks. The entire City of Boston Police Department is at your disposal. We've decided to give up crime-stopping altogether."

"Probably just as well," I said. "You weren't making that much progress anyway."

"And you, hot shot?"

"Less," I said.

Chapter 42

THE FISH PIER FINGERS OUT INTO BOSTON HARBOR ABOUT opposite Logan Airport. You get to it by going out Northern Avenue past Pier Four, which squats at the harbor edge like some vaguely Mayan temple to expense accounts, and is to restaurants what the Grand Canyon is to valleys. Most of Northern Ave. is seedy and barren with piers in various stages of disrepute and warehouses designed for function rather than beauty. There were a number of seafood restaurants in addition to Pier Four, and just before you got to one of them, Jimmy's Harborside, you found the fish pier.

The pier was lined on either side with fish-packing facilities that were undergoing restoration. The brick was getting sandblasted, the trim was getting painted. Two shirtless body-builders were retarring a section of the roof, and pausing every few minutes for a pose-off. There were probably going to be ferns hanging in macrame holders by next tourist season.

At the end of the pier was a building called the New England Fish Exchange, Members and Captains Only. It formed the dead end of the wharf, enclosing the long court-yard and blocking off the view of the harbor. In this interior courtyard, trucks and forklifts and tourists mingled with seagulls and food wrappers and the smell of dead fish and diesel fuel and the No Name restaurant where fish were frying. Water from melting ice formed puddles near the packing companies and stood stagnant, luminous with oil slick.

Behind the pier buildings, the fishing boats were tied to the pier, tossing on the baleful harbor water, rusted and dirty-looking with arcane equipment for dragging and trawling, and other things that a landling couldn't identify. After the noise and movement of the interior courtyard, this outback strip along the ocean was silent and almost empty of life. A crew member hosed down one of the trawl-ers, two guys in rubber boots and dirty white T-shirts sat on the edge of the pier eating fried fish from a paper container and drinking something from large paper cups. Across the harbor, planes sat waiting on the taxiways at Logan.

Hawk and I stood near the land end of the pier, looking down the length of the pier behind the buildings.

"If I were doing this I'd come in by boat," I said.

Hawk nodded. He was looking, in a relaxed way, every-where.

"Behind the Exchange Building, right?"

"Un huh."

"So they could come in from the harbor, do it, go back down into the boat and be gone before we hit the pier."

"If they could get a boat," Hawk said.

"Costigan can get a boat," I said.

Hawk nodded again, his eyes moving along the roof line of the row of buildings nearest us.

"And they only have to go over behind the next pier and get out and into a car and make good their, uh, escape."

"You eloquent bastard," I said.

"Be the best way," Hawk said.

I nodded. "Okay," I said. "We got about a half hour. Let's go next door to Commonwealth Pier and reconnoiter."

"Reconnoiter?" Hawk said.

"If you can say 'make good their escape,' I can say reconnoiter."

"True," Hawk said.

We went back through the short parking lot in front of the fish pier and walked maybe a hundred yards to the Commonwealth Pier Building, which had recently been an exhibition hall and was now being converted to some kind of computer center. The noise from the power tools was loud, and the rubble of interior demolition made it hard going. Workers in yellow hard hats moved about and a couple stared at us as we walked through hard hatless, but no one bothered us. The huge interior of the building was nearly gutted. A small yellow front-end loader was scooping rubble into a container to be skidded out to a truck. At the end of the pier we could look through the window openings in the gutted building and get a clear view of the fish pier behind the Fish Exchange. There were a lot of white seagulls with gray wings, and a few brown seagulls, the color of sparrows. There was nobody else.

"You figure they know what we look like," Hawk said.

"Probably got descriptions. Maybe pictures. Costigan owns Mill River and they had pictures of us."

"Or maybe they just got orders to blast every handsome black man they see with an ugly honkie."

"We'd be safe," I said.

An open-topped Art Deco speedboat with a very large outboard engine idled slowly past us and edged in toward the fish pier. It was a new boat, with very raked-back lines and a metallic-looking gray paint job with red trim. There were four men in it. The guy steering wore a white captain's hat. The other three were Oriental, wearing nondescript black pants and matching black T-shirts. The guy in the white hat brought the boat to a gentle idle beside the fish pier, on the outside harbor edge, behind the Exchange, eight feet below the surface of the pier, and tied up to a rusted metal ladder that reached almost to the water line. The three Orientals went up the ladder, almost it seemed without touching it. One of them stood in the center of the dock, moving his head back and forth. He carried a blue gym bag. The other two took a place at opposite corners of the Exchange Building. Below, the speedboat idled quietly, and the guy in the white hat leaned on the steering wheel with his folded arms and gazed out toward the open sea. I looked at my watch. They were fifteen minutes early.

"The revenge of the Ninja," Hawk said.

"Somebody's doing somebody a favor," I said. "Somebody must owe Costigan."

"Maybe everybody owe Costigan," Hawk said.

"We do," I said. "What do you suppose he's got in the gym bag?"

"Sophisticated kung fu weapons," Hawk said. "Like maybe a Uzi."

"Or a sawed-off," I said. "Where's Bruce Lee when you really need him."

"We could use a boat," Hawk said.

"Can you swim?" I said.

Hawk looked down at the murky harbor water and then looked at me. "In that?"

I nodded.

"That like swimming in a sewer," Hawk said.

I nodded again. Hawk shook his head.

"Man was right 'bout you blue-eyed satans," he said.

"We won't swim across," I said. "We'll drop off the fish pier and edge around below them."

Hawk didn't say anything.

We went back out of the construction and walked to the fish pier. On the Boston side a big trawler lay against the pier empty. Hawk and I dropped onto it. I took off my blazer, my shirt and shoes. I checked that the snap on my holster was tight. Hawk had a shoulder holster, which he removed and readjusted over his bare upper body. He looked down at the water.

"Least there no sharks," he said. "Pollution would have killed them."

We left our clothes in a pile on the trawler and went over the edge into the cold ugly water. Treading water we pushed along the hull of the trawler and around its stern and moved along the pier, holding the rough stones and pressing close, out of sight from the pier ten feet above us. A radio played on the pier someplace and I could hear Willie Nelson. Debris bumped against us as we edged along the pier. I didn't look. I didn't want to know what it was. The water was cold and harsh and black. There were barnacles here and there on the stones of the pier. Not many, and probably from another time. Not much could live in the water these days. Now and then half-rotten seaweed made the stones slimy and made me slip as we edged along.

Hawk said very softly, "You figure this stuff flotsam, or jetsam?"

There was a second fishing boat, smaller than the first,

with a narrow gush of water occasionally belching from the bilge pump. We went outside it. There was room inside but we didn't want to risk getting crushed if the boat drifted in.

At the end of the pier we paused, Hawk behind me. I edged my head around the corner. The stern of the speedboat rolled gently five feet in front of me. I looked up. The Orientals weren't visible. In the speedboat, from my ocean-going angle, I could see only the back of the driver's white yachting cap.

I turned and put my mouth next to Hawk's ear.

"You take the captain," I said. "I'll go up the ladder." Hawk nodded, only his head and one arm and shoulder showing above the water. We edged around the corner of the pier. Three gray and white seagulls bobbed on the water near the speedboat. They looked at us with what seemed to be annoyance.

I went inside the speedboat and caught the lowest rung of the rusty pier ladder. Hawk went past me, outside the speedboat. I looked back as he disappeared from view and then I took out my gun, and holding it in my right hand I went up the ladder. The man at the far right corner of the Exchange Building saw me as my head and shoulders cleared the floor of the pier, and went for his gun under his shirt. I shot him and he doubled up and dropped forward on the ground. The other two turned toward me.

"Freeze," I said with a lot of sincerity. I had the GI .357 leveled and moving in a small arc between the two of them. The man closest to me had his hand inside the gym bag. I felt a tremor on the ladder below me. I stepped up onto the pier, the gun still leveled and moving in its little arc. The fallen man by the edge of the building was doubled up, his knees drawn to his chest. He was grunting with pain. There was movement in the left edge of my peripheral vision.

"It's me, bawse," Hawk said.

"Never thought it wasn't," I said.

Hawk stepped to the man with the gym bag. He took a handful of hair in his left hand and caught the man's right wrist with his right hand. He eased the hand out of the gym bag.

"Anything in that hand, and you dead," he said.

The hand came out empty. Hawk kicked the gym bag toward me. He slid his hands over the man's body, took a big gravity knife out of the man's right-hand pocket and stepped away. He turned toward the other man, by the edge of the Exchange Building. He pointed at him.

"You," Hawk said. "Walk over here, hands on your head."

The man looked at Hawk and shook his head slightly and shrugged.

Hawk jerked his thumb toward us, and put his hands on top of his head for a moment. The man nodded once and put his hands on his head and walked toward us. I held the gun steady on him. When he reached Hawk, he launched a karate kick with a movement so fast and precise it was almost immediate. Hawk leaned back out of the way and the kick missed. The man landed and spun and launched another kick almost before he'd landed, elevating like a spring.

Hawk caught him.

Hawk got the kicking foot around the ankle with his right hand and locked a handful of T-shirt with his left. He held the man motionless at eye level for a moment then pivoted and threw the man spinning into the harbor.

The man with the gym bag said, "Jesus Christ."

"Yes," I said. "Exactly." I put my gun back in my holster

and picked up the gym bag. It said NIKE on it, in white script.

The kicker floundered below in the water, thrashing after the speedboat, which was drifting twenty yards from shore, the captain slumped facedown in the cockpit. I took off my holster and put it in the bag.

"Take him with us," I said to Hawk. "Around that way. I'll meet you at the car."

Then I headed down the right side of the pier carrying the gym bag. Down the pier I saw a Port Authority cop in a blue baseball cap walking rapidly along with two fishermen behind him.

"Officer," I yelled, "quick. A man's been shot."

The cop broke into a jog, one hand resting on his holstered gun, the other holding the walkie-talkie. As he ran he spoke into it.

"I got him out," I said. "He's back there."

"Stick around," the cop said. "I'll want to talk with you."

He went on past and the two fishermen followed.

"Yes, sir," I said. I cut through one of the fish-packing bays and walked swiftly to the parking lot. People stared at me, shirtless in my soaked jeans. Hawk was sitting in the backseat with the Oriental man. I got in front, started the car, and we drove away. Halfway down Northern Avenue we saw an ambulance coming with its lights flashing, and behind it, two Boston Police cars.

"Fearsome doings on the fish pier," I said.

"What's in the gym bag?" Hawk said.

I fished into it, on the seat beside me, and came out with a modified shotgun. No shoulder stock, and the barrels sawed off even with the remains of the stock.

"Inscrutable," Hawk said.

Chapter 43

I DROVE BAREFOOTED ALONG STORROW DRIVE TO SOLDIERS Field Road. I parked in a parking area opposite the Ground Round, not far from Channel 4. Then I turned and rested my right arm on the seat back and smiled at the Oriental man.

"What's your name," I said.

"Loo," he said. "Richie Loo."

"Chinese?"

"Yes."

"Where you from?"

"I'm from here," Richie said. "The two coolies were from Taiwan."

"Maybe they still are," I said.

Richie shrugged. "You gut shot one of them," he said. I nodded.

We were silent. Bicycles went past along the river. Across the way on the Cambridge side there were joggers. A white cabin cruiser with mahogany trim moved up the river. I looked at Richie Loo. He nodded slightly, as if he'd been in conversation.

"I don't know nothing about you," he said. "I work for a guy here who works for a guy in Hong Kong who owes a favor. The Hong Kong guy sent the two goons over and I met them. They don't speak English. We're supposed to kill you. I'm supposed to guide and interpret and be backup, but they're supposed to do it."

"Who you work for," I said.

Richie Loo shook his head. "Won't do you any good. You want to know who wants you killed. Connection's too complicated. Guy I work for don't even know."

"I know who wanted it done," I said. "I want to know where he is."

"Same answer," Richie said. "Won't do you no good."

"Tell me who you work for," I said. "It's a start."

Richie shook his head. "Can't do that. I tell you stuff, I'm dead. Maybe you'll kill me if I don't. But they'll kill me if I do, and they'll do it slower."

More silence. The traffic hum was steady behind us on Soldiers Field Road. Back toward the bend in the river, two kids were playing Frisbee with a golden retriever, the dog tearing off after the disk and sometimes catching it in the air.

"Get out," I said.

Richie Loo got out of the car.

"Close the door," I said.

He did. I put the car in gear and backed out and drove away.

Chapter 44

WE WERE IN TWO CONNECTING ROOMS IN THE HOLIDAY INN ON Blossom Street, back of Mass General Hospital. Belson was sitting in an armchair with his feet up on the bed watching a Popeye cartoon when Susan let us in. She raised her eyebrows at our half-naked wetness.

"What did they say at the desk," she said.

"Came straight up," I said. "Quirk gave us the room number."

Rachel Wallace came out of the adjoining bedroom.

"Did you learn anything?" she said.

"Don't swim in Boston Harbor," I said.

"Was it a trap?" Susan said.

"Yes."

"And you're all right?"

"Yes."

"We packed," Susan said. "For all of us."

"You suggesting I change?"

"And shower," Susan said. "You smell like a fish."

Hawk took our two handguns and the sawed-off from the

gym bag. Popeye sent Bluto spinning into outer space, and Belson looked over.

"Do I see an illegally modified weapon," he said.

"No," Hawk said.

"I didn't think I did," Belson said. He stood up. "You folks going to be all right for a while by yourselves?"

"Who knows we're here besides you and Quirk?"

"Nobody."

"Let's keep it that way," I said.

"What do I tell Ives?"

"Tell him you don't know," I said.

"Lie?" Belson said. "To the representatives of a federal agency?"

"Yes," I said.

"My pleasure," Belson said.

"Tell Ives I'll call him."

Belson nodded. "Better clean those pieces," he said. "Salt water will raise hell with them."

He took Susan's hand and squeezed it. She kissed him on the cheek. He said, "Ms. Wallace."

Rachel Wallace said, "Thank you, Sergeant," and Belson went out.

Hawk and I showered and put on clean clothes. Then I called Ives.

"Where the hell are you," he said.

"Shangri-la," I said. "Somebody in your organization is talking."

"Impossible," Ives said.

"Some people knew where we were, knew we had reason to look for Costigan, knew the phone number at the safe house."

"Perhaps the maiden has made some phone calls," Ives said.

"Her name is Ms. Silverman," I said. "If you call her maiden again I am going to put you in the hospital. Also if you call me Lochinvar. Some asshole in your asshole operation is on Costigan's string."

"Your threats don't scare me," Ives said. "And I can't run an operation like this without keeping track of the agents."

"My threats should scare you, and you will have to learn to run this operation without keeping track of us. We'll find Costigan, and we'll kill him like we said we would. But we'll do it without telling you where we are. Because you will probably run it live on the *Today* show."

I hung up.

Hawk had broken down the two .357's and was wiping them down with baby oil.

"Ives ain't happy 'bout us going underground," he said.

"I think that's right," I said.

"We need him to get off the hook in California," Hawk said.

"We'll do what he wants done," I said. "And he's too far into this to pull out now."

" 'Cause we'd blow the whistle on him?"

"Yes."

Hawk nodded. "So we on our own," he said.

"Who better," I said.

Rachel Wallace was sitting on the bed with her briefcase open beside her on the bed.

"Perhaps we should begin," she said, "by learning a bit more about our adversary."

"Can we eat and drink while we do it?" I said.

"Certainly."

I ordered some sandwiches and beer from room service, and Hawk reassembled and loaded one of the newly cleaned .357's and stood just inside the door in the other room when the waiter came. I paid him in cash and he went away.

"Whose name we under," I said.

"I don't know," Susan said. "Frank simply brought us here and opened the door with a key."

"We'll move on soon, anyway," I said.

I reassembled the other handgun and loaded it.

"We got money left?" Hawk said.

"About run out," I said.

"Gonna need money," Hawk said. "Airfare, cars, food, lodging, champagne."

"I know a man who has some," I said. "I'll ask him."

"Hugh Dixon," Hawk said.

"The man whose wife and daughter were killed in London?" Susan said.

"He said if I ever needed help to ask him. I think this is the time."

"Sho nuff is," Hawk said.

Chapter 45

I ATE HALF A CLUB SANDWICH. RACHEL WALLACE GOT HER notes in order and began to talk.

"To begin with you'll have to accept some things," she said. "For instance, you'll have to accept the limits of research. I have accumulated a lot of facts about Jerry Costigan, but he remains, in the way that you are probably most interested in, an enigma wrapped in a mystery."

"Nice phrase," I said.

"I did not originate it," she said, "as you well know. Why Costigan is as he is, and therefore, how you will best be able to bring him down, is beyond my skills. Perhaps Susan can help in that area."

Susan nodded. She was sipping a Miller Lite. She ate her club sandwich by taking off the top slice of bread and nibbling on the ingredients one at a time. I could eat a brontosaurus in the time it took her to eat a club sandwich that way.

"His holdings are large and various, but his current interest lies primarily in international commerce in arms. He seems without politics in this, selling arms and equipment to all shades of the political spectrum, without regard to their position vis-à-vis the United States."

"A citizen of the world," I said.

Hawk drank some Heineken from the bottle. "Wendell Willkie," he said.

"More than that," Rachel Wallace said. "He supplies not only arms and equipment, but personnel. He maintains a corps of trained mercenaries, for example the group you encountered in Connecticut, and supplies them as well as materiel to whomever."

"Rent-a-troop?" I said.

"In a sense," Rachel Wallace said, "but it's more interesting than that. As far as I can tell, and obviously I am interpreting data here, and may sometimes misinterpret, he uses some of his personnel to foment, and then sustain, conflict, thus creating a market for his product."

Hawk and I looked at each other. Hawk nodded his head. "Elegant," he said.

"Good old Yankee know-how," I said.

"As I say, Costigan seems to favor no position in this. He will sell arms to rebels, to governments suppressing rebels, to oligarchies, communists, democracies and dictatorships, people yearning to breathe free, people eager to prevent it. He often supplies both sides, and sometimes supplies personnel to both sides. He operates through a number of differently named companies. His sole interest appears to be creating a market for his product."

"This make sense to you, Suze?" I said.

"So far. I never knew too much about Jerry's business."

"Anything to add," I said.

"Let Rachel finish, then I'll offer whatever I can. If I hear anything I know to be wrong, I'll say."

"Okay." I looked at Rachel Wallace. She swallowed a bite of a chicken salad sandwich. She poured some Lite beer in her glass, about two inches, and sipped some.

"In his pursuit of profit and power, Costigan seems entirely amoral. Each has a salutary effect on the other. The more profit he makes the more powerful he becomes, the more powerful he becomes the more profit he makes. All evidence suggests that he is wealthy beyond calculation. He has no need to pursue either profit or power. He seems to pursue them because"—she made an I-give-up gesture with both hands—"because they are there."

"Maybe there's a point where if you don't pursue it, you lose it," I said.

"Perhaps," Rachel Wallace said. She finished her two inches of Lite beer. "And perhaps the process has become a purpose in itself."

She poured another inch of beer into her glass and took another bite of her chicken sandwich. We waited while she chewed and swallowed. Susan sat motionless, her club sandwich disordered and half eaten on her plate. She looked quietly at Rachel Wallace with the same inwardness that she'd maintained since I'd found her in Connecticut.

"However, in his personal life, and of this I know very little, he appears to be doctrinaire. He is entirely committed to the belief in some kind of frontier radicalism in which absolute individual freedom is life's greatest good. He is also a white supremacist."

"Him too," Hawk murmured.

Rachel Wallace smiled. "And an anti-Semite. He seems to believe that America is in danger of being overrun by blacks and Jews and foreigners and"—she smiled again—"lesbians."

"The lesbians are arming?" I said.

"And gay men," she said, "and feminists, and the IRS."

"How about the worldwide Roman Catholic conspiracy," I said.

"You get the idea," Rachel Wallace said. "Costigan appears to be fearful that America will be overrun by Americans. As a result he maintains not only a level of security commensurate with his wealth and power; but he keeps elements of his mercenary army on alert near him in anticipation of the forthcoming apocalypse."

"Where is he?" I said.

Rachel Wallace shook her head and smiled sadly. "Everywhere," she said, "nowhere. He has establishments and redoubts and hideaways and retreats and castles and keeps everywhere. I can, and will, add to the list I gave you by phone in California, but there's no way to know that the places I know of are all there are and less way than that to know if he's there, or when he will be. We know for sure only that he's not here in this room."

"Gee, that a start," Hawk said.

"Christ," I said, "we've got him cornered."

"Perhaps the government people can add to what I've got," Rachel Wallace said.

"As far as I can tell," I said, "they wouldn't even be certain he wasn't in this room."

"But they'd manage to let Costigan know that we were," Hawk said.

Rachel Wallace nodded. "So we're on our own," she said.

"I appreciate the *we,*" I said.

"I had occasion to appreciate it some years ago," she said. "Susan, do you have anything to add."

Susan was looking at her sandwich. She picked up a half slice of tomato and ate it carefully.

"I don't know where to look either," she said.

We were quiet. Hawk began on his second sandwich. Corned beef. I finished my beer and opened another.

"I don't want to talk about Russell," Susan said.

"Talk about whatever you want to," I said. "Anything we know will put us ahead of where we are now."

"Russell is not like his father," Susan said. She foraged a small piece of bacon from the sandwich and ate it. "I . . ."

I leaned a little forward toward her. "I won't hurt him," I said.

"Do you promise," Susan said.

"I just did," I said.

Susan raised her eyes from her plate. "Yes," she said. "You did. I'm sorry." She shifted her glance to Hawk. He was lying on the bed fully invested in his corned beef sandwich. He looked back at Susan.

"You tough lady," he said.

Susan was silent.

Hawk grinned. "Okay, since you put it that way. I won't hurt him either."

Susan nodded her head, almost as if to herself.

"Less of course you change your mind," Hawk said.

Chapter 46

"IN HIS PERSONAL HABITS JERRY IS QUITE ASCETIC," SUSAN said. "He doesn't drink, he doesn't smoke. He doesn't drink coffee or tea. Of course he does not ingest drugs. He runs five miles every morning. He avoids red meat. He is self-educated, and quite well. He reads a great deal, and he is very intelligent, but very rigid. He is devoted to his son, and devoted to his wife. Other than those two devotions, I have no reason to think he has any feelings whatsoever."

"How did he treat you?" I said.

"His anti-Semitism is virulent. It must have deeply offended him that I was with his son, though it's probably one of my charms for his son, but he never showed it. He was always polite, almost courtly, to me. If his son chose me, then he could forgive even my Jewishness."

"My son right or wrong but still my son," Rachel Wallace said.

"His love for his son is unflinching," Susan said, "and his son often did not make that easy."

"And his wife?" I said.

Susan shook her head. "Grace," she said.

"He not infatuated with her beauty," Hawk said.

Susan continued to shake her head. "I've always known that love was a compendium of needs. You learn that in your introductory psych course, but what complex of needs and pathologies binds those two people together . . ." She shrugged. "Yes, he loves her."

"And she loves him?"

"I don't know. She needs him, she manipulates him. She loves Russell," Susan said. "I don't know all the dynamics in that family. But I know . . . I *know* that Grace is the worm in that apple."

Susan's club sandwich lay unattended on her plate. I eyed it. Maybe if I reassembled it. No, it was hers. I looked at the sandwich platter. It was empty. I looked at Susan's disorganized sandwich again. Hell, she wasn't going to eat it. Susan took a piece of lettuce in her fingers and tore off a small triangle and ate it. She held the rest of the leaf poised in front of her.

"Talk a little more about Grace," I said.

"She's not very bright," Susan said. "And she affects a kind of little-girlishness that is simply incongruous with her bulk. She's . . . what is the phrase Jerry used about her once . . . often wrong, but never uncertain. She's overbearing and full of fear. She's infantile and tyrannical at the same time. She's weak and silly and her husband and her son are neither and she controls both of them."

Susan shook her head. "Remarkable," she said.

"Why," Rachel Wallace said.

"Why does she do that?" Susan said.

"Yes."

Susan tore off another edge of lettuce and ate it. The

large remainder of the sandwich lay nearly pristine if confused on her plate.

"To be taken care of, probably."

"She doesn't trust them to do that," Rachel Wallace said.
It wasn't a question. She and Susan were beginning to work
on a puzzle. People who were therapists or had had a lot of
psychotherapy tended to do that. To get interested in the
problem for its own sake, to work wondrous patterns out of
human behavior. Sort of like close reading a poem. I
couldn't see where this would take us, but I didn't have
anything else to listen to that was more likely to help.

"No. She's scared, it's maybe the central fact about her.
She doesn't understand life and it scares hell out of her.
She needs to be taken through it by the hand and she
doesn't trust anyone to do it unless she can control them."

"Her husband doesn't understand this," Rachel Wallace
said. "How about her son?"

"He hates her," Susan said.

"Without ambivalence," Rachel Wallace said.

Susan smiled. "And loves her."

"Powerful father," Rachel Wallace said, "seductive and
susceptible mother."

"Seductive?" I said.

"To Russell," Rachel Wallace said. "Classic pattern."

"Classic," Hawk said.

"Of course it sounds like psychobabble," Susan said.
"But she's right."

I reached for one of the best-organized remnants of
Susan's sandwich. She slapped my wrist. I pulled my hand
back.

"Is this getting me a shot at Jerry Costigan," I said.

Susan shook her head. "Probably not," she said. "But

that's really your area. What we can do is report what we know. You and Hawk are the ones who are supposed to see what can be made from it."

"True," I said. "Are you going to finish that sandwich?"

"In time," Susan said.

"Grace always travel with them?" Hawk said.

"No, she's afraid to fly," Susan said.

Hawk raised his eyebrows and nodded his head once.

I sucked my lower lip in and worried it a little. "Okay," I said. "Say we can get her alone, once we've got her what do we do with her?"

"He love her like he supposed to we can make him swap. Him for her."

I said to Susan, "When he travels does she normally stay in Mill River?"

"Yes."

"He knows we're looking for him. Richie Loo knew it so Costigan knows it."

"Ives know it," Hawk said. "Everybody know it."

"He loves her like he's supposed to he won't leave her alone."

Hawk nodded. "A point," he said.

"So he stays in Mill River with her, or he insists she go with him, scared or no." I looked at Susan.

"Yes," she said. "He wouldn't leave her, and he wouldn't force her to fly, maybe couldn't force her to fly. But she'll ride in a car."

"We've already gotten inside the Mill River place once," I said.

"Want to bet they've improved security," Hawk said.

I nodded. "Still, if he had a better place."

"That he could drive to," Hawk said.

"So we narrow it to the West Coast," I said.

"More or less," Hawk said.

All of the tomato was gone from Susan's sandwich. She was nibbling the last piece of bacon.

"Say, arbitrarily, a day's drive at fifty miles an hour."

"How long a day?"

"Say twelve hours," I said. "Six hundred miles. Draw a circle around Mill River with a sixteen-mile radius, what have you got?"

"A equals π th," Hawk said. " 'Bout 3,600 square miles."

"Search a square mile a day and, if he doesn't move, we'll have him within ten years."

Hawk looked at me in amazement. "My God," he said in a flawless English accent, "Holmes, you're incredible."

"Elementary," I said.

"So what we know about Grace leaves us no better off than we were," Rachel Wallace said.

"Only technically," I said.

" 'Fore we discovered about her," Hawk said, "we thought we have to search three million square miles."

Chapter 47

NARROWING THE SEARCH AREA TO 3,600 MILES WAS ABOUT AS well as we did for the rest of the afternoon. When we finished trying at six o'clock, we were no closer to finding Costigan than we had been at lunch. But dinner was closer. No cloud is all dark.

"I need a drink," Rachel Wallace said. "Or maybe twelve."

"I go out and get a bottle," Hawk said. "Stretch my legs."

"Why not have it sent up," Rachel Wallace said. "You might be spotted."

Hawk looked at her as if she'd said the world was flat.

"Or someone might follow you back here," Rachel Wallace said.

Hawk looked at her as if she had just fallen off the edge of the world.

"Scotch?" he said.

"And soda and ice and glasses," I said.

"Hotel will send them up," Hawk said. "I don't do set-ups."

He opened the door quietly and went out.

"Why," Rachel Wallace said.

"He feels like it," I said.

"But we all feel like things, he could cause trouble, he could jeopardize . . . it's childish."

"I know," I said. "Why don't you call and have set-ups delivered."

Rachel Wallace looked at Susan.

"They understand each other," Susan said. "Something about not letting the world dictate to you. As you said, it's childish."

Rachel Wallace shook her head and reached for the phone on the nightstand.

Susan said to me, "I need to talk." I pointed to the connecting room.

To Rachel Wallace, I said, "When they deliver, let me know before you open the door. And don't stand in front of it when he knocks."

She smiled and nodded. Susan went into the connecting room. I followed her and closed the door. She sat on the bed. I sat beside her.

"I need to talk with Russell," she said.

I nodded.

"I am clear on what I want. I don't want to be with him again. But I can't just end our relationship like we did. Just drive away and leave him standing by the side of the road."

I nodded again. "You know if you want to be with me?" I said.

"I know I don't want to be without you," she said.

"You know a number to call him?"

"Yes."

"Why don't you do it in here," I said.

She nodded. "If you had the number Martin Quirk could probably get the location."

I nodded. "I can't," she said.

"I know," I said. "I didn't ask."

"He may not be with his father," she said.

"Maybe not," I said.

"Even if he were," Susan said, "I couldn't . . ."

"No," I said, "you couldn't. You couldn't use your private knowledge of him to get his father killed. Even though Russell might like it."

"You understand that?"

"Yes."

"You understand that I can tell you about Jerry and about Grace and that sort of thing. But I can't give you his number that he trusted me with."

I nodded.

"You see the difference," Susan said.

"Yes," I said.

She took my right hand in both of hers and leaned forward and kissed me on the lips. Lightly.

Rachel Wallace tapped on the door. "Room service is here," she said. I took my hand from Susan's and patted her on the cheek. Then I went into the other room, and took my gun out and stood half into the bathroom door with the gun out of sight and said to Rachel Wallace, "Okay."

When the waiter left there were glasses and soda and a large bowl of Smokehouse almonds. "Ice down the corridor," Rachel Wallace said.

I was gazing at the almonds. "I'll get some when Hawk comes back."

Rachel Wallace grinned. "The almonds were with you in mind," she said.

"If you weren't a pervert," I said, "I think I'd marry you."

There was a tap on the door and Hawk's voice said, "Booze patrol."

I opened the door and Hawk came in with two bottles of Glenfiddich and a bottle of Domaine Chandon Blanc de Noirs champagne.

"Let the good times roll," he said.

I looked at the champagne. "Domestic?" I said.

"French house, California grapes," he said. "Top shelf."

I went down the hall for ice. When I came back into the room Rachel Wallace was talking to Hawk.

"And he knew that you were alone at the door. How could he know someone wasn't forcing you to lie at gunpoint."

Hawk looked at me sadly.

"If I understand your question," I said, "Hawk wouldn't do it."

"Even under threat of death he wouldn't betray you?"

"I doubt that either of us has thought of it that elegantly, but no, he wouldn't."

"And you know that?"

"Yes."

"How can you be sure?"

" 'Cause he know he wouldn't," Hawk said.

Rachel Wallace shook her head impatiently. "That's what I'm trying to get at. How do you know he wouldn't? How do you know he knows he wouldn't? Do you discuss these things?"

"One doesn't," I said.

"Oh, God, spare me the Hemingway posturing," she said.

I grinned. "We don't," I said.

"But damn it, why don't you?"

"One doesn't," Hawk said.

"Oh shit," she said and began putting ice cubes in a glass.

Susan opened the door of the adjoining room. "We need to talk," she said.

I went in and closed the door again. The phone lay on the bed, the receiver off the hook.

"He wants to talk with you," Susan said. Her face was pale and tight.

I picked up the phone. "Yeah?"

"With Susan," Russell said, "it looks like I lost and you might win. She wants it, she should have it. I wish her well."

Costigan's voice was hoarse, but steady. I knew how he might be feeling. I was quiet. My knuckles on the receiver were white.

"You and I aren't friends," he said, "but we got a special connection. We know things most people don't know."

I said, "Un huh?"

"You're trying to kill my old man," Russell said.

"Un huh."

"He's trying to kill you."

"Un huh."

"He's in Boise," Russell said. "Him and the old lady. They've been there since you broke into The Keep."

"Boise, Idaho?" I said.

"Yeah. There's an old silver mine that he's recycled."

"Recycled?"

"Yeah, he's turned it into a fortress. You get him in there and you're the best that ever lived."

"He know you're telling me this?" I said.

"No."

"You there too?" I said.

"I will be."

"See you there," I said.

He hung up. I stood for a moment listening to the empty sound of the incompleted circuit. Then I hung up too.

Susan was sitting on the bed with her back against the headboard and her knees hugged up to her chest. She stared at her kneecaps. I reached over with my right hand and softly massaged the back of her neck.

"Worse and worse," she said.

I was quiet. She reached behind her neck with her left hand and took my right and held it against her cheek.

"You and me, babe," I said.

She nodded, holding my hand as hard as she could.

Chapter 48

AN ASIAN MAN ANSWERED HUGH DIXON'S DOOR. WITHOUT ANY hesitation he said, "Come in, Mr. Spenser," and I stepped into Dixon's baronial foyer. It was as I remembered. Polished stone floor, a grand piano in the center. There aren't that many foyers big enough for a grand piano. The Trump Tower was the only other one I'd seen in recent memory.

"I'll tell Mr. Dixon you're here," the Asian man said, like I dropped in regularly and he'd seen me since 1976.

"Thank you."

He was gone maybe ninety seconds and came back and said, "This way, please." It wasn't the terrace this time, it was the study, or library, or office, or whatever people in Dixon's income bracket called it. Bookshelves, leather furniture, Oriental rugs, a huge and ornately carved mahogany table with a phone on it and a green banker's lamp. Behind it Dixon sat in his wheelchair.

"It's good to see you again," he said when I came in. The Asian man left silently.

"I need help, sir."

Dixon nodded his head toward one of the leather chairs. "Sit," he said.

"I'm afraid I might not find my way out," I said. "I've lived in places smaller than that chair."

"As you wish," he said. "What do you need?"

Dixon looked better than he had eight years back. His face was calmer, his eyes had less ferocity in them, and more life. But his massive upper body still loomed in profound stillness in the wheelchair as it had since the bomb blast took his legs and family in London.

"I need money," I said. "A lot."

Dixon nodded. His head was grayer than I remembered. "Easy," he said. "I have more of that than almost anything else."

"It is better that you not know why," I said.

"Don't care," Dixon said. "When you have little else to care about, you care about yourself, or try to. You care about your word, things like that."

"Yes, sir," I said.

"I told you if you ever needed help I'd give it to you. You and the black man."

"Yes, sir, in Montreal."

"Is the black man still alive," Dixon said.

"Yes, sir, he's in this too. The money is for both of us."

"How much?" Dixon said.

"Ten thousand dollars," I said.

Dixon nodded. "Will you have a drink?" he said.

The Asian man had come in. He went to a sideboard and brought a tray from it to Dixon. On the tray was a cut-glass decanter, and two brandy snifters.

"Sure," I said.

The Asian man poured two glasses of brandy and gave

me one. He gave the other to Dixon and left the decanter on his desk.

"Lin," Dixon said, "I want ten thousand dollars in"—he looked at me—"small bills?"

"Tens and twenties and hundreds," I said.

Dixon nodded and said, to Lin, "To go."

Lin left. Dixon and I drank some brandy.

"I can't pay you back, sir," I said.

"You may or may not be able to," Dixon said. "I don't expect you to return the money."

I nodded. We drank some more brandy.

"How have you been, sir?" I said.

"I am better," he said. "Time helps. And"—he took some more brandy, and nearly smiled—"I have remarried."

"Congratulations," I said. "That's very good to hear."

"Life goes on," he said. "And you?"

"Lately it's been complicated, but . . ." I shrugged. "In a while it will uncomplicate, I think."

Dixon picked up the decanter and gestured toward me with it. I stepped over to his desk and he poured some more brandy into the snifter. He put more into his glass and put the stopper back in the decanter. We drank.

"Will I have to wait to see you again until you need another ten thousand," Dixon said, nearly smiling again.

"Probably, sir," I said. "I'm not too sociable a guy."

Dixon nodded.

"A man who has as much money as I do is used to people who make it a point to keep in touch in case they do need ten thousand dollars. It is a great pleasure to see someone who doesn't."

"I took you at your word, sir."

"Many people say that. You seem actually to do it. I don't assume you take everyone at his word."

"Or hers," I said. "No, sir. Just people who can be taken at their word."

"And how do you distinguish which are those people," Dixon said.

I tapped my forehead. "A piercing intellect," I said.

"Or luck," Dixon said.

"That helps too," I said.

The sun was coming in from my right as it set, and where it hit the rug it made the colors seem almost translucent. We drank our brandy quietly. The house was still. It was so big it would seem still if someone were building a nuclear submarine in the other wing.

Lin returned with a square package the size of a shoebox, wrapped in brown paper and tied neatly with brown cord. He handed it to me and left.

"I have other resources," Dixon said. "In addition to cash in small bills." He took a small engraved card out of a drawer in his table. It had a telephone number on it and nothing else. Dixon held it toward me and I took it and put it in my shirt pocket.

"Thank you," I said. I drank the rest of my brandy.

Dixon said, "Good luck."

I said thank you again and left.

Chapter 49

THE TRANSPAN MINE WAS NORTH OUT OF BOISE ON ROUTE 55 toward Placerville. We parked our lease car on the shoulder of a barren stretch of road and looked down into a valley in the rolling foothill terrain.

"Map say here," Hawk said. He held a U.S. Topographical Survey map with detailed directions written in Rachel Wallace's neat circular hand. The valley ran north and south and the road curved along the rim of the eastern slope. A stream ran along the valley floor and along its west bank a narrow road curved with it toward a stand of western pine that obscured the north end of the valley.

"That end," Hawk said. "Behind the trees." He sat in front with me. Susan sat in the back wearing enormous sunglasses with lavender rims. I put the car in drive and we moved along the rim until we could see around the trees as the valley turned slightly east and the road followed.

I stopped the car and we sat looking down maybe half a mile at the mine entrance. It was square and dark, and even from here looked newly timbered and shipshape. To the right was a helicopter pad, and to the left a wide parking lot. A hundred yards down the road toward us from the entrance was a high chain link fence that encircled the entry area and was manned by a guardhouse. There were concrete vehicle barriers set up in front of the gate in a kind of labyrinth, so that a vehicle could get through, but only very slowly, to the gate. Around the mine entrance the face of the hill had been sheared so that it rose straight up for maybe a thousand feet and some kind of steel wire mesh had been stretched over it to retard erosion. There was a large sign outside the guardhouse but it was too far away to read.

"Bet it doesn't say 'Welcome,' " I said.

"Might say 'Step into my parlor,' " Hawk said.

We sat quietly looking at the mine entrance.

"We could go down the cliff face," I said.

"If they don't have people on top," Hawk said.

"Or if they do and we can take them out," I said.

"Without they let anybody know down below," Hawk said.

"Or we could land in a helicopter inside there," I said.

"If we find a guy willing to fly one in there and get shot dead," Hawk said.

"Pilots charge an arm and a leg for that," I said. "And even then we're only inside the fence."

We looked at the mine some more. On the crest of the hill above the mine, across the valley, a man appeared with a dog and a rifle. He stood looking across at our car.

"They got people on top," Hawk said.

"Time to go," I said and put the car in drive.

"What I wonder," I said as we headed back toward Boise, "is if Jerry Costigan knows we know where he is." I looked back briefly over my shoulder at Susan.

"I don't know," Susan said. "I can't figure out what he's doing." *He* always meant Russell. I didn't question it. "He's ambivalent about his father."

"How so," I said.

"He loves him and hates him, wants to be him, fears he isn't man enough," Susan said. "The other side of Oedipus."

"You shrinks ever look for motive?" I said.

"Yes, but not always in the same place you do," she said.

"What's he get out of this? Out of telling me where his father is holed up?"

"Maybe he lying," Hawk said.

"Right," I said. "Maybe he is. Maybe it's a way to steer us away from Jerry and out here in the great West where we're easy to find and make a good target. But the only way we find that out is to test it, and we have to test it by assuming Jerry's here."

Hawk said, "Un huh."

"So back to the question. What's Russell get out of helping us?"

"The good feeling that comes from being a nice person," Hawk said.

"Besides that," I said.

Hawk looked back at Susan. I glanced back at her. She nodded at Hawk.

"If you get killed," she said, "he has no competition for me."

Hawk nodded.

"And if we kill Jerry?" I said.

"He has no competition for Grace," Susan said.

Hawk and I were silent as we came into Boise. Susan didn't add to her comment. In downtown Boise I pulled the car in and parked on the street outside the Idanha Hotel. I looked at Susan.

"Is there any chance," I said, "that Russell might have been found on a hillside with his ankles pierced?"

Susan smiled painfully and shook her head. "I can't joke about it, even a little," she said. "I know you're trying to make it easier."

"Okay," I said. "You're saying that whether I get killed or Jerry gets killed, or we both get killed, Russell wins."

The afternoon was beginning to darken. It was autumn in Boise. Actually it was autumn in most of the hemisphere, but I only noticed it in Boise. The sun still shone full on the upper stories of the low downtown buildings, but the streets were shadowed. There wasn't much traffic. I had a sense that maybe there never was much traffic in Boise.

"This is the first time my ass may depend on whether Freud was right."

"And Sophocles," Susan said.

"Him too."

Chapter 50

"IF THE MINE DEPENDS ON OUTSIDE FOR POWER OR WATER WE could cut it off and force them out," Hawk said. We were eating dinner in the Idanha dining room.

"If we could find a way to do it," I said. "But when they came out they'd have such security around Costigan that we'd be no better off."

"And they'd know we here," Hawk said.

Susan was quiet, eating some cutthroat trout amandine. Hawk had ordered a Sokol Blosser Pinot Noir and I sipped some. I made a pleased motion with my head.

"Oregon," Hawk said. "Best Pinot Noir comes from Oregon."

"Who knew?" I said. I poured a little into Susan's glass. She smiled at me.

"Also," she said, "the Costigans aren't officially doing anything illegal. They can, and probably will, call the cops as needed. You would end up in trouble with the law again and you already have too much of that."

"Also reasonable to assume that Costigan has some influence with the law wherever he is," I said.

"Okay," Hawk said, "so we don't force him out. Mean we gotta go in."

I nodded. "At least he won't expect us in there," I said.

"Hell," Hawk said, "I don't expect us in there."

"We can't force it," I said.

"True," Hawk said. "Eighty-second Airborne couldn't force it."

"Guile," I said. "We've got to think our way in."

"We may be in trouble," Hawk said.

"Best we can do," I said, "is poke around and see what develops and keep thinking."

Susan looked up from her trout. "That's your master strategy?" she said. "Poke around and see what happens?"

"It's all anyone can do," I said. "The thing about us is when we start poking around we are hard as hell to discourage."

She put her hand briefly on my forearm. "You are that," she said.

We had some dessert, and some coffee, and some pear brandy, and after dinner Susan and I took a walk around downtown Boise. We stopped to look in the window of a bookstore on Main Street. Across the street a western-wear store showed a collection of high-heeled boots, and big-brimmed hats, and long-skirted canvas dusters. Just down from the hotel a storefront restaurant advertised steak, eggs, and fresh biscuits. There was a pawnshop where everyone seemed to have pawned a shotgun or a hunting knife. Everything was closed and there was around the small city a dark starlit sense of space running off in all directions under a high disinterested sky.

"Not like Boston," Susan said.

"No," I said.

"I've never been in the West before," she said. "Have you?"

"In a sense," I said. "I was born here."

"In Boise?"

"No, next state, Laramie, Wyoming."

"I never knew that," Susan said.

"My father and my two uncles and I moved east when I was small."

"Your mother died when you were small," Susan said.

"No," I said. "She died . . . actually she died before I was born."

Susan looked at me in the light from the streetlamp. She raised her eyebrows.

"She was in an accident," I said, "when she was nine months pregnant. She died in the emergency room and the e/r doctor took me by cesarean section."

"So in some sense you never had a mother," Susan said. "You were posthumous."

"Un huh. Not of woman born."

"What kind of accident," Susan said.

"I don't know. My father never spoke of it. Neither did my uncles."

"Not your father's brothers, as I recall."

"No," I said, "my mother's. It's how my father met her. The three of them had a little carpentry business."

"And your father never remarried."

"No. He and my two uncles brought me up."

"Is he alive still?"

"No."

"Your uncles?"

"No."

"You never talk about them."

"I'm interested in what's going to happen tomorrow," I said.

"But what's going to happen tomorrow grows out of what happened yesterday," Susan said.

"Maybe," I said, "but I can't control what happened yesterday. Leo had looked amazed when the bullet hit him."

"But you can change what yesterday did to you," Susan said.

"Yes," I said, "I guess you can."

We were back at the hotel. I held the door for her. We went in and walked up to the room.

Hawk was lying shirtless on the bed, reading the local paper. When we came in he put it on his chest and smiled at us.

"Guile paying off already," he said. "Russell called up and say he can get you into the mine."

Chapter 51

"HE IS A VERY COMPLICATED PERSON," SUSAN SAID. "HE MAY be doing it for me because he thinks I want it. Or because I'll be grateful and be with him again, or for the same reasons he might have had to get us out here in the first place."

"To get me killed," I said.

"Or his father. Or both."

"Or kill me himself," I said.

Susan looked at her hands folded in her lap. "Maybe . . . no. I won't believe that. He's dangerous. He's violent. Never with me. But . . . he wouldn't do that. He wouldn't."

"We'll see," I said.

Susan put her arms around me and rested her head against my chest.

"Time to go," I said.

She nodded, her head still against my chest. Then she stepped away.

Hawk handed me the .357 in a shoulder holster and

helped me as I slipped into the harness. I hiked up the right leg of my jeans and Hawk taped a sheathed hunting knife to my calf. I shook the pants leg down over it. I was wearing gray Nike running shoes, and a black T-shirt. I put the black and gray Windbreaker top to a jogging suit on over the T-shirt and shoulder holster. I put the government black-jack in my right hip pocket. The jacket had a zippered pocket across the front and I put a handful of shells in and zipped it up. I turned and walked three steps toward the other side of the hotel room. The shells jingled like change in the pocket. I shook my head and Hawk said, "No," at the same time. I took the shells out, and Hawk went to the bathroom and returned with adhesive tape. I pulled up the jacket and T-shirt and Hawk taped a dozen .357 shells across my stomach. I dropped the T-shirt over the ammo, letting it hang out over my belt so I could get at the shells quicker. I walked across the room again. Quiet.

"Okay," I said. "I'll see you here afterwards."

"I wish you weren't alone," Susan said.

"Me too," I said. "But it's his rules."

Susan nodded. I looked at Hawk.

"You got to kill him," Hawk said, "kill him. Don't die 'cause you think you promised her."

I nodded.

"She don't want that," Hawk said.

I nodded.

"Do you?" Hawk said to Susan.

She shook her head. "No," she said. "God, no, I . . . no. No promises. You do what you must do to come back." She was sitting on the bed, her hands rubbing both temples. "I want you to come back."

I took in a big drag of air through my nose. I put my hands on either side of her face and tilted it up and kissed her gently on the mouth. She put her hands on top of mine for a moment and held her mouth against me. Then we stopped kissing and I straightened up and stepped away. Her look followed me, but she didn't speak. I looked at Hawk. He nodded once, a short nod. I opened the door and went out.

Russell Costigan picked me up in a Jensen-Healey convertible with the top down. He had on a silver racing jacket and backless pigskin driving gloves and Porsche sunglasses. His longish hair was disarranged by the wind and I could see that he was balding. I was pleased.

"You pumped up?" he said.

I didn't say anything.

"You wonder why I'm doing this?" he said.

"No."

He grinned. The grin was wolfish, like a carnivore curling back its lips. "The hell you don't," he said.

We were heading north out of Boise, but on a different road. It was a little late in the year for a convertible and the air was cold. I sat and looked at Costigan, feeling tightness in the muscles along my spine and across my shoulders. Costigan glanced at me as he drove. He looked back at the road and then glanced again and then back at the road. He nodded his head slowly.

"Yeah," he said, "I know. I know the feeling. You want to kill me. But you don't. You hate my ass, but there's this connection. Right? There's this special connection."

I nodded without speaking.

Russell drove with one hand on the wheel and one arm resting on the door. But there was nothing relaxed about him. He was all sharp edge and strung wire.

"Think you could kill me?" he said. He glanced at me,

shifting his eyes more than his head. "You think you could?"

"Anybody can kill anybody," I said.

He nodded to himself. "What's she say about me," he said.

I didn't answer. He shook his head. "You're right," he said. "Question was out of line." He shook his head again. "Bush," he said. He tapped the door where his arm rested with his fingertips, as if he were listening to music I couldn't hear.

We were quiet for maybe ten minutes until Russell pulled the Healey, too fast, into a left turn, tires squealing, and onto a dirt road that headed west through the grasslands. We followed that, too fast, so that the Healey bumped and rocked like a jackass, for nearly a mile. Behind a low hill, Russell slowed up, braked, and parked.

"We walk a ways," he said.

He got out and started around the hill. I followed him. It was late afternoon, and the sun low in my face as we rounded the hill told me that we were heading west. There were small blue flowers on the grassland. Hills rolled away to the west, getting slightly higher in the distance as they mounted toward the Rockies. Russell was wearing lizard-skin cowboy boots, and the high heels made him pitch slightly side to side as he walked. They also made him about my height.

We went down the modest slope of the hill we'd parked behind, and up the modest slope of the next hill. At the top we looked down into a somewhat deeper valley. The valley wall across was scarred with rock outcroppings, and there was some scrub growth in among the rocks. We went down into that valley and maybe five yards up the opposite slope.

Russell paused by a jut of ledge and took a pack of Lucky

Strikes from his shirt and lit one with a butane lighter, not the cheap disposable kind, but one in gold and pigskin. Or maybe that was the kind of disposable lighter people in Russell's tax bracket bought. He dragged a big lungful of smoke in and let it out slowly in a thin stream through puffed lips. The smell of cigarette smoke was strong in the empty landscape.

"How'd you know I wouldn't have ten guys waiting with guns," Russell said.

"I didn't."

"You must have thought of that," Russell said.

"She said you wouldn't."

"And if she was wrong?"

"Maybe ten of your friends get hurt," I said.

Russell grinned his wolfish grin again. "When my old man built this place," he said, "he didn't trust anybody. The place is impregnable, but he didn't take chances. He had a private escape route built."

He took another deep suck on the cigarette. It was a short one, no filter. He held the smoke in for a long moment and let it dribble out as he talked.

"Family only. Nobody else. Just me and the old lady and him."

He dropped the cigarette onto the ground and rubbed it out with the toe of his right boot.

"And I'm going to show it to you," he said.

"And?"

"And then stand around and see what happens," he said.

"Fun?" I said.

"Fun," he said. "Help me move this rock."

We leaned our weight against a narrow piece of rock that jutted up out of the grass. It gave grudgingly, then easily, and a big outcropping behind us moved forward away from the valley wall. Russell grinned and bowed toward me and made a flourishing gesture like a maître d' ushering in a baron. There was a dark opening behind the ledge.

"Voilà," Russell said.

I walked to the opening.

Russell said, "Spenser."

I turned and looked at him.

"I've loved her since I've been with her," he said. "And I still love her."

"That's the special connection," I said. "I do too."

Then I went into the dark tunnel and heard the hydraulic sound of the ledge closing behind me.

Chapter 52

IT WAS DARKER WHERE I WAS THAN INSIDE OF A DRAGON, AND achingly silent. Where the hell is Reddy Kilowatt when you really need him. I would have traded some of my armament for a flashlight, but there seemed no interest in the trade so I began to feel along the walls, easing one foot ahead of the other carefully, the way you do going down strange stairs in the dark. If I had much distance to cover, at this pace, I'd have plenty of time to plan my strategy. So far the ploy I had devised had me feeling my way along in the dark until something happened. Then I'd react to what happened. It wasn't a hell of a plan, but it had the advantage of being familiar. *Life its own self,* I thought.

I moved along, one sliding foot at a time, carefully. I kept waiting for my eyes to get used to the dark. But of course they didn't. They don't in total dark. They adjust to dimness but black is black is black. I reached out with my left hand. I couldn't touch the other wall. I reached up. I could touch the ceiling. I ran my hand along the ceiling and down the wall. I felt no corner. The tunnel was probably a tube.

The walls felt like corrugated steel. Probably seven feet around. The floor was flat. I squatted and touched it. Probably concrete. Poured in the tubes after they'd been laid, and leveled, enough to make a flat footing. I straightened up and felt along farther. Nothing was certain. Without sight to confirm what I felt I wasn't sure of my sense of touch. I paused again and listened. Only my breathing. I sniffed. No scent. The temperature was neutral, neither hot nor cold. There was neither dampness nor a sense of dry. I moved on, sliding one foot at a time out ahead of me, feeling for the possibility that a cavern measureless to man might open beneath me and I would plummet down to a sunless sea. Probably not many sunless seas in Idaho, probably not even that many caverns measureless to man. If this were in fact the family escape hatch there was no reason to doubt its safety. I continued to inch along. I couldn't guarantee that it was the family escape hatch. But if it wasn't what the hell was it. It was obviously built. It was not, obviously, a mine shaft. It seemed to have no function beyond running from the inside to the outside. Or, vice versa. My foot hit the edge of a drop. I stopped, pulled back. Stairs? Bottomless pit? I guessed stairs. I dropped on my stomach and inched forward. A guy paranoid enough to build this underground fortress, and then a private escape hatch, was paranoid enough to booby trap it coming in. I dropped my hands over the edge and felt. A stair. I reached farther. Another stair. I stood and felt along the wall and stepped one step down. There was a railing. I hung on to it. A railing. Life was good. I held the railing with both hands and took another step. And another. Joy is relative. Right now the railing was better than sex and almost as good as love. I went a third step and a fourth. And each time there was a stair. I relaxed a little. I let go of the railing with my left hand and held it only with my right and went down the stairs carefully, bumping my heel against each riser as I stepped, feeling each stair as I went down, holding firmly to the railing with my right hand, but descending upright, like a man, or at least like a primate, resisting the temptation to descend backward, hands and feet. There were thirty stairs down and the floor leveled. I went forward, still feeling, but moving with new confidence. There was still no sense data but feel. I was moving encapsulated in myself and wrapped in the dark neutral stillness. Un-oriented. The world of light and sound and smell and color was above and behind. The world where Susan was seemed last year's world, and distant. This was the world now. I moved through it like some of those cave creatures who live blind in the earth's innards. Following the endless tube down and forward and down again and forward again deeper and deeper into the belly of the beast. Would I have to cross a river? Would there be a dog with several heads? Was I getting goofy? I thought about Susan, about her odd stillness and her deep interiority and her steadiness and pain. I thought about her strength and how good she looked with her clothes off, and the intellect and compassion in her face. I thought about forever and how we were forever. Forever. In my black, silent, senseless progress *forever* was like a clear beacon and I thought about it again. *Forever.* It was a fact. The fact. Susan and I were forever. What that meant, what it implied, what it required, were a way down the road yet, but the fact existed, changeless as eternity. We'd get down that road just as soon as I killed a guy at the bottom of the world. And got back up. More stairs. Down slowly. Hand on the railing, feeling with my foot, tapping the riser with my heel. Silent as a salamander, breathing softly, ammunition taped to my belly. Level off again. Slide along the wall. My eyes wide, searching, sightless. The habits of a lifetime. Useless in the absoluteness of the dark. *Forever.* I smelled hair spray.

Hair spray?

I smelled hair spray. My time in the labyrinth had sharpened my senses. I smelled the chemical banana smell of hair spray and then I realized that the darkness was no longer absolute. That I couldn't quite see anything but looking was less hopeless. Then there was light. I saw a thin pinstripe of light at floor level. I inched to it. No hurry. Don't gain anything by being sudden at the end. There was no moat. No monsters, not at least on my side of the door. I reached it and touched it. The line from beneath it seemed all one would ever need, after my time in the tunnel. I ran my hand slowly over the surface. It was smooth and metallic. Like a fire door. With a knob. I pressed my ear against the door and listened. I could hear a quiet hum, the kind a refrigerator makes, or a dishwasher on dry cycle. Maybe also a sound of voice or music, too faint, but there was something besides the quiet hum. I touched the .357 in its shoulder holster and changed my mind and left it there, under my arm, inside my jacket. No one expected an intruder. If I went in quietly they might not notice. Or they might. In which case I could then take out the gun. I took hold of the knob and turned it. The door opened and I stepped through the looking glass.

Chapter 53

I WAS IN A CLOTHES CLOSET. THE DOOR WHEN I STEPPED through it was a full-length mirror on the other side. I felt along the edge and found the latch and felt along the jamb where the door fitted and found the release. I closed the door and it fit smoothly against the wall and looked simply like a full-length mirror. The smell of hair spray was stronger. I tried the catch and the door released smoothly. I shut it again. If I had to go out that way hurriedly I needed to know how the door opened. I tried it again. It worked. I closed it again and moved toward the front of the closet. It was a big one, a deep walk-in with women's clothes hanging along both sides. It was the clothes that gave off the scent of hair spray. The front of the closet was a louvered door. I listened through it. The hum was still there. The sound I'd heard below the hum was a television set. I listened for movement, breathing, sound. The television was tuned to a game show. But the sounds of a game show are not human sounds.

There was no movement outside the closet. I opened the

door. I was in a bedroom. A woman's bedroom, obviously. There were two twin beds in there. One was neatly made, in fact immaculately made. Hospital corners, bounce a quarter on the taut gray blanket. The other was unmade, a huge aqua-colored puff was turned back in a sloppy triangle, aqua flowered sheets were rumpled and a pillow with an aqua slip was rumpled and stained with mascara and lipstick. A stiffly ribbed girdle complete with garters was draped over the foot of the bed and a pair of stockings, not panty hose, but stockings that went with garters, was bunched on the floor. The floor was carpeted in lavender. *Nice,* I thought. *Nice with the aqua.* There was a heavy mahogany bureau with curving drawers. The top was covered with makeup and perfume bottles and big rollers and several prescription drug containers, the amber kind with the childproof caps that only strong men can open. There was a television set on a stand next to the bureau, but it was silent. The game show came from the next room. Above the bureau was a mahogany-framed mirror and on walls to either side of the beds were portraits of big-eyed children. On the left wall a door opened into a bathroom. There was no one in the bathroom. I stepped to the bathroom door. It was ajar. Two nightgowns, one pink, one yellow, hung from a hook on the back of the door.

It had to be Jerry and Grace Costigan's bedroom. But except for the scrupulously made bed there was no sign of Jerry. Unless I read it wrong and Jerry was sleeping on the aqua sheets in the unmade bed. And wearing a corset and stockings.

I edged my head around the door and looked into the next room. It was empty. The television was tuned loudly to a soap opera. If a soap opera plays in an empty room, does it make a sound? I moved across the room full of wing chairs and overstuffed couches and out through the far door and left the slow-phrased agony of the soap behind me. The room I entered was the living room, leather furniture, Oriental rugs, brass, walnut, and, like all the subterranean rooms, low-domed. To the right an archway into the dining room, to the left a solid metal door. I went for the metal door and was out in a domed, bright corridor. It probably looked just like the dark one I'd felt my way through to get here, except it was lit. Ahead the tunnel widened enough for a desk to be set up. On the desk was a telephone and a looseleaf notebook in a blue leather binder. Behind the desk, facing away from me, was a big dark-haired guy in a white short-sleeved shirt with a shoulder holster on. The family receptionist. As I walked toward him he turned and stared at me.

"I came in last night," I said. "With Russell."

The gun in the shoulder holster was a Browning .45 automatic.

"Nobody told me," the guard said.

I shrugged. "You know Russell," I said.

The guard made a small half laugh and nodded. "Everybody does," he said.

I grinned. "Jerry wants to see me," I said. "Which way?"

"Probably in the office," the guard said. "Second door, down the tunnel, speak to the guard."

"Thanks," I said. "Place is a real maze, isn't it."

"First visit?"

"Yeah."

"Takes a while," the guard said. "You'll get used to it."

I made a friendly salute, put my hands in my hip pockets so he wouldn't see the blackjack sticking out, and sauntered on down the tunnel. Periodically there were the blank steel doors cut into the steel tube. I opened the second one, into another tunnel, and headed on down. Out of sight of the guard I tucked the blackjack into my belt, under the T-shirt, and zipped the jacket halfway up so the bulge wouldn't show.

The corridor was long and straight with a dwindling perspective. There were doors punctuating it too. As I walked along, looking like a friendly visitor, I figured that the layout must be a series of chambers connected by tunnels. Always the low hum of the life-support machinery made a quiet white sound, which probably no one heard once they'd been in here a day or so. Ahead was a crossway where two tunnels intersected. In the widened area was another guard. He had on a work shirt and cords. His gun was a big Colt magnum in a western-style holster.

"I'm staying with Russell," I said. "And Jerry wants me to come to the office."

"Yes, sir," the guard said. "You know the way?"

"No, Russell and I just came in last night. I haven't got a clue."

The guard smiled. "It's confusing at first," he said. "Jerry's down this tunnel. Third door on the right."

"Thanks," I said.

"No problem," the guard said.

Three doors down, about a hundred yards, walking casually maybe a minute. I wasn't getting enough oxygen. I was having trouble swallowing. Probably because there was no saliva to swallow. My mouth tasted like an old penny. Do or die. Do and die. Don't and die. Swell options. I flexed my hands. Above ground Susan.

I clamped my jaw a little tighter. The muscles ached. I came to the third door and opened it and walked in. There was a woman. A middle-aged secretary at a desk. Christ, she was my age. Blue framed harlequin-shaped glasses hung on a gold chain around her neck. She looked friendly and firm, like someone in a coffee commercial.

She said, "May I help you?"

I said, "Yes, is Jerry in?"

"His family is with him," she said warmly. "Perhaps you can wait."

"Sure," I said. "Actually he wanted me to show you something."

I walked to the desk and held my clenched left fist out in front of me, low near the desk top. "Watch," I said, "when I open my hand."

She smiled and looked down. I took the sap out from under my shirt with my right hand and hit her low on the back of her head. She sprawled forward onto the desk and was still. I put the sap in my back pocket and took out my gun and went past her to the inner office door and opened it and stepped in. Jerry was there at his desk with his feet up smoking a thin good-looking cigar. Grace sat in a leather chair near the wall and Russell leaned on the same wall next to her, his arms folded.

"Ah, Kurtz," I said.

Jerry swiveled slowly and stared at me. He saw the gun before he saw who held it and he recognized the gun before he recognized me. But he did recognize me. The stages of surprise and slow recognition played on his face.

Grace said, "Oh my God, Jerry . . ."

Russell had an odd tight grin. His face looked shiny. He didn't move or speak. Jerry stared at me.

"Jerry," Grace said, "Jerry, for heaven's sake do something. What's he want, Jerry?"

Jerry stared at me for a moment then turned his head and looked at Russell.

"You let him in," Jerry said.

Russell grinned at him. "Not me, Pop," he said.

"You Jew-loving little bastard," Jerry said.

"Jerry," Grace said.

Jerry kept looking at Russell.

"You sick Jew-loving little bastard," he said. His voice quivered slightly.

Grace said, "Jerry," again, louder.

Costigan looked back at me. "Fuck it," he said, "get it done."

I shot him. A hole appeared in his forehead and the impact spun his swivel chair half around. He fell sideways and lolled out of the chair draped over one of the black leather arms. Neither Russell nor Grace moved. I stepped around the desk and shot Jerry again, behind the ear, to be sure. Then I turned toward his widow and orphan.

Russell still had the fixed shiny grin. His arms were still folded across his chest, he still leaned against the wall. In the acrid silence I could hear his breathing, shallow and fast. There seemed to be spots of color on his cheekbones. Grace's face was squinched up like a withered apple, a trace of saliva was at one corner of her mouth, and her entire posture seemed to have bunched up like a fist.

"Don't you touch me," she said. Her voice had a raspy sound to it. "Don't you dare touch me. Don't you dare come near me," she said.

"We'll go out together," I said. "We three. If I get out you get out. Otherwise you're dead."

"You better not touch me," Grace said.

Russell said, "No. I'm not going." His voice was tinny.

"I shot him," I said, "I'll shoot her. We're going out together."

Russell shook his head. "You're on your own now, Superman."

"Rusty," Grace rasped. Her voice was electric. "You do what he says."

"Like hell, Ma," Russell said. "He won't shoot me."

"And your mother, do you care about your mother," she said.

The spots of color on Russell's cheeks deepened and enlarged as if a fever had begun to spread.

"Ma," he said.

She clapped her hands together once, sharply. "Rusty Costigan, you listen to me. You still belong to me. And now that Dad's dead, you're all I have. You do what he says. Don't you let him hurt me."

The rasp in her voice came and went, replaced at odd moments by a lisping little girl sound full of lateral *L*'s and infancy. Russell's breathing was even shallower. His face was fully flushed now.

"Move it," I said.

Grace stood and took Russell's arm, and turned him toward the door.

"I know you want to sit in that chair," I said to Russell. "But unless we walk right out of this mine without any sweat," I said, "I promise to kill you both."

"You just don't touch me," Grace said. She had her hand firmly clamped on to her son's upper arm. "You just behave," she said.

The secretary was still sprawled on the desk in the outer office. I slid the .357 back in under my arm as we went into the corridor.

"So much as look funny at this guard," I said, "and everybody's dead."

Grace squeezed her hand on her son's arm and pushed her shoulder against him.

"We'll go straight to my room," she said. "There's a way out that way."

As we approached the guard I said to Russell, "You catch the Cubs on cable? How 'bout that Sandberg?"

Grace said to the guard, "How is your family, Ralph?"

He smiled and nodded, "Fine, Mrs. Costigan."

"That's nice," Grace said.

I nodded as if Russell had spoken. "Still, I think it's probably Bobby Dernier that makes them go, you know?"

Out of earshot, down the tunnel, Grace said, "You saw what your father did, your father died for me, died to keep this man from hurting me. Now it's up to you. You do exactly what this man says. You do it just like your father would. You do what I say."

"Just like my father would," Russell said. We both knew that wasn't why his father died. When we came to the second guard we went through the same rigamarole. This time Russell said yes he had seen the Cubs on cable.

Then we were in her apartment. I took my gun out. "Back here," Grace said. "In the back of my closet. Don't look, I haven't had a chance to pick up today."

There was a way to light the tunnel from the inside, and Russell knew it. What had seemed like a Dante-esque descent in the darkness became a few hundred yards of banal corridor in the fluorescent brightness. Outside on the grassy hillside under the high stars the journey underground seemed an eternity that happened long ago.

Grace said, "There, we did just what you said." She held Russell's arm. "Rusty and I helped you escape."

I nodded. I was looking at Russell. He looked back, the stiffness in his face clear in the bright harvest moon. He stared back at me. Our eyes held. He seemed to be waiting.

I did too. Neither of us knew quite what we were waiting for.

"You have to let us go," Grace said. "You said that if we helped you you wouldn't hurt me. That's what you said."

Russell and I looked at each other some more. I could smell the grass as the minimal night wind moved over it.

"That's what you said," Grace said. "Rusty. He said that."

"Go ahead, Ma," Russell said without moving his eyes. "He won't stop you."

"Alone?" she said. "Out here? In the dark? I can't go alone. You have to take me."

The smell of the grass was released by the dew that had gathered on it while I was underground. It was the smell of spring mornings when I was small. I nodded slowly.

"Good-bye," I said and turned and walked away.

"Spenser," Russell said.

I turned. He had a gun, a short automatic.

Grace said, "Rusty, you put that down."

I still held my own gun. We stood ten feet apart.

"What would she say if you killed me?" Russell said.

Grace said, "Rusty."

"I won't kill you," I said.

"She make you promise?" Russell said.

"I promised," I said.

"Stop it," Grace said. "You stop it right now. Rusty?"

"I didn't," he said.

I put the .357 back under my arm. "She needs both of us alive, so she can make the choice," I said. "Unless she can choose she's lost."

Grace clapped her hands sharply, the way you do at a puppy. "Russell Costigan," she said.

Russell held the gun in front of him at arm's length and

aimed over the barrel at me. Grace stood about five feet away, rocking slightly with her hands clutched over the back of her head. Russell moved the gun back and forth in a small arc.

"She chose already," he said, moving his head very slightly to continue to sight over the moving gun barrel. "She told me in Mill River that she was going back to you."

The gun was a Beretta, nine millimeter.

"She said she loved me, but she loved you more," Russell said. The tinniness was gone from his voice. "She said the shrink had helped her, and that you had changed some."

Peripherally I could see Grace stop rocking and stand motionless with her hands still on her head.

"I couldn't let her leave," he said.

I nodded.

"I got some of my old man's people and had them watch her," he said.

"Your father was opposed," Grace said. She dropped her hands. "He wanted to let you work this out yourself. But I said, 'Jerry, he's our son. If you love me you'll do it.' "

The gun moved still in its small arc.

"They didn't really prevent her," he said. "But she was so fucked up . . ."

"Rusty."

". . . that she couldn't oppose me alone. So she called the black guy. And we had a tap on the phone." Russell shrugged. "And it got out of hand."

"Hawk's sort of quick," I said.

Russell nodded.

"I wanted to get her away from you, and I wanted to get her away from the shrink."

"She needs the shrink," I said.

Russell nodded again. "I know," he said. "She needs you too."

The gun stopped moving and held motionless on me. "I love her," he said. "As much as you do."

"Yes," I said.

"And she's destroyed you," Grace said. "She took you for all she could get and then wants to go back to this man who killed my Jerry."

"If I kill you she'll never forgive me," he said.

"This man killed my Jerry," Grace said. "You don't have to be forgiven."

"But I've lost her anyway," Russell said, looking at me over the gun.

"There are plenty of girls, Rusty," Grace said. "A boy with your looks and money. Come on."

He turned his head toward his mother slowly, and the gun followed, arm still outstretched, until it pointed at her. Grace opened her mouth and no sound came out. No one moved for maybe ten seconds. Then Russell dropped his arm to his side and walked away into the dark with the gun hanging at his side. Grace and I watched him silently for a moment and then Grace rushed after him.

"Rusty," she shrieked. "Wait for your mother."

I walked back to town and got to the hotel at sunrise.

Chapter 54

IT WAS SUNDAY AFTERNOON AND SNOWING GENTLY IN BOSTON. There was an applewood fire going in the fireplace, and bread baking in the oven, and my apartment smelled like Plimoth Plantation. On television the Redskins were pasting the Giants. I stood at the front window and looked down at Marlborough Street as the snow began to accumulate. A brown and white taxicab pulled in off Arlington Street and parked and Susan got out and paid the driver and walked toward the front door carrying a lavender garment bag and a dark blue suitcase. I buzzed her in and in a minute she was at my door. I opened it and took her suitcase and put it on the floor behind the couch. She put the garment bag carefully over the back of the couch and turned and smiled at me.

"This is the way my grandmother's house was supposed to smell," she said.

"But it didn't," I said.

"No," she said. "It smelled mostly of mothballs."

"So I don't remind you of your grandmother," I said.

Susan came and put her arms around me and put her head against my chest.

"You don't remind me of anyone," she said. "I've never met anyone even a little like you."

I held her lightly against me. "How's your mental health?" I said.

"I'm all right," she said. "Nobody's a hundred percent. But I'm in the high nineties."

"You through seeing Dr. Hilliard?"

"Yes, at least for now. Maybe forever."

"And we don't have to get the children off the streets?" I said.

She shook her head against my chest. "I may get occasionally restless," she said, "during the time of full moon, but I don't think I'm a danger to anyone."

"Russell?" I said.

"I saw him once, right after Boise. He came to my condo in Mill River and we said good-bye. And he left, and I haven't seen him or heard from him."

"He going to run the family business?" I said.

"I hope not," Susan said.

"Maybe he'll go back to his wife," I said. "He has before."

"I hope he does. I hope he doesn't destroy himself. His life has been . . ." She shook her head again. "I don't want to talk about that relationship anymore."

"Okay," I said. "How about this one? How are we doing?"

"We are doing very well," she said. She raised her face and I kissed her. When we stopped kissing she said, with her face still very close to mine, "Are you okay? Is anyone going to arrest you?"

"Not for Mill River," I said. Our lips brushed lightly as we spoke. "Ives actually fixed it."

Behind me on the television Dick Stockton described John Riggins running twenty yards for a score.

Susan kissed me again. It was not a sisterly kiss.

"I have flown six hours," she murmured with her mouth against mine. "I need to take a bath, fluff up my body a little."

"Un huh."

"And then maybe we might make love," she murmured.

"Un huh"

"And drink champagne."

"Un huh."

"And make love again."

"I take it we are together again," I said.

"Yes."

"Forever?" I said.

"Yes," Susan said. "Forever."

"Go run your bath," I said.

Chapter 55

IT WAS EVENING AND THE SNOW HAD STOPPED. THE BREAD WAS cooling on a rack in the kitchen and my fire continued to warm the apartment. Susan and I lay naked in bed together drinking Domaine Chandon Blanc de Noirs from narrow fluted glasses and holding hands.

"How did you know I'd have champagne handy?" I said.

"You would be prepared," she said.

The bedroom door was open to the living room. I held the champagne glass away from me and looked at the pink amber tone of it in the diffuse light of the fire.

"Hawk sent us a case of this stuff," I said. "It's good, isn't it."

"Lovely," Susan said. "You have some new scars."

"I'll say."

"New physical scars," Susan said. "Here." She traced the healed bullet wounds in my chest.

"A young woman shot me," I said, "last year."

"And you never told me?"

"No need," I said.

"Was it bad?"

"Yes," I said. "Almost killed me."

Susan put her head against my shoulder. Her glass was empty. I reached the champagne bottle from the floor beside the bed and poured more. It had to be done carefully and a little at a time to keep it from bubbling over. Susan watched.

"It's like us," she said.

"The champagne?"

"You have to pour it so carefully. It's like our lovemaking. Careful, gentle, delicate, being careful not to spill over."

I nodded. "It's sort of like the first time."

"It is the first time," Susan said. "These two people, the people we are now, have never made love before."

"But will again," I said.

Susan smiled. "Practice makes perfect," she said.

We drank.

"Or nearly perfect," I said.

"Hell," Susan said, "we're that now."